Luke released a harsh breath as he watched Carlie walk away.

While he'd already noticed she was attractive, this time her appeal was striking a primal chord.

There was nothing indifferent about Carlie; she was passionate, vital and far more beautiful than he'd recognized at first. She reminded him of being in the desert after a spring thunderstorm, where everything had been dry and desolate, only to awaken with a roar after a dose of life-giving rain.

A wry smile curved Luke's mouth—flash floods through an arroyo weren't uncommon after a spring storm, either, and they could be lethal. Besides, he wasn't a desert—he was a man who'd lost his wife.

The last thing he needed was to get fanciful about someone like Carlie.

Dear Reader,

Christmas is a cherished time of the year and I love writing stories based around the holiday. In *Christmas with Carlie* I indulged in creating a setting filled with evergreen swags and twinkling lights, along with the scent of baking cookies and wassail.

For my first three stories placed around Poppy Gold Inns—my imaginary bed-and-breakfast complex—I wanted to include a military theme to honor the men and women who serve their country. And it occurred to me that a wealthy hero, who'd lost his wife in the army, would be interesting to explore. Luke Forrester has two small girls who are struggling to understand why Mommy never came home. In helping them, he discovers love again with a special woman who creates her own place in his heart.

Classic Movie Alert: There's a wonderful 1988 TV movie called *I'll Be Home For Christmas* starring a host of talented actors, including Hal Holbrook, Peter Gallagher and Eva Marie Saint. The title is shared with multiple holiday films, but this one is set in the last days of WWII. I haven't had luck getting this on DVD yet, but I keep hoping!

I enjoy hearing from readers and can be contacted c/o Harlequin Books, 225 Duncan Mill Road, Don Mills, ON M3B 3K9, Canada.

Julianna Morris

JULIANNA MORRIS

Christmas with Carlie

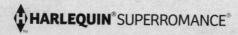

HARLEQUIN® SUPERROMANCE®

Recycling programs
for this product may
not exist in your area.

ISBN-13: 978-0-373-61014-3

Christmas with Carlie

Copyright © 2016 by Julianna Morris

Printed in U.S.A.

Some of **Julianna Morris**'s most cherished childhood memories are of sitting by the fire and listening to Christmas music as she crafted gifts for her family. Since then Julianna has experienced Christmas in many different parts of the United States. Traditions vary, but she finds the spirit of the season wherever she travels. Perhaps one of her most unique memories is Christmas Eve in Albuquerque, New Mexico—spent, of all places, in the old cemetery, where people light luminarias to remember family and friends. She'll never forget the warmth and love found in the flickering glow of thousands of candles.

Books by Julianna Morris

HARLEQUIN SUPERROMANCE

Honor Bound
The Ranch Solution

Those Hollister Boys

Winning Over Skylar
Challenging Matt
Jake's Biggest Risk

Poppy Gold Stories

Undercover in Glimmer Creek

Other titles by this author available in ebook format.

To all the men and women who serve their country.
May you find peace.

PROLOGUE

"MR. FORRESTER?"

Luke jerked, realizing he'd been staring into space, thinking about Erika again.

"Yes, Tilly?" he asked, shaking his head to clear it.

"I've made all the holiday arrangements you requested, but I wish you'd reconsider."

Her face was tense and she only called him Mr. Forrester when she was annoyed. Tilly Robinson had been with him since soon after he'd started his business and often acted more like a mother hen than an executive assistant. Most recently she had been encouraging him to take his daughters away for Christmas. Maybe she was right. Beth and Annie were hurting over their mother's death and no words seemed to comfort them.

Hell, *he* didn't understand.

He'd never expected to fall in love with a soldier, but he hadn't been able to ask Erika to give up something she'd believed in, even after their twin daughters were born. Her father and grandfather had served in the army and she'd prepared her whole life to follow in their footsteps. The night he'd proposed, Erika had reminded him that it couldn't always be someone else's husband or wife or daughter who served.

The sound of a throat clearing made Luke realize his thoughts had drifted yet again. He looked into Tilly's determined eyes. "Why are you so sure that going away is the right idea? Even the grief therapists I've consulted can't agree."

"I'm not sure, but hanging around Austin hasn't done you much good," she replied bluntly. "How long has it been since you got a full night's sleep?"

Longer than he could remember.

If he slept, he dreamed about his wife, especially their last vacation. The twins had been five and Erika had managed to get leave from her unit in the Middle East. She'd met them in Italy. They'd spent two weeks with the girls, exploring Tuscany. Three months later, an army notification team had shown up, regretfully informing him that his wife had died in the line of duty.

Telling Annie and Beth had been the hardest thing he'd ever done in his life. The look on their faces had haunted him ever since. It was as if they'd retreated into themselves and he didn't know how to bring them back.

"I've never slept that much, Tilly, you know that. And it's Beth and Annie that matter." Luke tossed his pen onto the desk. "Do you have a place in mind for your great plan?"

"I'm sure we can come up with something."

His first thought was the large villa he'd rented for the family in Tuscany. The twins had enjoyed the indoor pool and the villa had come fully staffed. He shook his head. What was he thinking? Italy was the last place they'd seen Erika. It would simply remind them that she wasn't there.

"Maybe the Caribbean," he mused.

"Absolutely *not*," Tilly told him sharply. "That's where you went that time Erika's leave was revoked. And don't suggest the French château you went to three years ago, either. You should go somewhere completely new. Take a look at this." She slapped a paper down on his desk.

It was a printout from the website of a place called Poppy Gold Inns on the West Coast.

"California?"

Tilly's eyes narrowed. "There's nothing wrong with California. As a matter of fact, General Pierson's aide recommended Poppy Gold the last time we spoke. I'm sure I can clear your appointment and meeting schedule for the next month."

"A month?" he repeated. "How did we go from getting out of town for Christmas to a whole month?"

"It has to be long enough to do some good. Better yet, stay a week or two into the New Year. They have a fully equipped business center, so you'd be able to handle anything urgent that comes up."

"Let me take a look."

Luke turned to his computer and pulled up the website for Poppy Gold Inns, where the holidays—both Thanksgiving and Christmas—were the main theme. According to the description, the entire historic district of a town in the California Gold Country had been converted to a group of bed-and-breakfast inns. In the pictures, Poppy Gold Inns was a quaint Victorian village, decorated to the nines with holly, evergreen and red velvet bows.

"I don't see any snow," he said, "so it obviously wouldn't be a white Christmas."

Tilly snorted. "When was the last time we had a white Christmas in Austin, Texas? Down here, it's Santa Claus in a cowboy hat, driving a stagecoach. Stop procrastinating. I've checked and one of the houses is available."

"You've already checked? Let me guess—you've already reserved it, too."

"Of course. I didn't want anyone else to take it while you were dragging your feet. It needed a referral from General Pierson's office, so the clock was ticking."

Luke's jaw tightened. Maybe a change *would* be best for the girls.

For him, too.

"All right, clear my calendar from the last week

of November through the first week of January," he told her. "We'll take the jet and leave the day after Thanksgiving."

Tilly pursed her lips. "What about your parents? They planned to be in Austin until the twenty-fifth."

Luke loved his mother and father, but they could be something of a trial. Craig and Heather Forrester both had generous trust funds, but when he was a kid, they'd always spent their annual allowance within nine or ten months. He'd hated the way they lived off their wealthier friends the rest of the year. Luke's grandparents on both sides had given up on them before his sister, Nicole, was born, being people who heartily disapproved of a frivolous lifestyle. He barely remembered them.

"Get my parents invited to an embassy dinner in Washington. They'll regretfully call off their trip to Austin."

Craig and Heather's latest goal was getting appointed to a diplomatic post. They were effortlessly charming, so it was possible, but he doubted they understood that being in the diplomatic corps required actual *effort*. Work wasn't a concept they grasped well.

"Which embassy?"

"It doesn't matter. Just find one that's having a party. I'll ask my sister if she wants to come with us to California."

"You'll also need a tutor for the girls so they don't get behind in school." Tilly made a note on her pad. "Anything else?"

"Not right now, but I hope this bed-and-breakfast place has decent plumbing."

Tilly looked smug. "If they don't, you can fire me."

"I've fired you a hundred times. You refuse to go."

"That's what makes me such a valuable employee... I don't listen to a word you say."

He smiled faintly. Tilly was more valuable to him than a thousand other employees and she knew it.

As she walked out of the office, he closed his eyes, wishing he could go back to when life had been simpler. But life never got simpler. It just got harder.

CHAPTER ONE

CARLIE BENTON BREEZED through the back entrance of Old City Hall. No longer a civic building, it housed the reservation hub and guest reception area for Poppy Gold Inns and Conference Center, along with various offices and other useful spaces.

"Good morning," called a familiar voice.

Carlie grinned at her aunt. "Good morning, Aunt Polly. Wasn't Thanksgiving terrific?"

"It was wonderful. I think we broke a record for everyone getting back home to Glimmer Creek for the holiday."

"That's because they wanted to see Tessa's baby."

Polly Murphy beamed. "I don't think Tessa and Gabe got to hold their daughter the entire afternoon, even to change Meredith's diapers."

"Tessa was able to nurse Merri, that's all." Carlie glanced at the clock. "Oops, I've got to go. Busy day. See you later."

Until sixteen months ago, Carlie had been working in the San Francisco Bay Area, only returning to her hometown for visits. Then she'd been hired as the Poppy Gold Inns' activity director. Carlie loved it and in many ways working at the historic bed-and-breakfast facility was like attending a family reunion every day. Her cousin Tessa McKinley was the owner-manager along with her father, Liam Connor, and half the employees were related in one way or another.

If only her *own* father...

A hint of melancholy went through Carlie. Dad had been injured the previous summer while laying down asphalt on a road as a highway worker. An impatient driver had sped around some slow-moving cars and plowed into him, permanently damaging his leg. Mike Benton now worked as a traffic flagger at road construction sites, which he hated. But he also wouldn't take a job at Poppy Gold, no matter how much the family cajoled him.

"I don't want anybody's pity," he'd declared on more than one occasion. He didn't understand that it wouldn't be pity; it would be giving Poppy Gold the benefit of three decades of practical, hands-on civil engineering experience.

Carlie shook the thought away and greeted the members of her staff who'd already arrived.

"Did you hear...?" Joan Peters started to say, only to stop and blush.

"Hear what?" asked Carlie.

"Nothing," Tracy Wade said hastily.

Tracy and Joan exchanged glances and hurriedly

went back to making holiday name tags for the staff.

Carlie frowned.

She'd sensed an air of anticipation in Old City Hall after arriving, but had put it down to adrenaline. They had to hit the ground running to get ready for Christmas, so there was little time for day-after-Thanksgiving relaxation. For the next six weeks, Poppy Gold would be devoted to the Christmas and New Year celebrations. The Victorian village was ideally suited for strings of lights, electric candles in the windows, mistletoe, evergreen swags and everything else that was bright and cheerful.

"Is something going on that I should know about?" she asked.

"Uh, no. We mustn't gossip."

Especially here at work, Carlie added silently.

Gossip was a form of entertainment in the small town of Glimmer Creek, but it was discouraged at Poppy Gold, particularly when it came to their guests.

Carlie didn't have time to think about anything new, regardless. The basic holiday schedule had been established long before she'd begun working as the activities director, but that didn't mean she wouldn't be busy implementing her own ideas. Traditionally, the autumn decorations came down the morning after Thanksgiving, with Christmas arriving with a vengeance the next day. Well, it would arrive with a fervent festive spirit.

Poppy Gold Inns had guests who booked years in advance for Christmas kickoff day, as the regulars called it. Visitors didn't have to participate, but being able to join in as part of the "work crew" was why many of them came for the extended Thanksgiving weekend, saying it got them in the mood for the holiday. Some loved decorating trees, some preferred making wreaths, while others strung evergreen garlands on fences or lampposts or worked on the public areas of a specific Victorian. There were lots of things to do for all ages.

In her office, Carlie pulled up a list of the expected Friday check-ins on the computer, her eyebrows shooting upward when she saw that the largest suite at the John Muir Cottage had been reserved for the next month by the Forrester family. Actually, for the next month and a half.

Forrester?

The name seemed familiar, but she couldn't think why.

Carlie dialed her cousin's number. Tessa was Poppy Gold's manager, and if anyone knew what was going on, she was the one. After all, the John Muir Cottage was special. Poppy Gold reserved it for active service members, as well as veterans and military families who were going through a difficult period.

"Hi," she said when Tessa answered. "I wanted to check with you about the John Muir Cottage. The Yosemite suite has been reserved through January 7. What if you get an urgent referral for someone else?"

"We'll put them in the Gold Strike House or find something else. You know we always keep a certain percentage of space available for emergencies, though nothing the size of the Yosemite suite. It should be okay. Referrals for families are rare at Christmastime."

"But a month and a half? That's longer than normal."

"It's an unusual situation. I, um…" Tessa sounded distracted, probably because of the baby crying in the background. A moment later, she came back on the line. "Sorry, Merri needed some attention. Anyway, Mrs. Forrester was an army major who died in the Middle East. The father wants to get away from home with his twin daughters to help them through the holiday season. Apparently they're still having a rough time dealing with their mother's death."

Forrester?

Carlie's jaw dropped as she realized why the name was familiar. The year before it had been on magazine covers, scandal rags, newspapers…*everywhere*. There weren't too many wealthy men whose wives had died wearing army fatigues and the media had covered the story for weeks. She'd felt terrible for them. Grief should be a private thing.

"Uh…oh, I see," Carlie said. "Are they staying under the usual terms?"

Poppy Gold's policy was to offer military families seven days of rest and relaxation at no charge, and a substantially reduced rate for longer visits, but Luke Forrester could probably *buy* Poppy Gold with his pocket change. She remembered the articles about him saying he had the Midas touch for everything from real estate to investing to manufacturing. Basically, he ran a huge conglomerate of different companies.

"It was a regular referral from General Pierson's office, so it wouldn't seem right to treat them differently from anyone else who's stayed there."

"Right. Thanks."

Carlie hung up. Her staff had left on various tasks, giving her a quiet moment to think. Celebrities often visited Poppy Gold, so she couldn't be sure the air of anticipation she'd noticed was because of Luke Forrester's imminent arrival. It seemed possible, though. He was a different *kind* of celebrity and female employees were bound to see him as a romantically tragic figure, particularly the unmarried ones.

She shook her head and went to the storeroom to finish checking the contents of the shipment received on Wednesday. This year, she'd suggested they give a uniquely designed Poppy Gold Christmas ornament to the guests and volunteers for kickoff day. But the ornaments had arrived late and she and her staff were still checking for quality and putting them back into their gift boxes.

Two hours later, she got up and stretched. She wasn't done, but she wanted to attend a noon luncheon at the concert hall catered by Sarah's Sweet Treats. Sarah was one of her cousins and a fabulous cook and baker.

It was a fun event, featuring dishes made with "leftover" turkey. Of course, they weren't actually *leftovers* because the catering staff had been baking turkey all night, but the guests wouldn't care. They could enjoy "leftover" Thanksgiving dishes, but also curried turkey salad, turkey croquettes, turkey sandwiches...along with a huge number of other inventive offerings.

Creative Turkey Bites had started nine years ago when Tessa's mother decided a few of their stay-over guests might miss leftovers. Because of that, Poppy Gold had begun serving a second turkey meal on the Friday *after* Thanksgiving. The tickets were expensive, but worth twice the price in Carlie's opinion.

"Carlie, Bill Blalock just phoned," Tim Mahoney called out from his cubicle. "Your presence is requested in Guest Reception."

Because her office was located in Old City Hall,

she was sometimes asked to help out with public relations issues. On the few occasions when her presence was "requested," it meant they had a difficult guest. She headed to the reception area, only to stop and blink when she saw Luke Forrester standing near the curved mahogany reception counter.

His pictures hadn't done him justice. He was the most gorgeous man she'd ever seen—and the most grumpy-looking one, too. Two little girls stood nearby. Both seemed solemn and anxious and one had tearstains on her face. Plainly they weren't experiencing any warm, after-Thanksgiving glow.

Carlie stepped forward. "Hello, I'm Carlie Benton. May I help you?"

"Yes. We've been up since two this morning and now I've been informed we can't get into our accommodations for several hours," Luke Forrester snapped, ignoring her extended hand.

"I see."

So much for romantically tragic; he was more like the Grinch who'd stolen Christmas. Carlie cast a look at the clock. It was shortly before noon and check-in started at 4:00 p.m. unless prior arrangements had been made. Both the website and any employee Mr. Forrester talked to would have made that clear.

Carlie walked around to a registration monitor

and confirmed they had a standard reservation, with no special requests.

"I'm sorry, but your rooms aren't ready yet." She smiled at the two girls, who had to be identical twins—they were as alike as two peas in a pod. "In the meantime, would you like to have a yummy lunch?"

The one whose cheeks were tearstained ducked her head while the other offered a tiny smile in return. "Yes, thank you. I'm Beth," she said. "And this is my sister, Annie."

She nudged Annie, who wiggled her fingers in a small wave.

"It's great to meet you both. I'm Carlie."

"Excuse me, you haven't explained why you weren't ready for us when we arrived," Luke Forrester interjected impatiently.

Carlie fixed him with the steady gaze she'd cultivated dealing with newspaper reporters at her old public relations job. It was never easy for her to stay calm, though. She had a terrible temper.

"Mr. Forrester, I'm very sorry, but check-in time is 4:00 p.m. We had visitors at the John Muir Cottage last night. They left on schedule and our housekeeping staff is working to get everything ready for you. In the meantime, there's a special luncheon being served down the street. You and your daughters are welcome to eat as our guests while you're waiting."

A muscle ticked in his jaw and she expected further demands, but he finally said, "Fine," in a sharp tone.

Carlie glanced at Bill Blalock. He was excellent with people, so it was unusual for him not to be able to handle a difficult client. Of course, no matter how skilled he was, a few guests always insisted on speaking to someone with more authority. In most cases, she'd discovered they'd caused their own problem and didn't want to take responsibility.

"Bill, please call me when Mr. Forrester's accommodations are ready," she asked, giving him a significant look that suggested putting a rush on the cleaning crew.

Poppy Gold Inns allowed guests into their rooms early when feasible, but first they had to be properly prepared and approved by a housekeeping supervisor. While Carlie didn't believe that bad manners and arbitrary expectations should be rewarded, the Forrester family was obviously under a great deal of strain. Quickly getting them into their suite would be best all around.

"I'll take care of it," Bill promised. "Don't be concerned about your luggage, Mr. Forrester. We'll secure your bags here and deliver them later."

LUKE NODDED CURTLY.

He still questioned whether this trip to California was the best idea for the girls, and being told the house wasn't available hadn't helped. A part of him knew it was unreasonable to be upset, but nothing was going well.

Flying at night was his preference since it saved time, but the jet's copilot had been rear-ended while driving to the airport. Though she'd escaped injury, Luke had insisted she take a few days off. Not wanting to wait for a replacement, he'd taken the copilot's seat himself rather than working during the flight as planned. He held a pilot's license for emergencies, though this had mostly qualified as an inconvenience.

His sister was still in Austin; she was being treated for an ear infection and couldn't fly until the doctor said it was okay. Luke had hired a backup copilot and sent the jet back to Texas so Nicole could come once she was well enough for travel.

The limousine service had been late meeting them at the airport and the drive to Glimmer Creek on the small curving roads had upset Annie's stomach. She'd cried and gotten sick, only to push him away when he tried to help.

On top of everything else, the private tutor he'd hired had canceled just hours before their departure, so now he'd have to get someone local.

A polite throat-clearing sound drew his attention. "This way, Mr. Forrester," said Carlie Benton.

She was holding Beth's hand, and though her expression was pleasant, Luke suspected she wasn't impressed with him. That was okay. He hadn't gotten where he was without making a few enemies.

"Do either of you skate?" Carlie asked the girls as they walked down the front steps. "Ice skating, I mean."

"Yes, but not like Aunt Nicole," Beth told her. "She's awfully good. She can spin and twirl and *everything*."

"Aunt Nicole was s'posed to come with us in Papa's jet, but her ear got sick," Annie half whispered, making Luke's eyes widen. Annie was shier than her sister and rarely spoke to strangers.

"That's too bad. Is she coming later?"

"Uh-huh."

"I'm glad. We have a skating rink starting tomorrow after the water freezes, so you'll have a chance to skate if your papa doesn't mind." Carlie stopped and pointed across the street to the park. "It's going to be right over there, past that little white bandstand. And you know what else we're having this year? A sledding hill. That is, we'll have one when the temperature is cold enough to make snow."

"Yippee," cried Beth.

Carlie grinned at both girls and continued walking. Down the street was an attractive building with a historic marker on the front lawn saying Glimmer Creek Concert Hall. It reminded Luke of the concert hall at the historic Stanley Hotel in Estes Park, Colorado.

Where he'd stayed with Erika on their honeymoon.

Hell, how long would everything remind him of what he'd lost?

Frustrated, Luke directed his thoughts elsewhere as they climbed the steps. On the pillared veranda, he read a freestanding sign next to the door. "Creative Turkey Bites?" he asked wryly. "So your 'special' luncheon is recycled Thanksgiving leftovers."

"We don't serve leftovers at Poppy Gold," Carlie said, her blue eyes glittering coolly. "The meal showcases the ways leftover turkey *could* be made into something new and different. In addition, traditional Thanksgiving dishes are provided for people who still want them. But everything is freshly prepared."

Inside, there was a buzz of conversation and Carlie was greeted by one guest after another. She introduced Beth and Annie by their first names only, for which Luke was grateful. While it was entirely possible nobody would recognize their names, he preferred to avoid awkward moments. Privacy was important, particularly for his daughters.

A barbershop quartet in red-and-white-striped jackets was entertaining in the front of the hall, their mellow tones resonating around the room. While pleasant, the decorations were still autumnal in theme and Luke worried the girls would be disappointed. He'd told them that spending the holidays in California would be like going to a Christmas wonderland. When would he learn not to promise something he couldn't control?

"Good afternoon, Sarah," Carlie said to a slender blonde woman wearing a chef's apron. "This is Luke and his two daughters, Annie and Beth. They're Poppy Gold's guests today for lunch."

Sarah beamed. "Welcome. Just get in line and tell the servers what you want to try."

"Thanks." Carlie crouched so she was level with Annie. "Would you like to wash your face before you eat?" she asked gently.

"Okay." Annie put her fingers in Carlie's outstretched hand.

"Is that all right?" Carlie queried, looking up at him. "I can take her through the food line when we get back. Just let me know if she has any allergies."

"It's fine. Neither of the girls have allergies."

Yet Luke was perturbed as he watched his daughter leave with her. Damn it, he was Annie's father, but she'd refused to let him help her, either in the limousine or after they'd arrived.

Sometimes he questioned whether Beth and Annie blamed him for their mother not being there. Sometimes he even wondered that himself.

If he hadn't been so open-minded about Erika staying in the service, she might still be alive.

Open-minded?

He snorted at the thought. Hardly. More than anything he'd wanted to keep Erika at home. Even the *media* had known he wasn't open-minded. What was the headline that had become so popular...the Beauty and the Autocrat?

It hadn't been fair to his wife. While beautiful, she'd also been a brilliant, decisive army officer. Luke didn't see himself as autocratic, either—he just tried to make sure the people he cared about were safe and didn't lack for anything. There was nothing wrong with that. Nonetheless, he'd wanted to be supportive of Erika's career choice.

The irony was that his wife had raised the question of resigning her commission after the girls were born. He'd tried not to influence her, so now he would always wonder what might have happened if he'd followed his instincts and asked her to stay home.

"Is that better?" Carlie asked Annie, drying her cheeks with a towel.

The youngster heaved a sigh. "I guess. But my eyes are scratchy."

"You'll probably forget about it when you eat."

They were in the lounge area of the restroom

and Annie patted the cushion she was sitting on. "This couch is funny."

"It's called a fainting couch. They used to be popular back in the 1800s, which is when the concert hall was built. What do you know about Poppy Gold? That's the name of this place."

Annie shrugged. "Papa told Aunt Nicole that it's a tourist town."

Carlie knew she was biased, but Poppy Gold was a whole lot more than just a tourist town. "It's a Victorian village, Annie, which means it was built long ago when Queen Victoria ruled England. People visit here and stay in our homes and hotels. We have lots of fun things to do and I think you came at the best time of all. Christmas is my favorite time of year."

"I used to like it, too. But, um, I'm not sure anymore."

"Maybe we can make it your favorite again. Will you give Poppy Gold a chance?"

Annie chewed her lip for a long minute. "I'll try."

Sadness went through Carlie. The child couldn't be more than six, yet her eyes were much older.

Out in the main hall, Carlie took her through the food line, letting her carry her plate to the table where Beth and her father were sitting.

Luke murmured a "Thank you," along with his daughter.

"You're welcome to eat all you like," Carlie said, winking at Beth and giving Annie a smile meant just for her.

Over at the serving table, she got back in line.

"Lots of turkey curry salad," she told the server, someone on Sarah's staff she didn't know well.

"It's my favorite, too." The woman put three large scoops onto the plate and sprinkled them with roasted cashews. "What else can I get you?"

"One of the turkey-and-cranberry-cream-cheese sandwiches. And some green salad so I can pretend I'm eating healthy again."

"You got it."

Plate filled, Carlie joined her aunt Polly at a table along the wall.

Aunt Polly clucked at her. "I was trying to ignore that curry salad. Your hips can stand it—mine can't."

"Sorry." Carlie ate a forkful. "Would it help if I said it was terrible?"

"Nope, because I'd know you were lying."

It *was* a lie. The food that Sarah and her catering staff prepared was always fabulous.

Carlie periodically looked over at the Forrester family, noticing that Annie and Beth were talking to each other, but Luke didn't seem to be talking to anyone. He was eating, though, and drinking large amounts of the specially blended Poppy Gold coffee.

Carlie's tension grew as the meal progressed. Being six-year-olds, Annie and Beth were slow eaters, but they would finish eventually. If they weren't in their suite soon, she'd have to go to plan B to keep them busy. Fortunately, her phone rang as she was swallowing a last bite of custard-rhubarb pie. It was Bill Blalock saying the Yosemite suite was ready for the Forresters.

"Thanks, Bill. Great timing—they just finished."

"Their luggage is already in the cottage and Christine will personally escort them in a guest shuttle. She's outside the concert hall as we speak."

"Terrific. I'll let them know."

She got up and crossed the hall to where the Forresters were sitting. "Hi. I just got the call that your rooms are ready. A shuttle is waiting outside to take you there."

Luke Forrester nodded. He wore a slightly mellower expression, possibly aided by food and coffee.

Time would tell what kind of guest he'd be. But at least he *did* have two adorable daughters.

CHAPTER TWO

"YOU'RE IN THE Yosemite suite," Christine Saunders explained as she stopped the electric shuttle in front of a Victorian. "The door opens off the garden on the south side. Breakfast will be delivered by our caterer, Sarah's Sweet Treats, and Housekeeping will come each morning to clean. Is anytime after eight too early, or would you prefer later?"

Luke stared at the young woman who'd driven them from the concert hall. "Are you saying we don't have the entire house?"

"Er, no, Mr. Forrester. The John Muir Cottage is divided into several different suites, but the Yosemite is the largest and has private access. Please be assured, the walls are well insulated, so it should be very quiet."

His temper began to rise again. It had been on a short fuse for the past year, and when he was particularly tired, it was even worse.

"It was my understanding I'd rented the entire house."

Confusion flitted across her face. "Did someone at Poppy Gold tell you that?"

"I didn't speak to anyone here. My executive assistant made the arrangements. She said—"

Luke stopped abruptly and gritted his teeth. Actually, all Tilly had said was that they were staying at the John Muir Cottage. Which, despite being called a cottage, was actually a large, rambling Victorian. He'd simply assumed they'd have the entire house and all the amenities he was accustomed to having when he traveled.

Damn it, Tilly knew the locations where he took the girls always had a full staff, from housekeepers to nannies. She'd mentioned they'd have to eat out for lunch and dinner, but that was all.

"Mr. Forrester, I assure you the Yosemite suite is quite spacious," Christine explained earnestly. "There are three bedrooms upstairs, and downstairs you have a smaller bedroom, a family room, front living room, powder room, kitchen and laundry. Each bedroom also has a private bath."

The comment Luke had made to Tilly about modern plumbing flitted through his mind. It hadn't occurred to him that some of the bedrooms might *not* have a private bath.

"Very well," he said tensely. There was little else he could do. It was unlikely that other suitable accommodations were available in the small town and returning to Austin would just upset the girls even more. "After eight is fine for Housekeeping, but I'd prefer breakfast earlier."

"Is the seven to eight time slot all right?"

"Yes." Luke lifted his daughters out of the shuttle.

"Would you like me to show you around the suite?" Christine asked.

"Thanks, but we'll be fine."

"I hope you enjoy your stay. Please let us know if there's anything you need." She drove away before he could get his wallet out for a tip.

"Let's go see our home for the next few weeks," he said to Beth and Annie.

They looked at him doubtfully. Perhaps he should have brought their nanny, but he'd agreed with Tilly that if the trip was going to do any good, a complete break was best. He just hadn't expected Nicole to get sick and the tutor to drop out at the eleventh hour.

He'd manage, though. His sister would be here in a few days, and however small the town of Glimmer Creek appeared to be, surely they had qualified tutors available.

The garden around the John Muir Cottage was trimmed and mulched for winter, but it was still attractive. A covered porch overlooked the garden and rolling hills beyond, and it was furnished with white wicker outdoor furniture.

The real disappointment started inside.

While the rooms had a pleasant Victorian flavor, there were no Christmas decorations in sight.

Granted, it was just the day after Thanksgiving, but he'd expected more. A thorough check of the premises also revealed there wasn't a single piece of office equipment, though he could have sworn that Tilly had mentioned a full business center.

Beth and Annie had slept on the plane, but they seemed half-asleep now—maybe the turkey lunch was making them groggy—so he hunted through the luggage for their favorite stuffed animals and they curled into bed for a nap. Down in the kitchen, he dialed Tilly's cell number. A chirpy voice-mail recording greeted him. Knowing Tilly Robinson and her determined attempts to manage his life, she probably planned to duck his calls for a few days until he cooled down.

"Tilly, it's me," he said after the beep. "I refuse to believe you didn't know this is a suite, not the whole house, *or* that there's no personal staff. Right now, it's just me and the girls. The tutor didn't come and Nicole couldn't fly with us because she has an ear infection. She won't be here for another few days. Get back to me."

Muttering beneath his breath, he called the front desk.

"Yes, Mr. Forrester?" Based on the British accent, it was most likely the employee who'd first greeted them.

"I'd like to speak with Carlie Benton."

"Certainly, but is there anything I can do?"

"I prefer dealing with Ms. Benton." Luke wasn't certain why except that she appeared to be the kind of person who could get things done. Besides, Beth and Annie had responded to her…a lot more than they'd responded to *him* the past year.

"Yes, sir." A moment later, the same voice came back on the line. "I'm sorry—Carlie is away from her desk. But I've called her mobile and she'll stop at your suite in a few minutes."

Luke had frowned the moment he heard "away from her desk," only to realize that a face-to-face discussion would be best.

CARLIE COULDN'T BELIEVE she already needed to deal with Luke Forrester again.

Though she was the Poppy Gold activities director, her responsibilities included public relations. The job had its challenging moments, but it was a big improvement over doing PR for a company with frequent product safety recalls. It was one of the reasons she'd resigned…along with not wanting to see her ex-fiancé every day. Especially after he'd gotten engaged to the owner's daughter.

July the previous year had *not* been a good month. First her wedding had been canceled at the last minute in the most embarrassing way, and ten days later her father was critically injured.

A friendly voice hailed her as she approached the John Muir Cottage. "Hi, Carlie."

It was Esther Perkins, one of their repeat guests. Esther lived in San Jose and stayed at Poppy Gold several times a year, but Christmas kickoff day seemed to be her favorite.

"What's up, Esther?"

"I just want to be sure that I can decorate at the Victorian Cat tomorrow. I like it best."

"Of course you can." Guests weren't employees; they could volunteer for anything they wanted to do.

"Do you think Moby Dick will let me put a red bow around his neck?" Esther asked. "It would look darling against his fur."

Poppy Gold tried to make something unique about each of the houses, and at the Victorian Cat mansion, each room was populated by an amiable feline. Moby Dick was a fluffy white cat with a talent for manipulating guests into giving him extra treats.

Carlie chuckled. "Moby is easygoing, but I wouldn't try making him wear a bow. Not to worry, though—Tessa found red and green cat collars from a specialty store and they'll be put on the VC cats tomorrow."

"That's wonderful."

With a wave, Esther hurried away and Carlie continued toward the John Muir Cottage, wishing all their guests were like Esther Perkins.

Bill had offered to give Luke Forrester her cell

number to save her a trip, but Luke was the kind of guy who wouldn't hesitate to phone at 2:00 a.m. to demand a cup of tea. The twenty-four-hour staff in Guest Reception could handle those kinds of calls and decide whom to contact in case of something more serious. She might do public relations work in addition to being the activities director, but she wasn't a frontline manager, thank goodness.

Trying to appear friendly rather than frustrated, Carlie knocked at the Yosemite suite.

The door opened almost immediately.

"Hello, Mr. Forrester. I understand you asked for me."

He cocked his head as if listening for something and then stepped onto the porch. "Yes, I have several concerns. For one, where are the decorations? I promised my daughters this would be a holiday extravaganza. Even though this is just the day after Thanksgiving, I expected to see a few signs of Christmas."

Carlie could see his concern and knew it wouldn't help to point out that the website listed the date when Poppy Gold was decorated. At any rate, it was Annie and Beth who mattered and Carlie didn't want them to be disappointed.

"I understand, but tomorrow should reassure the girls. Our guests call it Christmas kickoff day," she told him. "Members of the historical society will be in Victorian costumes and go around caroling in small groups. In addition, we'll have snack kiosks throughout the facility serving coffee, hot spiced cider, cocoa and a selection of cookies and other treats. It's purely voluntary, but guests are invited to help decorate trees, make wreaths, put up decorations and this ye—"

"You have guests do staff work?" Luke's tone was neutral, with only the faintest emphasis on the words *guests* and *staff,* but Carlie spotted a hint of derision in his eyes. Her temper rose, but she managed to squash it down again.

"Not staff work, just fun. Kickoff day is extremely popular. Most of our guests come for Thanksgiving weekend just to participate," she replied evenly.

The event was expensive for Poppy Gold since they needed an army of employees to keep an eye on things, do the heavy work, watch the treat kiosks and do the primary decorating. Getting everything done in one day would be impossible without the massive amounts of planning and prep work she and the other Poppy Gold employees did for weeks beforehand.

"I'm sure it's entertaining if you enjoy that sort of thing." Luke's expression suggested only a moron would enjoy "that sort of thing."

Her smile became even more strained. She loved Christmas…the colors, music, the warmth, the decorating and the way many people seemed to behave nicer in the holiday season. Though in Luke Forrester's case, she'd hate to think this was his "nice."

"As I mentioned, Mr. Forrester, participation is voluntary. If you aren't interested in decorating, my staff has planned a number of activities, as well. As for your suite, it will be dec—"

"Not by nosy guests, I presume," he said, cutting her off a second time. "I expect privacy. As a matter of fact, I expected to have the entire house, not just a section of it."

Muscles tightening, Carlie reminded herself again that Luke Forrester had lost his wife and no matter how wealthy and demanding, he was dealing with something traumatic.

She drew a deep breath. "Employees decorate inside the suites. As for having the entire house, I'm sorry for the misunderstanding," she apologized as cordially as possible. "But there are eleven bedrooms in the John Muir Cottage and dividing the space means it's available to multiple individuals or families."

"I see."

"Before I forget, I wanted to tell you that since we're supposed to have a hard freeze tonight, we're starting the snowmakers on the sledding hill as soon as the temperature drops low enough. Probably around eight. Spiced cider and other goodies will be served. I thought Annie and Beth might enjoy it."

"I don't think so. We've had a long day."

"Please, Papa, can we go?" asked a voice from the open door behind them.

Luke jerked around. "Beth, I thought you were asleep."

"I woke up. Carlie, can you take us to see the snow if Papa is too tired?"

Carlie made an effort to keep her face straight. "That's up to your papa." She'd hoped to be sliding into a warm bath by then, but couldn't resist the entreaty in Beth's eyes.

"I wanna go with Carlie," Annie declared, peeking around her sister.

Luke seemed thoroughly harassed. "Very well. That is, we'll all go. Now go back to bed. You'll need extra rest if you're going to be out late."

The twins instantly hurried away and Carlie tried to look innocent as he turned to her. "Shall I come by around seven thirty this evening?"

"No, we'll meet you there."

"Fine. Is there anything else?"

"Yes. I need a tutor for the girls. The one I hired in Austin quit at the last minute."

I wonder why, Carlie thought wryly.

"I also need a business center installed," he continued. "Desk, a computer with dual monitors, a minimum of two additional phone lines, printer-fax machine and satellite communications. The downstairs bedroom can be used since it won't be needed for a live-in tutor. I'll be managing my business concerns remotely for the next six weeks, and contrary to what your website claims, there aren't any business services in the suite."

She stared. Had he honestly believed those kinds of facilities were installed in every building at Poppy Gold?

"There's a courtesy business center available at Old City Hall," Carlie told him firmly. "That's what the website states. At this time of year we don't book any business conferences, so except for a few guests checking their email, it's empty most of the time."

"I need one here in the suite."

Carlie suspected her patience was going to be tested to the absolute limit by this guy.

"Mr. Forrester, the John Muir Cottage isn't wired for that kind of technology. However, Poppy Gold has Wi-Fi and we can provide a multifunction printer for your visit, along with a computer since you apparently didn't bring your own laptop. The existing phone line can be used to send and receive faxes."

His features tightened. "I *do* have a laptop with me, but I keep it off-line when I'm outside my company's firewall. I take it there isn't a business supply store in Glimmer Creek where a new computer could be purchased."

"No."

"In that case, I'll take the loaner until my assistant can arrange for the proper equipment to be sent."

She nodded. "All right. As for a tutor, the school district has a list of people who do that sort of work. I'll send a copy over and you can call them for interviews."

"I—"

"Have a good rest of the day," Carlie interrupted brightly. "I'm going back to my office now to get things started. If you get hungry, there are several restaurants that deliver. Just consult the information folder in the kitchen. We put a facility map in there, so you shouldn't have a problem finding the sledding hill later. See you then."

Carlie hurried away before she lost her cool and gave him a piece of her mind. Honestly, he wanted a full office in his suite? According to what Tessa had said, Luke Forrester was at Poppy Gold to help his daughters through Christmas, but how was he going to do that if it was business as usual for him?

LUKE CLOSED THE door and groaned. The coffee he'd drunk had carried him for an extra hour, but that was all.

At home he'd be working, no matter how little sleep he'd gotten the night before. Except for the rare times Erika had been on leave, he used the day after Thanksgiving to read reports and make calls to overseas associates who didn't celebrate the US holiday.

As for Beth and Annie, they would have gone to the Austin zoo or aquarium with his parents. Curiously, becoming grandparents had changed Craig and Heather Forrester. A little at least. They were still irresponsible in many ways, but they tried to spend time with their granddaughters every couple of months.

He appreciated it. When he was growing up, they'd acted more like reckless playmates than dependable adults. Money was no longer a problem for them, either, since he'd quietly tripled the size of their trust funds and arranged for the trustees to disburse the payments monthly, rather than annually.

Inexplicably, his thoughts drifted to Carlie Benton. Perhaps if he hadn't been so tired and distracted he might have handled their contacts with more grace. He certainly should have realized they wouldn't have a business center in every suite at Poppy Gold Inns, but he'd grown accustomed to the kind of services provided by Caribbean villas and French châteaus.

Tilly often claimed he'd been spoiled by success and needed a dose of reality… Maybe this was her way of giving it to him.

Luke got up and found the informational folder

Carlie had mentioned, flipping through it to acquaint himself with Poppy Gold's amenities and those of the local community. Then he saw a reminder of the check-in and checkout times and sighed.

Apparently he'd made an ass of himself in more ways than one.

NICOLE FORRESTER PUT a warm compress against her infected ear and wondered how Luke and her nieces were getting settled in California. The pictures she'd seen on the internet of the Victorian community looked wonderful.

She'd always wanted to explore the Gold Country; stories of the 1849 Gold Rush had fascinated her as a child. Well, a lot of things fascinated her. She'd just never found a vocation that compelled her. Instead, she worked for her brother as a computer programmer. Luke paid his employees well and provided excellent benefits, but she hadn't earned the job on her own merits. He also did ridiculously generous things like buying a new car every year for her birthday and paying off her condo, no matter how much she protested.

Her protective big brother. She adored him, though ever since Erika's death, he'd been different.

Everything had been different.

Depressed, Nicole stuffed another pillow behind her neck. Sometimes it seemed as if she hadn't achieved a single thing with her life. Certainly nothing like Luke, who'd made his first billion by the time he was twenty-seven. Everything he touched turned to gold. Soon afterward he'd gotten married and a few years later the twins were born. He seemed able to do anything, whether it was achieving wild success in real estate, playing the stock market or building a massive conglomerate company with dozens of subsidiaries.

Or finding someone who genuinely loved him.

Bored and vaguely discouraged, Nicole turned on the television and flipped through the cable channels. Finally she got up and put a DVD into the player. She hadn't watched *Forbidden Planet* in a while and it would be a distraction. Normally she wasn't so moody, but getting sick and being unable to travel with Luke and her nieces was lousy timing.

She was worried about Luke and just as worried about Beth and Annie. Annie was shy and introverted, while Beth plowed ahead, often thoughtlessly. They were young, but patterns were established early.

Nicole shuddered as she recalled a kid she'd met in childhood. The Forresters had been out of money as usual, so they'd invited themselves to stay with wealthy friends in South Carolina. Kira was the Lexingtons' only child and had demanded her own way in everything. She was still like that…which might explain her four divorces.

The opening segment of the film began playing and Nicole relaxed. Some of the special effects were poor, but she loved old science fiction movies and *Forbidden Planet* was one of her favorites. It was great seeing Walter Pidgeon and Leslie Nielsen on the screen together—one older, one younger, and both equally delicious.

Yet in a way, seeing the character played by Anne Francis was discouraging. The woman was fearless, even if she wasn't always likable. Nicole wished she could be more like that…strong, bold and unafraid. Instead, she tried to be invisible most of the time.

She pulled a lap robe over her legs. It was still just midafternoon and she ought to be doing something productive, but she wanted to recover and get out to California as soon as possible. Anyway, she was already packed and ready to go. She just needed the swelling in her ear to go down so it would be safe to fly.

CARLIE DROPPED BY the maintenance yard to see the loads of fresh evergreen that had been delivered that morning. The crew was sorting the branches, cutting them into usable sections and loading everything into containers for delivery to the various decorating work sites.

Lord, it really *would* be easier if Poppy Gold didn't invite guests to help decorate. That way the evergreen swags and wreaths could be made ahead of time and be ready to go up first thing in the morning. Of course, it wouldn't be as much fun, either.

Carlie inhaled the thick scent of pine and cedar. She loved Christmas and had always tried to be there for kickoff day. Her ex-fiancé's indifference to her favorite time of year should have been her first clue that he was the wrong guy for her.

"What are you doing here?" asked Uncle Liam. He smiled at her, almost the way he used to smile before Aunt Meredith had died. They'd shared a wonderful marriage and had created Poppy Gold together. "Don't you have enough to keep you busy?"

"I'm just stressed and wanted a sniff—nothing says Christmas like fresh-cut evergreen boughs."

He gave her a hug. "Anything I can do to help?"

"I'm okay, just feeling sorry for myself. It's an unattractive habit I'm trying to break."

Uncle Liam was less depressed now, but the family tried to keep things upbeat around him. He left managing Poppy Gold to Tessa, though he still looked after the maintenance department, while Tessa's husband had taken over the security division.

Thinking about it reminded Carlie that she ought

to give her cousin a heads-up about Luke Forrester. As the Poppy Gold owner-manager, she needed to know what was going on. So instead of going straight back to Old City Hall, Carlie stopped at Tessa's office in the train depot and found her cuddling little Meredith.

Carlie's throat ached. She was thirty-one, only a year younger than Tessa, and had hoped to be a mother herself by now. And she *might* be if Derek had been the man she'd thought.

Instead, the morning they were supposed to get married he'd told her it was a mistake. Yeah, a mistake...he'd asked another woman to marry him. Incredibly, he seemed to think it *wasn't* cheating since he'd decided to call off the wedding before sleeping with someone else. Or at least that was what he'd claimed.

She wasn't convinced. In the cold light of reason, Carlie suspected he'd seen an opportunity to marry into money and had taken it.

So instead of being a wife and mother, she was an honorary aunt to the younger members of the family. She'd have to be content with that for now, because she wasn't ready to let her heart get shredded again.

Tessa looked up. "Hey, you look frustrated."

Carlie determinedly pushed Derek out of her mind. He hadn't been a part of her life for more than a year and didn't warrant the kind of energy she was spending on him. Perhaps it was on her mind, seeing how happy Tessa was with her husband. Gabe McKinley seemed to be Tessa's opposite in every respect, but the way he looked at her and his new daughter…

"Carlie?" Tessa prompted.

"Sorry, my brain was somewhere else. I just wanted to give you a heads-up. Luke Forrester isn't particularly happy. Apparently he believed his family would have the entire John Muir Cottage. He also wants a full office installed in the Yosemite suite, including satellite communications."

Tessa blinked. "He couldn't have been serious."

"*Noooo*, he was quite serious. He plans to run his conglomerate from Poppy Gold while staying here. Anyway, I told him about the facilities we *do* have and that he's welcome to use loaner equipment."

"We don't expect anybody to take abuse from a guest," Tessa said quietly. "No matter what their circumstances."

Carlie shook her head. "He's just demanding and his daughters almost make up for him being difficult. They're adorable. I just wanted you to know since there's a good chance he won't be satisfied, whatever we do."

"Don't lose any sleep over it. Maybe Poppy Gold will work its magic on him."

"I hope the magic works fast."

They chatted for another few minutes before Carlie got up and said goodbye.

On the walk to her office, she called her parents, who expected her for dinner with her two brothers, home visiting from college over the Thanksgiving break. Between everything she had left to do and attending the snowmaking event with the Forresters later, she wouldn't be able to eat with them.

"I'll send Quinn or Russ over with something for you to eat," Mom offered instantly. When Leah Benton couldn't do anything to fix a problem, she fed people.

"No need. I have stuff in the office fridge and ate too much at lunch, anyhow. How is Dad? I wish he hadn't worked today."

"You know...the usual."

Yeah, Carlie knew.

Her father pretended everything was fine, but standing for so many hours as a traffic flagger made his chronic pain that much worse. He didn't *have* to work—the settlement from the accident was enough to cover lost wages—but Mike Benton refused to take things easy. To his way of thinking, men worked to support their families. They didn't live on insurance settlements.

"Okay, Mom. I'll talk to you tomorrow."

Carlie got off and hurried up the Old City Hall's front steps. Inside to the left was a broad, curving staircase that rose to an open, semicircular gallery in front of the ballroom. On the right, there was a pair of elaborate double doors set with an intricate pattern of sparkling beveled glass. They were a striking entryway into the guest reception area and original to the building, which made them even better. She waved at Bill and Christine through the clear oval center and headed through the rotunda.

Quickly she packed a spare computer from the storeroom into a box, along with a multifunction printer. Then she printed out the list of local tutors. Next to Luisa Cabrera's name she wrote that Luisa had taught first grade for thirty-five years.

"Tim, would you take this to the Yosemite suite for me?" she asked, putting the list into an envelope.

"No problem."

She sealed the envelope and then accessed her voice mail. There was only one message. It was from Luke Forrester and what he said practically knocked her to the floor.

"Ms. Benton, it's Luke Forrester calling. I failed to thank you for our lunch today. It was a nice gesture. I've read through the informational packet you mentioned and see that Poppy Gold Inns' standard check-in time is 4:00 p.m. So, um, it was good to get into our accommodations early. Have a good afternoon and we'll see you tonight."

Carlie blinked. All things considered, it was practically an apology.

THE TEMPERATURE DROPPED rapidly once the sun had gone down and Carlie shivered as she hurried across Poppy Gold to meet the Forresters at the sledding hill. Turning down the twins' requests had been impossible, but she hadn't expected to stay this late and had just worn a lightweight coat to work.

The sledding hill was in the more open section of Poppy Gold where a number of gold miners' cabins and other relics of the 1849 Gold Rush were preserved.

As the story went, a few of the miners had dug their heels in when the "townsfolk" wanted to buy them out and build fine homes on the rolling land above the creek. They'd hung on, forcing the town to build north of them on a flatter section. Most had been abandoned by the time James Connor bought the historic district of Glimmer Creek, but they'd been restored now. A few were even available for people who wanted to try sleeping in a primitive gold miner's shanty.

A number of guests had already gathered at the base of the hill, breath fogging as they sipped from paper cups. Cheerful greetings back and forth showed their spirits weren't dampened by the chilly air. Stacks of hay bales lined the gentle slope, creating a wide channel down to the flatter area below. Spotlights illuminated the scene, along with Christmas lights on the bare branches of the surrounding trees.

Carlie checked to see if the Forresters had arrived before getting decaf coffee for herself, grateful to wrap her fingers around the warm cup. If Luke and the twins didn't arrive soon, they might miss the first sprays of snow from the machines. Not that it was actually *snow* when it came out, but the water droplets froze almost instantly in the frigid air.

Hurry up, she urged mentally.

A couple of minutes later she spotted them coming up the lighted path.

"We're just about to start," she called.

The girls eagerly got cider and cookies and stood at the base of the slope with the other guests. They were just in time. Uncle Liam stood at the top with two large handbells. He raised his arms theatrically and shook them.

The snowmakers chugged into life, starting at the top of the hill and moving down, spewing white plumes across the grass. The onlookers cheered and someone began singing "Let It Snow." The others joined in and it was soon followed by "Jingle Bells" and other festive songs.

There were sixteen snowmakers altogether and they could put out a huge amount of "snow" by morning. In the meantime, the holiday lights sparkled brilliantly against the plumes of white.

Despite her awareness of Luke Forrester's brooding presence, Carlie smiled.

She really loved Christmas.

CHAPTER THREE

CARLIE GOT TO Poppy Gold early before six the next morning and went over her to-do list one more time. Her division wasn't in charge of decorating—they coordinated guest activities—but she still *felt* responsible for anything that would add to or detract from a visitor's experience.

She went upstairs to the ballroom where volunteers and employees had gathered. A cheerful babble of people talking greeted her, along with the scent of coffee and breakfast foods.

Uncle Liam and Tessa were talking to the supervisors assigned to the teams of decorators. Tessa's husband was also there. He managed security operations for Poppy Gold and was speaking to his staff, who would keep a careful eye on the buildings as they were decorated. Gabe was a former navy SEAL, so he was fierce about security. Poppy Gold had always felt safe, but with Gabe McKinley on the job, it was probably more secure than Fort Knox.

Carlie collected a cup of coffee and a bagel and gathered her own team for a chat. They'd already been over the day's plans, so she mostly wanted to be sure they didn't have any questions. It was her second Christmas as the activities director, but she was still filled with nervous anticipation.

Everything had been staged for kickoff day the night before, including putting out the kiosks to be used for treats and setting up the locations where the wreaths and evergreen swags would be made. The equipment and supplies to create and decorate the skating rink had also been moved into position.

"Okay, everybody," Tessa called twenty minutes later, clapping her hands. "It's nearly seven o'clock and some of our guests get out early. Let's go."

Employees and volunteers began streaming through the various doors. Poppy Gold tried to have everyone in position by the time the first guests had finished breakfast, but they never succeeded. Excitement trumped the desire to sleep. Some didn't even wait to eat breakfast, but that was all right—the treat kiosks would be stocked within the hour.

Work would also begin on filling the skating rink; it might have been better to set it up the previous evening and let the chilly weather help with the freezing process, but this way visitors could watch. As for the snowmakers on the sledding hill, they'd run all night and would keep going until the temperature rose too high.

Snow was probably coming out of their ears by now.

Carlie ate her last bite of bagel and hurried down the main staircase, humming. Yet her festive spirit faltered when she saw Luke Forrester and his daughters in the rotunda. She certainly hoped he was in a better mood this morning.

"Merry Christmas," she called. "I hope you didn't get too cold last night."

"It was *splendid*," Beth declared while Annie smiled shyly and ducked her head.

"This is better," Luke said, glancing around with visible approval. The night registration staff had started decorating after midnight and it *was* lovely.

"Thanks. What can I do for you, Mr. Forrester?"

"Well, I—"

"Papa, why does Carlie have to call you Mr. Forrester?" Beth interrupted.

"Uh, she doesn't." He focused on Carlie. "That is, please call me Luke. I'm afraid I spilled coffee on our list of activities for today. I came to get another copy."

Spilling coffee was such a human thing to do that Carlie grinned. "No problem—we have plenty. Just give me a moment." She went to the reception desk to fetch another list. She returned and held it out. "Here you go. Annie and Beth may also enjoy seeing how much snow has been made since last night. The temperature is still below freezing, so the machines should be operating."

Luke looked down at the cream-colored paper

with holly decorating the edges. He appeared more rested than he had the day before, but whether it would have a positive effect on his mood remained to be seen.

"Just in case, I also got you another copy of the events planned in the next week," Carlie added, giving him a second sheet. "Those are just the activities that have been scheduled. Other things occur spontaneously."

He frowned. "How can the girls join in if we don't know what's happening?"

What part of spontaneous didn't he understand?

"Don't stay in your suite," she replied. "Go sledding. Come out to the events. Then if something happens, you'll have a fair chance of getting involved."

And don't spend all your time working, she told him silently.

After getting home late the night before, she'd researched Luke Forrester on the internet. She'd felt guilty because it had seemed like reading petty gossip, but she'd figured that knowing more might help her deal with the guy. Descriptions like brilliant, decisive and confident had been mixed with less complimentary labels, such as ruthless and arrogant. While she certainly agreed with the arrogant part, he also appeared supremely confident.

Not surprisingly, numerous pictures of his wife had also popped up and she was as beautiful as

Carlie remembered. Society shots showed her in elegant evening gowns and expensive gems, while others were of her in uniform. She'd been stunning, even in military fatigues. Erika Forrester would have intimidated most women, no matter how sound their egos might be...and Carlie's ego wasn't particularly sturdy after the way Derek had treated her.

She glanced at Annie and Beth. In her brief acquaintance with them, she'd noticed they almost seemed disconnected from their father. There were few of the unspoken signals that usually flowed between parent and child. If she'd seen them somewhere and didn't know the family, she wouldn't have thought they were related.

Was it grief?

Tessa and Uncle Liam had grown even closer when Aunt Meredith died, but Tessa had been an adult. The girls being twins might change things, too.

Carlie checked the clock on the wall. She needed to be out, circulating through the different areas to be sure how the various activities her staff had planned were going. "Annie, Beth, would you like to start by making paper chains?" she asked encouragingly. "We're giving prizes for different designs."

"Goody," cried Beth, while Annie nodded.

Carlie led the twins outside, assuming Luke

would follow. Poppy Gold was abuzz with activity in the early-morning light. Mother Nature was cooperating when it came to the skating rink and sledding hill. Other than the rain forecast for Monday or Tuesday, the weather was supposed to be dry and unseasonably cold, which was ideal.

"Some of the kids' activities are in the concert hall today," she explained to Luke as they climbed the steps of the hall.

Only after Annie and Beth had begun work did Luke say something. "Paper chains?" he asked with eyebrows raised.

"It's a good holiday craft for young children."

"I guess. I just haven't seen anybody make them since I was a kid."

Carlie cocked her head. "Not even your daughters?"

"No, we have professional decorators. Ordinarily they come on November 30th and do the house inside and out."

A wry comment threatened to break through Carlie's diplomacy, so she pursed her lips and went over to check on Annie.

LUKE FOCUSED ON his daughters as they sorted through containers of colorful paper strips. He appreciated Carlie's restraint in *not* pointing out that he'd expected Poppy Gold to be decked out several days before when his own house would have been decorated.

Christmas music was playing, and despite the early hour, quite a few children were in the room, cheerfully making their chains. Lighted "pine" garland entwined with strings of silver beads and red velvet ribbons had been put up the day before. Each corner of the room had an enormous decorated tree, covered with twinkling lights and ornaments that fit the quaint, historic atmosphere.

He shifted uncomfortably. What had possessed him to come to California? He didn't *do* quaint. He didn't do charming. He didn't do cute. Erika hadn't, either.

Yet Beth and Annie seemed to enjoy that kind of thing, possibly because of their nanny. Dacia was from Kilrush in Ireland and he sometimes thought he caught the lilt of her accent reflected in his daughters' voices. When he'd interviewed her for the position, Dacia had announced she didn't hold with not telling young ones fairy tales, so they should expect her to share the old legends and myths with their girls.

Though Luke had appreciated Dacia's forthright honesty, Erika hadn't been as certain since she didn't want her daughters becoming fanciful. Yet even as infants, Beth and Annie had responded to Dacia far better than the other applicants. In the end, that had counted for more than anything else.

Luke read through the two activities lists. There were carol-singing parties, craft workshops to make Christmas ornaments, holiday scavenger hunts, a nightly parade of lighted historic vehicles and much more.

With any luck, the girls would react well. Otherwise, there wasn't any point to visiting Glimmer Creek in the first place.

His phone rang and he stepped into a quieter spot to answer. "Hey, Nicole. How are you feeling?"

"Much better. The doctor thinks I can fly Monday. What's going on there?"

He glanced around the room. "Quite a few things. They call it Christmas kickoff day, which means the entire historic district is being decorated. They surround it with activities and serve hot drinks and snacks at different locations. Last night they even made a production out of starting the snowmaking machines. There were treats and singing. Very...*traditional*."

"It sounds like fun," Nicole said, sounding wistful.

"The girls seemed to enjoy themselves. At the moment they're making paper chains."

"How are they doing?"

"It's hard to tell—with Annie at least. Right now she might be on the verge of tears," Luke said, worried again. "The activities director is talking to her. By the way, the tutor I hired couldn't come. I have an interview set up with a retired schoolteacher instead."

BACK IN AUSTIN, Nicole pressed a finger to her forehead. She wasn't great with children, but she certainly could have tutored her nieces. Why had Luke invited her to go with him to California if he didn't want her to help out?

"Maybe I could do it," she suggested.

"No, getting someone else will give you time to enjoy yourself. But be prepared. Glimmer Creek is even smaller than I thought. There isn't much shopping or other services."

"I don't have a problem with small towns."

"You've never spent much time in one, either," Luke retorted. "By the way, they're setting up an outdoor skating rink today, so bring your skates."

That was nice to hear about, but Nicole didn't know why she couldn't spend a few hours each day going over Beth and Annie's schoolwork. It might help them get closer. Yet there wasn't any point arguing with Luke once he'd made up his mind. Maybe she should cancel her trip altogether, but if there was the smallest chance she could do something to help her brother or nieces, she wanted to try.

"Okay. Anything else I should pack?" she asked.

"You may need your ski clothes. They're also offering a sledding hill when the weather is cold enough. I've arranged for skates and sleds to be sent by express courier."

"Surely the facility has sleds to go with the hill."

"Probably, but I'm more comfortable choosing ones I know are well constructed. We'll donate them when we leave."

"Beth and Annie might want to keep theirs."

"I can always get new sleds if needed."

Nicole hesitated. "What I *meant* is that they might prefer keeping their sleds for sentimental reasons. I realize you and, uh, that you aren't sentimental yourself, but your daughters might be." She'd almost said "you and Erika," only to catch herself. She never knew whether to talk about her sister-in-law or keep her mouth shut.

While Nicole had been fond of Erika, her sister-in-law hadn't been easy to know, probably because they'd had so little in common. Luke's wife had grown up in a military household, moving whenever her father was reassigned. From earliest childhood, she'd wanted to follow the family tradition of serving in the military. She'd been brilliant, courageous and dynamic. But having a conversation with her had always stymied Nicole.

"I don't see any point in being sentimental," Luke retorted, dragging Nicole's thoughts to the present.

"It isn't a crime."

"Are you trying to start something with me, sister dear?"

Nicole made a face. She wasn't bold or outspoken and it was rare that she "started" something with anybody, even her brother. On the other hand, this was something she felt strongly about. "No, but I have to defend Beth and Annie's right to be themselves. They aren't your clones. They're little girls."

A long silence followed until she heard a heavy exhalation through the receiver. "Is that what you think I've been doing—trying to make my daughters be like me?"

"I don't know, but please don't throw those sleds out before talking to them."

Nicole was actually more worried about Luke trying to make Beth and Annie into clones of Erika. She couldn't be sure that was happening, but she also didn't understand why her nieces were still struggling so desperately with their mother's death. Fourteen months wasn't long, but they were young and Erika had been stationed away from Austin for most of their lives. Sad to say, they couldn't have known her that well.

"If you think it's important, I'll ask before I do anything," Luke said. "I've sent the jet back to Austin, so it's ready for you to fly out. Let the captain know what time you want to take off and he'll notify the limousine service when to meet the plane."

"Maybe I should fly commercial and rent a car."

"Don't be crazy. This is much more convenient."

It *was* convenient, which was part of the problem. Letting her brother smooth the bumps in the road was very easy. Some people didn't realize how generous he could be. Nicole knew all too well… She also figured she *ought* to weather more of those bumps without his help.

"I'll be there soon, at any rate," she murmured. "Give Beth and Annie my love."

"Will do. Glad you're feeling better."

After saying goodbye, Nicole looked around her condominium. While it was attractive, she had to admit there wasn't a whole lot of individuality except for the shelves of old movies in her spare room. There hadn't been any point getting fond of belongings as a kid. Her parents' roving life-style hadn't lent itself to saving stuffed animals and dolls or other childhood mementos.

Nonetheless, she was a closet sentimentalist. She adored lemon drops because they reminded her of summer. Daffodils were also special. Her father had given her a bouquet of sixteen perfectly made sugar daffodil blossoms for her Sweet Sixteen birthday party. They'd been so pretty she couldn't bear to eat them, though it hadn't taken long before they'd crumbled into piles of yellow and green sugar.

Luke hadn't been kidding about his own lack of sentimentality. He loved his family, but Nicole doubted he'd kept private mementos of Erika, such as receipts from restaurants they'd visited or his boutonniere from the wedding. He and Erika had been alike in that way—too practical to invest emotional value in an inanimate object. After returning from her honeymoon, Erika had even donated her wedding gown to be used by military brides.

Nicole, on the other hand, had carefully dried the roses from her maid of honor bouquet and hung her dress in a protective garment bag in the back of her spare closet. She'd done it reasoning that Luke and her sister-in-law might have children someday who'd want a few keepsakes.

But no matter what she'd told herself, the truth was that the dress and dried flowers were reminders of a day when her brother had looked perfectly happy for the first time in his life.

CARLIE MANAGED TO slip away from the concert hall fairly soon, though not before she'd seen how differently Annie and Beth each approached making their paper chains.

Beth's were wild, gaudy with glitter, made with any color that took her fancy. Annie's color choices were green, red and white in a creative arrangement that included larger and smaller rings. Her sister had pestered her, declaring it needed more color and glitter, so Annie had begun carefully applying a dot of silver glitter to each ring, probably to stop her sister's nagging.

But she hadn't looked happy.

Around Poppy Gold, groups of Victorian-garbed carolers were out in force, singing carols such as "Good King Wenceslas" and "Jingle Bells." It added a lovely mood to the day, spiced by the fragrance of hot cider and other tasty snacks at the treat kiosks.

Poppy Gold didn't need guests to actually *do* the decorating, which meant they were all free to enjoy the benefits of kickoff day. Everyone would also receive one of the specialty gift ornaments, which were being placed in their suites.

"Carlie, I need to check with you about something," called a voice.

She turned and smiled at Gideon Cartwright, the new veterinarian in Glimmer Creek. He'd volunteered to coordinate the farm animals and help set up the living nativity scene they were having every Friday and Saturday night until Christmas. It would be staged in front of the small white church that served as Poppy Gold's travelers' chapel.

"What can I do for you, Gideon?"

"I just got a call. Thaddeus Baxter won't be able to bring his sheep tonight—he's got pneumonia. I'm going to see if any of my other clients have sheep they're willing to loan for the evening."

Carlie was instantly concerned. They'd lost Aunt Meredith from pneumonia. "I hope Thad will be okay."

"It's just a mild case and his wife tells me this has convinced him to get the pneumonia vaccine,"

Gideon assured her quickly. "But I'm not sure how long it will take to make the calls to other livestock owners in the area and I'm supposed to start my health exams of the VC cats at 10:00 a.m. I haven't been able to locate either Liam or Tessa to let them know I'll be late."

Traditionally Dr. Chevalier had come to the Victorian Cat to give the resident felines their quarterly health checkups, but he'd retired earlier that year. When Gideon had bought the practice, he'd continued the custom, saying it was easier for everybody to spend a morning at the VC examining the cats one after another than to do it at the clinic.

"I'll tell them," Carlie promised. "Another Saturday might be better, in any case. The cats must be stirred up with everything going on here."

Gideon looked rueful. "Probably. I hadn't realized kickoff day was such a big deal. I'll do my best to find another pair of sheep for tonight."

"I appreciate it."

The living nativity was Carlie's brainchild. It was the first time they'd had one at Poppy Gold, but she figured everyone would enjoy the event. Even if Gideon couldn't locate replacement sheep, it would be a nice tableau.

GIDEON WALKED QUICKLY toward the Poppy Gold parking lot where he'd left his car. He was thoroughly enjoying his move to Glimmer Creek, though after eight years of veterinary practice in Beverly Hills, he'd had to reacquaint himself with horses, cows and sheep. Not to mention llamas, pigs and a small, cantankerous herd of buffalo.

Yet even as pleasure went through him, his mouth compressed. He'd never wanted to live in the city, but had made an agreement with his wife. After qualifying, he would go to work at her father's exclusive Beverly Hills veterinary clinic for eight years. Then, if he *still* wanted to be a small-town vet, they'd pack up and move. But when the time came, Renee had flatly refused. Apparently she'd made the agreement never thinking she'd have to keep it, figuring nobody would choose to live anywhere else once they'd had a taste of Los Angeles.

In the end, Gideon realized they'd grown so far apart they really didn't have a marriage to save.

Back at the office he unlocked the computer and did a search for clients with sheep. Dr. Chevalier had disdained computers, keeping detailed paper records instead. One of the huge jobs still ahead was getting those files entered into the system, but at least Gideon's office manager had finally gotten the basic data input done on all their current clients. It would have to do for now.

He'd hate to disappoint Carlie. Her enthusiasm about the living nativity was refreshing.

Gideon made a couple of calls and found a teenager involved in the 4-H club who was thrilled to have her two sheep in the living nativity.

He'd just hung up the phone when a handful of mail was dropped through the slot on the door. He sorted through the envelopes until he reached one from Los Angeles.

Inside was his final divorce decree.

CHAPTER FOUR

LUKE WAS CONCERNED how the girls would react to the paper-chain-making contest, but since every kid won a prize—for one reason or another—it turned out all right. Beth was triumphant over getting "most colorful," while Annie appeared quietly pleased with "prettiest use of traditional Christmas colors."

Every award was "the best" or "the most" or another superlative, and he wondered how long it had taken Carlie or her staff to come up with enough prizes to be sure each child received an accolade of some type.

Once the ceremonies had been completed, the paper-chain-making supplies were moved to a single table and other crafts were set out.

"Look, Carlie is back," Annie cried and ran across the room, followed by her sister.

Luke watched, wishing his daughters would greet *him* with that much enthusiasm. They immediately grabbed the activities director by the hand and dragged her to where he sat with a cup of coffee.

Carlie's cheeks were pink from the cold air outside and he had to admit she was pretty with her blue eyes and long, golden-brown hair. *Wholesome.* Like a character from a Christmas film where true love triumphs. It wasn't any wonder the twins gravitated toward her, though Annie's instant attachment was unusual.

"What are you doing now?" Carlie asked the girls.

"I want to make origami birds," Annie said, pronouncing the new word with care. She pointed to a table where a woman was demonstrating how to fold paper into different shapes.

"*No.* That's dumb," Beth declared. "Let's go see how much snow there is."

Carlie looked at him. "Maybe Annie could learn to do origami while the two of you go out to the sledding hill. There are volunteers here to watch the children."

Luke hesitated. While marginally quieter now, the room was still busy with kids and adults coming and going. He couldn't see letting Annie stay by herself, even if someone was specifically assigned to watch her. "Maybe another time. I saw on the schedule that Poppy Gold has another holiday craft workshop next Saturday."

"*Yippee,*" Beth cried.

Annie was still hanging on to Carlie's arm, and Carlie was talking to her in a soft voice. He only caught a few words. "Only if you go, too," Annie said finally. "But I don't want to squish my chain." She held up the gift bag the children had been given to carry their paper chains and other belongings.

"You can put it in my office and come back for it later," Carlie offered.

"Let's just *go*," Beth implored, hopping impatiently from one foot to the other.

Carlie smiled at her. "It won't take long and this way you don't have to carry your bag around."

"Oookaaay."

As they stepped outside, Luke asked why the building used for Guest Reception had the words *City Hall* impressed above the main doors. Was it to add to the village atmosphere?

"It was Glimmer Creek's original city hall," Carlie explained when he asked. "James Connor purchased the town's historic district during the Great Depression, including all the civic structures except the Carnegie library."

"Sounds like the Connors are one of the early robber-baron families of California."

Carlie looked annoyed. "Actually, James Connor paid top dollar, donated a boatload of money to the town and allowed residents to live in their homes rent-free for five years. He didn't buy the property for profit. He did it to preserve history and help Glimmer Creek get through the Depression. Personally, I don't think the town was properly grateful—they called it Connor's Folly for decades."

"Oh."

"Why did you assume he was out for himself?" she asked.

Luke made a noncommittal gesture, though he couldn't remember a time when he hadn't questioned people's motives. Growing up, he'd seen too many people taking advantage of others, his parents included. It had made him determined to make a different life and to take care of his sister. Nicole kept saying she needed to take care of herself, but that was nonsense. She *was* independent. While he'd paid for her college expenses and given her a job, she worked hard and was a terrific computer specialist, in her own right. Nobody could accuse her of being a freeloader.

CARLIE UNLOCKED HER private office. It was quiet in this part of the building; on such a busy day all available staff members were out, handling various responsibilities.

"Just put your bags on my desk," she told the twins, who'd gone instantly to look at the decorated tree in the corner, seeming to forget everything else.

The branches were adorned with white lights, delicate crystal icicles and the wild-animal ornaments she'd collected since she was a little girl. Raccoons, squirrels, mountain lions, rabbits, foxes, birds of every variety, mice, deer and other animals adorned the branches and she loved them all. They sat on beds of "snow" as if in their mountain home.

"It's the bestest tree *ever*," Annie said solemnly.

Beth nodded, but Carlie suspected she normally preferred something flashier. That was okay. Sometimes Carlie enjoyed flashy, too, though they tried to keep the decorations at Poppy Gold restrained.

Perhaps the girls would like to have a Christmas tree in their bedroom. Actually, *two* trees. They could do the decorating and make them as individual as they liked. She scribbled a note and put it on her computer monitor, not wanting to mention it to Luke until she'd collected a selection of ornaments that reflected both Annie's and Beth's apparent tastes.

It wasn't in her job description, of course, which was mostly to entertain the guests. Decorating wasn't an "activity" like scavenger hunts and hayride parties, but Tessa gave her a lot of leeway. If Carlie saw a way to enhance a guest's visit, she could act on it without getting permission.

"These must be your parents," Luke said, looking at a framed photo on the wall, taken shortly before her father's accident. In it, he was hale and hearty, and looked half the age he did now.

"Yes. Shall we go to the sledding hill?" Carlie prompted.

"Sure."

When they arrived, she was pleased to see the snowmaking machines were still running and the guys in parkas and heavy gloves were out grooming the slope. A line of kids, both young and old, were queuing at the top in anticipation. There were so many, in fact, that Carlie excused herself to go talk with her uncle about creating a separate snow field for making snowmen.

"Splendid idea," Uncle Liam said enthusiastically. "We've got more than enough snow for sledding today. The water hoses are long enough. We'll just move the snowmakers over to the open area and hope it stays cold enough for a couple of hours."

The snowmakers were shifted and Carlie called to see if the local grocery store could deliver a rush order of carrots, prunes and other environmentally friendly items for the snowmen's features. They promised her everything would be there within twenty minutes.

Before long, the overflow of sledding enthusiasts were making snowmen and women, including Beth and Annie.

"This is what I meant by spontaneous," Carlie

told Luke as she brushed snow from her hair after a trek through the wide circle of snowmakers. While she was trying to sound innocent, a part of her was smug that he'd been present for one of the impromptu events. "Why don't you help Beth and Annie build their snow person?"

"They probably want to do it alone."

"Why wouldn't they want their father to help?"

A mix of emotions flitted across his face. "No reason, I suppose."

LUKE APPROACHED HIS DAUGHTERS. It was difficult to acknowledge, even to himself, but he didn't know if they *wanted* him around. They were unusually self-sufficient for their age. The evening before he'd asked if they needed help getting ready for bed or for him to read a story, but they'd refused. And that morning they were already dressed and playing a game by the time he came out of his bedroom.

Snow was still shooting out from the machines and the girls were enjoying the artificial blizzard. Annie kept putting her head back and letting the flakes settle on her closed eyelids, while Beth danced around, trying to catch them in her mittens.

The thought flitted through his head that he could have tried renting a ski lodge in Tahoe or somewhere else for the holidays, but he shook it away. They were at Poppy Gold, and though the place wasn't what he'd expected, it could work out. With that thought, he glanced at Carlie, who was setting out piles of fruits and vegetables for everyone to use creating the snow people's features. Surely she would become less important to the girls once Nicole arrived.

"Sorry, everyone," an older man called from the opposite side after another hour. He was the same man who'd signaled for the snowmaking machines to be turned on the night before. "The temperature is starting to rise. We have to shut everything down."

Almost immediately, silence descended, followed by good-natured groans. Beth stuck out her lip in an undeniable pout and even Annie seemed a bit sulky.

"Okay, let's build that snowman," Luke said to them, trying to sound enthusiastic. "I haven't made one since I was your age."

He began gathering snow into a mound when Beth fixed him with a stern gaze that reminded him of Erika. "Papa, you have to *roll* it around. See?" She and Annie demonstrated, rolling a small ball of snow around the white ground. It picked up layers, slowly becoming larger.

"And we're building a snow *girl*, not a snow-*man*," Annie added.

"Oh." He hid a smile. "I'm glad you told me."

BEFORE GIDEON RETURNED to Poppy Gold, he took
the divorce decree upstairs to his apartment, glad
it had come on a Saturday when the office was
closed. Until things settled down more, he was living in one of the two apartments above the clinic.
He'd finally gotten a post office box for his personal mail, but he must have forgotten to update
his address with the court and his lawyer in Los
Angeles.

Intentionally?

He considered the possibility and then shook his
head. The divorce bothered him, but it was for the
best. He and his ex-wife had never valued the same
things and it was hard to base a marriage on such
a poor foundation. In their last argument, Renee
had even snapped that she'd done her best, but he
was still a clod-hopping Nebraska farm boy who
didn't deserve her.

They were just too different. Once she'd thought
it was charming that he'd grown up on a farm,
while he'd been proud of her stylish sophistica-
tion. Now he saw women in designer clothes and
wanted to run the opposite direction.

Gideon tossed the paperwork in a drawer.

At least Renee's parting retort had reminded him
that he was proud of who he was and where he'd
come from. The only reason he hadn't returned to
Nebraska after Beverly Hills was because of the
long winters. Going away to college hadn't been

about changing into a different kind of person. It had been about learning to be the best vet he could be.

Now that his foster parents had sold their farm, he was trying to convince them to move to Glimmer Creek. Helga had asthma and Gideon hoped she'd do better in a milder climate. At the very least he wanted them to come out for a few months to see if they liked it here. That was one of the reasons he'd started looking for a house. Lars and Helga hesitated to accept anything from him, but he might be able to convince them to stay in the apartment above the clinic if it was empty.

NICOLE PUT HER skates with the other luggage in the foyer of her condominium. Her restlessness and uncertainty had increased after talking to Luke. Granted, he and the twins had only been in California for a day, but she hadn't liked hearing Annie was tearful in the midst of all the holiday cheer.

Belatedly she remembered she hadn't packed her digital camera and got even more depressed. Wouldn't a proper aunt have thought of that first?

She padded up to the spare room and collected her camera and charger, along with a handful of new SD cards, trying to think if there was anything else she might need. From Luke's description of Glimmer Creek, it might be difficult to get some items and she didn't want him making an extravagant gesture to get her lip gloss or something.

Laundry soap, Nicole thought. She used an organic, unscented variety. It raised the question of whether there were any laundry facilities at Poppy Gold Inns, or would they need to use a community Laundromat?

She looked up the phone number and called California.

"Poppy Gold Inns. Can I help you?" a man's friendly voice said.

"I hate to be a bother," Nicole apologized, "but I'm flying out Monday to stay for a few weeks. I'm meeting my brother and his family, who have already arrived. I wanted to find out if you have any laundry facilities or what other plans I should make. Oh, and is there a dry cleaner in town?"

"There's a dry cleaner that will pick up and deliver. We also have laundry facilities on-site and a limited number of suites have them, as well. May I ask your name?"

"Sorry—Nicole Forrester."

"Er, right. Mr. Forrester mentioned your arrival had been delayed. The suite where you're staying includes a full utility room with a frontload washer and dryer. There's also a nicely equipped kitchen."

It was probably her imagination, but something in the man's tone made Nicole wonder if Luke had made a nuisance of himself. She was the first to admit her brother wasn't always the most sensitive guy and he liked having things his way.

"I don't cook, but that sounds wonderful," she replied brightly. "And I'm sure there are restaurants in town."

"Yes. A hot breakfast is also delivered each morning from a local caterer. The food is freshly prepared, with a different central dish every day."

Nicole had stayed at bed-and-breakfast inns where breakfast was little more than Danish and coffee, so she'd wait and see what Poppy Gold actually provided. In the meantime, the tension in the polite conversation was uncomfortable.

"I don't want to take any more of your time," she said. "But thank you for the information."

"Of course, Ms. Forrester. Have a safe trip. Happy holidays."

"Happy holidays to you, too." She gratefully hung up the phone.

Anyhow, her questions had been answered, so Nicole packed a supply of laundry soap. She turned around, looking for something else to do, and her gaze lit on the space in front of the window. She'd always put a Christmas tree there the day after Thanksgiving and now she thought the condo was lonely without it.

Even knowing she was being silly, she took her tree out from the storage area under the stairs and assembled it, stringing lights and hanging ornaments. At least she could enjoy the cheerful lights and tinsel until she left.

THE BEST VANTAGE point for the official "lighting" of Poppy Gold was at the city square park. Carlie had noted the information on the activities sheet for everyone, though most of the regulars already knew. The townspeople of Glimmer Creek knew, as well, and were all welcome to participate.

Of course, not everything was controlled by the master switches. The electric candles in the windows operated by sensors, so they'd turned on when the sun set. The same was true of the lights on the wreaths and assorted other decorations. But lights on the houses, trees and buses would go on when the switches were thrown.

Between the singing and eating and general bonhomie, the park resembled a block party. People were tired and it had been a long day, but the payoff was at 6:00 p.m. when Poppy Gold would go "live" for Christmas.

"Is it soon, Carlie?" asked Beth, hopping from one foot to the other in excitement. She looked bright and lively, probably because she and her sister had taken naps that afternoon. Luke had insisted over their protests, saying they needed rest to enjoy the evening events.

Carlie checked her cell phone. "Twenty-five more minutes.

"Did you know your new tutor taught me in first grade?" she asked Beth, hoping to distract her. While the girls were napping, Luke had interviewed Luisa Cabrera and hired her as their tutor.

"Honest?"

"Honest. Mrs. Cabrera was one of my *favorite* teachers."

From what Carlie could see of Beth's expression, she seemed content with the comment, while Annie was harder to read. But they were obviously accustomed to employees in their lives. Their artless chatter throughout the day had included numerous references to their nanny and assorted other household staff.

Erika Forrester *hadn't* been mentioned, though that wasn't necessarily strange since according to what Tessa had said, they were still having trouble dealing with their mother's death. Carlie hadn't lost a parent, but she'd come close when her dad was injured. She didn't know how she would have handled losing him and she was much older than the twins.

"Um, I'll be back in a few minutes," she said, her stomach rumbling. She walked over to one of the treat kiosks.

"Hey, Sarah," she said, seeing her cousin put out a fresh platter of cookies. "You look bushed."

Sarah chuckled. "That's the catering business. Sixteen-hour days and never enough sleep."

"I'm glad it isn't me—I'm devoted to sleep."

Carlie grabbed an empty cup and stuffed it full of apple wedges and cheese.

"Hey, you're still here, too," Sarah pointed out. "And I'm guessing you haven't eaten all day."

Carlie grinned. "I had a bagel this morning." She crunched down a bite of apple, followed by a cheese cube. "Besides, my job is to help people have fun. What could be better than that? Today I was just too busy enjoying myself to eat."

"We can't have you passing out from hunger or dehydration." Sarah held out a cup of warm cider.

Carlie glanced toward the Forresters as she drank thirstily. It wasn't unusual for certain guests to gobble up a lot of time. Tessa liked the personal touch at Poppy Gold and had given her a staff, so if some guests were more demanding, the others weren't neglected. Of course, they'd never had a guest stay for six weeks, either.

But Luke had mentioned his sister would be arriving Monday, which meant Annie and Beth should be better occupied. It was just as well. The twins were sweet, but surely they needed family, not a stranger.

After gulping the rest of her apple slices and cheese, Carlie circulated through the crowd of people, chatting and offering reminders about the living nativity that was starting in another forty-five minutes. But she quickly held up her hand when the reporter-photographer from the *Glimmer Creek Gazette* raised his camera.

"Please, Perry, I don't want to be in the newspaper. Surely you'd prefer a photo of Uncle Liam or Tessa."

"I didn't say anything about putting it in the *Gazette*." He winked and took a quick shot. "You were always my dream girl. If I can't have you, at least I can put your picture under my pillow."

Carlie laughed. They'd gone to high school together and had even dated as juniors, but she'd *never* been his dream girl; Perry Fisher enjoyed playing the field too much. Still, he was a fun guy and a volunteer fireman with a reputation for going beyond the call.

"Keep talking, Perry. You're good for my ego."

"Does that mean you'll finally go out with me? How many times have I asked since you came back to Glimmer Creek?"

"I'm just so busy," she said, wishing she hadn't brought it up. "You know, with everything..."

Perry's face sobered. "I know. We miss Mike down at the fire department. How is he?"

"About the same." Her dad had been forced to resign as a volunteer firefighter after his accident. "Why don't you take pictures of the carolers in their costumes for your article?" she suggested, eager to change the subject. "I'd also love a plug for the living nativity. Remember, every Friday and Saturday night until Christmas, six thirty to nine."

"Anything for you, sweetheart."

A few minutes later, she circled around to Annie and Beth and smiled at them. "We're getting close."

"I don't think they believe you," Luke murmured.

"When you're six, minutes can seem like hours. By the way, I want to ask you something later."

He instantly looked suspicious. "I don't do interviews and the girls are off-limits at all times."

Carlie blinked, confused. "What makes you think I'd want you to do an interview?"

LUKE WAS ANNOYED that he'd said the first thing to pop into his mind. "I've been watching that photographer, the one with the press badge, and saw you talking to him."

Carlie's lips tightened. "I asked him to do extra promotion for the living nativity. It's a new event and I want it to be a success. An interview was my last thought. For your information, Poppy Gold frequently has high-profile guests. We have an agreement with the *Gazette* and local radio station to leave them alone. Perry is taking pictures and writing a story about kickoff day. That's all."

"Oh."

"We've had much more interesting people stay at Poppy Gold, by the way. I don't think you need to worry."

From her flashing eyes, Luke suspected Carlie would have loved to tell him off, but was constrained by her position working for the bed-and-breakfast complex. Not that she'd done a bad job of knocking his ego down a peg with her polite comment about "much more interesting" people staying at Poppy Gold. Luke didn't mind; honesty was a quality he valued as much as his privacy.

"We're starting, everyone," a voice called above the carol singing, which quieted instantly.

A count started in the crowd, reminiscent of Times Square on New Year's Eve.

"Five, four, three, two…"

As the final number rang out, the rooflines, windows and doors of the Victorians were suddenly outlined with strings of lights. The trees lit up a moment later, along with bushes and the poles of lampposts that looked like they were converted gaslights.

Beth and Annie squealed with excitement and clapped their hands. Carlie Benton's face reflected their blissful pleasure, and even Luke, who wasn't big on showy displays, thought it was attractive.

Christmas had arrived with a splash at Poppy Gold.

CHAPTER FIVE

EARLY TUESDAY MORNING, Nicole got dressed and walked quietly down the stairs of the Yosemite suite. She hadn't gotten much chance to explore the suite after arriving the previous afternoon and wanted to indulge her curiosity.

She'd taken an architectural history class in college and particularly loved homes from the Victorian period.

From the little Luke had said, she'd expected a pokey set of rooms carved out of the servants' quarters of an old house. It was nothing of the kind. Everything was lovely. The rooms were spacious—not the size of Luke's home in Austin, but very nice—with great architectural details. The overall feel was gracious comfort.

Nicole looked out the windows and took in the garden and hillsides beyond. It seemed fitting that the John Muir Cottage was on the edge of town since it was a huge, old Victorian farmhouse.

A faint smile curved her mouth as she thought about the families that must have lived there, expanding the building to accommodate new generations of married children and grandchildren. She hadn't resented their nomadic childhood the way Luke had, but having a real home with roots was immensely appealing.

Curiously she looked around the kitchen. It was nicer than the one in her condo, but since she didn't cook, she hadn't looked for a place with a show-case kitchen and appliances. The real-estate agent had objected, talking about resale value, but Ni-cole wasn't worried about that. The condo met her needs and she didn't expect to get married or sell anytime soon. Dating tended to be casual since she'd discovered that some men felt her connection to Luke Forrester was her biggest appeal.

With the ease of long practice, she pushed the thought from her head. She couldn't regret being Luke's sister, but it brought challenges.

A tap sounded on the front door and she remem-bered Luke mentioning that the catering service delivered breakfast between seven and eight in the morning. She peeked out to be sure it was them and opened the door.

"Hi," said the woman carrying two insulated containers. "I'm from Sarah's Sweet Treats Cater-ing Service. I'm a couple minutes early, but I saw the light turn on in the kitchen. May I come in?"

"Oh, yes, of course." Nicole stepped back and the catering employee walked briskly inside. "I'm

Nicole Forrester. You've probably met my brother and nieces."

"Yes—cute kids. Did you get in yesterday?"

"Midafternoon."

"Welcome to Poppy Gold. I'm Mariko Kirahara." Mariko put the insulated containers on the counter. "Cold items are in the bag with the blue tag and hot in the other. Instructions are on the labels."

"Don't you need to take them with you?"

"Nope." Mariko opened a cupboard door and removed identical bags. "These are from yesterday. The housekeeping staff puts them here for us. Have a great day."

"You, too."

Mariko left quickly, probably because she had other food to deliver. Poppy Gold was huge and must provide accommodations for hundreds of guests each day.

After Nicole had arrived the previous day, Luke and the girls had shown her around the Victorian village. The sledding hill and skating rink were huge attractions, along with the lighted historic vehicle parade that occurred each evening.

But Beth and Annie's greatest excitement had been introducing her to Carlie Benton, the Poppy Gold activities director. Carlie seemed to have instantly inspired pure adoration from the twins.

Nicole sighed and investigated the coffeemaker. It was similar to the one she used at home, so she quickly filled the filter with coffee and poured water into the reservoir. Soon a rich fragrance filled the air.

Mmm. Making coffee was one of the few domestic skills she possessed. When she and Luke had talked late Saturday evening, he'd mentioned that Poppy Gold Inns had their own special blend. His description of "remarkably flavorful" had made her look forward to a taste. Her brother didn't bestow praise lightly.

There were unopened containers of cream in the fridge and Nicole made her cup rich and sweet. But before she could take a sip, Luke appeared at the kitchen door.

"Did I wake you up?" she asked.

"It wasn't you. I haven't slept much since…well, for over a year." He rubbed his face.

Nicole poured him a cup of coffee and sat in the picturesque breakfast nook, unsure how to respond. His reluctance to say Erika's name was the reason everyone else danced around it, as well.

Understanding Luke seemed impossible. Maybe part of the problem was the age and experience gap. She was thirty; he was nine years older. By the time she'd started college he was already wealthy and successful. She hadn't married, while he was a widower with two children. He was fearless; she was practically scared of her own shadow.

Still, even as a child, Luke had kept a piece of

himself separate, watchful, as if holding off the world. Perhaps it was because she'd always had him to depend upon, while he'd only had himself. Nicole didn't count their parents as reliable support; as Luke said often, Craig and Heather had a long way to go before they became responsible adults.

Luke sat down and stared into the steam rising from his cup.

"How late were you up?" she asked.

"I'm not sure. I was working. Three or four, probably. Tilly didn't want to send anything for me to look at, but I insisted."

Nicole pressed her lips together. Tilly Robinson was probably the only person in the world who would challenge Luke. Sometimes she won, sometimes she didn't. Nicole envied her, and at the same time was frustrated that somebody else could be closer to Luke than his own family.

"Surely your business interests could survive a few weeks without your spending so much time on them," she suggested carefully.

"If I can't sleep, I might as well work," Luke murmured, still looking only half-awake. "Oh, the tutor started yesterday. She's coming weekday mornings at eight thirty to work with the girls for a few hours and will stay if we're out for some reason. Beth and Annie are playing in their room. I'll call them down for breakfast."

Wanting to be useful, Nicole set the table and

then unpacked the two insulated bags. The food smelled delicious. Everything was out on the table when Beth and Annie appeared and sat quietly. In a sad way it reminded Nicole of her own childhood, when they'd stayed with other families and were expected to be invisible. Luke had rebelled, but she'd learned the lesson all too well.

"Would you like orange juice?" she asked.

Beth shrugged, while Annie gave a small nod. Restraining another sigh, Nicole poured juice and glasses of milk. The silence bothered her. Surely childish chatter was normal, yet her nieces said little except "Please" and "Thank you" and "May I have some more?"

After several stabs at conversation, Nicole gave up. She wasn't accustomed to a large breakfast, but the ham-and-asparagus frittata was delicious, along with the rich cheese sauce, cinnamon rolls, fluffy biscuits and sausage gravy. A fruit compote of melon and assorted fresh berries accompanied the meal.

Gradually Luke began looking more alert, but Nicole didn't attempt any more conversation. It was too much like talking to herself.

WITH CHRISTMAS KICKOFF day over, Carlie was both relieved and regretful. It was a huge amount of work for everyone, but also a gloriously fun event. The one spot of not-so-much-fun had been Luke Forrester.

I don't do interviews.

Honestly, how fatheaded could someone get?

They'd had former US presidents stay at Poppy Gold, also members of Congress, rock stars, actors, a few high-profile writers and other people worthy of interest. And *none* of them had ever been interviewed by the *Glimmer Creek Gazette* unless they were the ones who initiated the contact.

Carlie might not particularly like Luke, but the thought of asking a grieving widower for an interview was appalling.

"Carlie, I'm getting coffee. Want some?" Tracy called from the outer office.

"No, thanks. I'm going out for a while."

Despite Luke Forrester's egotistical assumptions, Carlie hadn't forgotten her idea about Annie and Beth each having a Christmas tree in their room. She wanted to check the storage areas for appropriate decorations; it would be important to have a variety to satisfy Annie's and Beth's individual tastes.

From the computer inventory she could tell that most of the decorations stored in the top floor of the El Dorado Mansion hadn't been used, so she went there first. Unlike some attics in old houses, the ones at Poppy Gold were clean and organized.

It wasn't long before she'd put together a large assortment of ornaments and had selected two artificial Christmas trees.

Outside she found the sun had vanished and clouds covered the sky. Spats of rain were coming down and Carlie hoped it wouldn't be a big storm. Uncle Liam probably had his crew out already to cover the sledding hill with tarps to help preserve the thick layer of snow.

It took several trips to get everything to her office, but Carlie was happy with the mix of ornaments she'd found. While Poppy Gold favored Victorian-style decorations, they tried to mix things up year to year.

Now she just had to discuss her plan with Luke. Normally talking to a guest wouldn't be a problem, but he had a talent for rubbing her the wrong way.

WITH HER BROTHER working again and her nieces studying with the retired schoolteacher, Nicole finally left a note saying she didn't know how long she'd be gone and went for a walk. It had become cold and gray with a light drizzle coming down, but as if to brighten the day, the lights on the houses, trees and bushes suddenly switched on.

It was pretty, but even though she didn't have any clothes for hiking, she was more intrigued by the wilder countryside she'd seen from the front porch of the suite. She decided to head in that direction.

Nicole went southeast and after a mile or two encountered a country road. It was quiet with little traffic except an elderly couple who stopped to ask if she needed assistance. After she assured them that she was all right, they waved and drove away.

Once they were gone, Nicole debated whether to continue or return to the house. The house, she decided. Yet as she turned back toward Poppy Gold, a faint "miiiaaaw" caught her attention.

Nicole looked around nervously, her pulse leaping before settling down again. While she wasn't familiar with the wild animals in California, she was reasonably certain the cry had come from a domestic feline.

"Kitty, kitty?" Nicole called, scouting around the edge of the road. It was ridiculous to think cats automatically responded to "kitty, kitty," but surely they could recognize a welcoming voice.

Under a bush, she spotted a kitten, thoroughly bedraggled in the light rain. It looked at her and shrank backward.

"No, no, no, no, *no*," she whispered frantically, fearful it would run away. "It's okay—I'm not going to hurt you."

She extended a hand and the kitten closed its eyes, as if resigning itself to its fate.

Nicole crawled far enough under the bush to get

hold of the small thing. It trembled at her touch, though whether from cold or fear, she didn't know. Close up, she saw fur was matted over a wound on its leg, but she didn't have anything to use as a bandage.

Whispering a string of soothing words, she took off her jacket and tucked the baby in the middle, cupping it gently to her stomach. At the moment, all she could do was provide some warmth.

She got out her cell phone to call for a taxi, but there was no signal.

"Drat," she muttered.

Trying not to jostle the kitten too much, she hurried toward Poppy Gold. But when she reached the Victorian village, she found herself at one of the outer parking lots, rather than the John Muir Cottage. She picked up one of the facility's courtesy phones.

"Poppy Gold front desk. May I help you?"

"I found a kitten out in the brush. The poor thing is half-starved and needs a veterinarian, but I don't know where to take it," she said, the words spilling out with an undeniable edge of panic. "I'm not even sure where I am. I meant to go back to the John Muir Cottage, but I only arrived yesterday and I—"

"It's all right, ma'am," the man interrupted soothingly. "You're calling from the Jumping Frog parking area. I'll dispatch a shuttle to take you to the veterinarian we use at Poppy Gold. The clinic is just a few blocks away."

"Thank you. I apologize for being, um, hysterical." Nicole peeked inside the fold of her jacket, trying to see how the kitten was doing.

"Don't be concerned. Dr. Cartwright will take good care of your new friend."

Maybe it was the hint of an English accent or his composure, but Nicole realized her pulse and breathing had slowed to a more normal rate.

They talked for another couple of minutes until Nicole saw one of the Poppy Gold courtesy shuttles drive into the parking area.

"It's here," she said into the phone. "Thanks again."

As she sat in the vehicle, Nicole reached into the warm nest she'd made of her jacket. She was reassured when the kitten licked her finger, but it seemed to take ages before she saw a sign for the veterinary clinic. Apparently they treated both small and large animals, which bothered her. Wouldn't it be best to have a specialist?

She mumbled her appreciation to the shuttle driver and rushed inside. Luckily the waiting room was empty.

The receptionist smiled. "You must be the guest from Poppy Gold. They gave us a call that you were coming. Is the blood from you or the cat?"

Distracted, Nicole looked down at her hand. There were streaks of red, smeared by the misting rain, where tiny claws had dug into her skin. "Me, I think. It has a wound, but it wasn't bleeding."

"All right. Dr. Cartwright and his technician are finishing up in surgery, so let me get some basic information for the file."

Nicole provided her name, address and cell number, which were entered into the computer. She couldn't say much about the kitten, other than that she'd found it outside the town.

"I was out walking, so I don't have my wallet," she explained. "But I'll pay the bill, whatever it is."

"We can worry about that later," said a deep voice. "I'm Dr. Gideon Cartwright."

The tall, dark, unsmiling man was the last thing Nicole had expected. Weren't country vets supposed to be white-haired and kindly looking? Her knowledge of animal care was limited to the *All Creatures Great and Small* stories by James Herriot, but this guy seemed too grim and handsome to be someone who birthed cows and horses and that sort of thing.

"Um, Nicole Forrester."

"You can wait out here while I treat the patient, Ms. Forrester. It may take a while since my technician is with a dog coming out of anesthesia."

Nicole bit her lip. Despite her limited experience, she knew staying in the reception area wasn't usual. People generally stayed with their pet unless they were having surgery or something.

She wasn't good at standing up to anyone, but she gulped. "I'm going with you."

His face tightened. "Very well." He gestured toward the interior door.

In the exam room, Nicole tried to set the kitten and jacket on the table, but the kitten dug its claws into her blouse, connecting with the skin beneath. She winced and gently unhooked the tiny, very sharp scimitars.

The veterinarian reached out a hand. "Let's see what we have, then."

Nicole wouldn't have thought the baby cat had enough energy to react, but it looked at the tall man and spit.

"Male, three to four months old," the doctor murmured. He swiftly snipped the sharp ends of the baby's claws before probing the kitten's partially healed wound.

In repayment, his patient gave him a swat.

"Feisty, aren't you?" Dr. Cartwright observed without heat. He put a clear gel into a syringe and squeezed a few drops onto the baby's gums.

"Wh-what's that?" Nicole asked.

"Glucose. I want to get some calories into him. This little guy is half-starved. By the way, did he bite you?"

"No. He hooked his claws into my hands and

clothes, but he hasn't bitten or done any real scratching."

The examination continued, punctuated by additional doses of the glucose. A blood sample was taken and the doctor left for a short while. Nicole let out a breath and put the baby back on her jacket, figuring it was warmer than a stainless-steel exam table.

Then she called Luke to let him know what was going on, but his phone immediately rolled to voice mail. "Hi, Luke, it's me," she said. "I don't know how long I'll be gone. I've rescued a kitten and have taken it to a veterinarian. See you later. 'Bye."

Nicole sat in a chair, looking into the kitten's eyes and rubbing his neck.

"I'm sorry," she whispered. "This is to help you. I'm not trying to be mean."

A tiny pink tongue appeared. He licked his jowls, appearing quite disgusted by the flavor of the glucose gel.

They both jumped when the door swung open and Dr. Cartwright burst into the room. "Other than being malnourished, he seems to be okay. The blood tests came back clear. I'm going to treat that wound now."

A couple of times Nicole wanted to snatch the kitten away, especially when the doctor shaved the fur around the injury. The little cat was hissing and sending looks that accused her of major betrayal.

"Maybe it would be easier if I helped hold him," Nicole offered shakily.

"You'll ruin your clothes."

She glanced down. Her blouse and slacks were already snagged and covered with dirt. Her shoes were soaked with mud and deeply scored from the rocky terrain. "I'll have to toss everything, anyway."

"Fine." He gestured. "Put your hands here and grasp firmly."

When the injured area was finally shaved, Nicole let out a relieved breath. Dr. Cartwright didn't seem bothered by the kitten's distress, but it nearly broke her heart. Maybe a veterinarian *had* to be tough and not allow things like that to get to them.

"Where did you find him?" the doctor asked.

"By the road leading out of town, under a bush with shiny red bark. I was hiking and heard him cry." She wasn't sure why she'd mentioned the bush, but she was flustered by how stern and unfriendly Dr. Cartwright seemed to be.

"Manzanita," Gideon said absently, cleaning his patient's wound, which seemed to be healing well, with no signs of infection. The one trouble spot proved to be from a piece of embedded glass, suggesting the injury had come from a broken bottle. Cats had impressive recuperative ability, which was how they'd earned a reputation for having nine lives. Still, the little guy had gone through more than enough.

"Manzanita?" Nicole echoed.

"The bush. Manzanita bark is unmistakable. You must not be from around here."

"I live in Austin, Texas."

Gideon flicked a glance in Nicole Forrester's direction. Who in *hell* went hiking in a silk blouse, linen slacks and Prada shoes? Not to mention diamond solitaire earrings that were at least two carats each. His failed marriage to a fashion maven had taught him enough to recognize that hefty price tags had accompanied his new client's clothes and accessories, yet she'd casually talked about tossing the outfit.

He dodged another swat from the kitten's claws. "Austin is a big city."

"I, um, think it's the eleventh-largest population center in the United States. And the fastest growing. It's beautiful and there's always something to do," she said, her voice stronger and more enthusiastic than before.

A true Texan.

He'd known several people from the Lone Star State and they were proud of all things Texas, whether they'd had anything to do with it or not. Now, Gideon *liked* Texas. As a twelve-year-old kid he'd vacationed there with his foster parents and the state had a huge amount to offer in entertainment and things to see. But he was done with cities, even nice ones.

"What tempted a city dweller to go hiking?" he asked.

"I was restless. I'm not outdoorsy, but it was pretty and fresh in the rain. Look, I don't understand how a kitten this size got out that far. There weren't any houses nearby."

Gideon finished his exam. "He doesn't have a microchip and he hasn't been neutered. It's almost certainly a case of abandonment."

"That's awful."

Gideon agreed. Animals could be brought to the local shelter without any cost; they'd never turned one away, though it often stretched the private rescue group's resources. But the responsible party wasn't necessarily local. Sadly, some people would drive quite a distance, just to dump an unwanted pet.

The faint fragrance of an expensive perfume drifted into his consciousness and he scowled. He respected Nicole Forrester's willingness to help an animal in distress, but he refused to find her attractive. For one thing, his divorce from a similar city woman with expensive tastes had just become final. And for another, he'd just bought the veterinary clinic and couldn't afford distractions.

"We've done as much as possible for today," Gideon said briskly. "I'm only giving him the core vaccinations. The others can wait until he's in better shape. No sense in overloading his body too much."

"But he's going to be all right?" Nicole asked.

"Barring complications. This isn't the city. Life after being dumped is rough."

Nicole gritted her teeth. Gideon Cartwright seemed competent and was the handsomest man she'd met in ages, but the kitten didn't like him and she was in wholehearted agreement. The doctor's brusqueness made her want to shrivel; it was only for the kitten's sake that she'd stood up to him earlier.

"I'm sure life is rough for abandoned animals in a city, too," she managed to say.

Dr. Cartwright just shrugged and put a stiff cone around the kitten's neck. The kitten meowed in displeasure and pawed at it.

"What's that for?"

"To keep him from fussing at his injury."

Great, he'll just scratch his head off, instead.

"Haven't you ever dealt with animals?" the vet asked with a patronizing expression.

"No." Nicole didn't want to admit that anything larger than a small cat made her nervous. Loud dogs were particularly bad. Being a coward wasn't something she was proud of and the veterinarian's superior attitude was particularly hard to take. He didn't seem like someone who'd ever doubted himself for a minute, while she doubted herself all the time.

"Well, we'll transfer this guy to the local animal rescue. He mostly needs love and good food to recover and he'll get it there."

Nicole's shoulders straightened. "What makes you think he couldn't get that with me?"

"You're an out-of-state visitor and hardly equipped to take care of an animal at Poppy Gold. But don't worry—rescued animals have a home for life at the Glimmer Creek shelter, even if they aren't adopted. He'll be fine."

She pushed down her tremors, flattened her hands on the exam table and leaned toward Gideon Cartwright for emphasis. "*I'm* not *abandoning him.* I'll ask the Poppy Gold housekeeper to provide whatever is necessary. It can't be much—you said yourself that he mostly needs food and love."

GIDEON'S JAW HARDENED.

He'd known Nicole Forrester was trouble the minute he'd spotted her in his waiting room. However mussed from rain and the rigors of rescuing a kitten, she'd radiated an aura of money and privilege. And her casual assumption that she could call upon the Poppy Gold housekeeping staff to provide supplies was just further proof she didn't live in the real world.

"Poppy Gold is a Victorian village, filled with antiques and architectural treasures," he said through clenched teeth.

"How much damage can a little kitten do? Anyway, I'm keeping him. We're staying through the first week in January, which should be enough time for him to recover and get to know me. He won't have to fly in the cargo hold on the way home, if that's what you're concerned about. We'll return in my brother's private jet."

Thoroughly frustrated, Gideon stomped out to the empty waiting room and called Poppy Gold to get her a ride, deciding not to warn them ahead of time that she expected to keep the cat in her suite. They promised someone would arrive within a few minutes.

Then he grabbed a cardboard animal carrier and bag of kitten food, glad it was lunchtime and no one was there to witness his foul mood.

"Here." He returned to the exam room, put the food on the table and assembled the carrier. The kitten went inside, complaining loudly.

"Maybe I could carry him in my jacket," Nicole said tentatively. He'd noticed she seemed a bit nervous most of the time, but maybe it was the unfamiliarity of a vet clinic.

"A closed carrier is safer." Gideon made several notes in the computer medical file, hoping the shuttle would arrive quickly. He couldn't shove

Nicole and his patient out in the cold *or* leave her alone in the waiting room.

He held up the bag of food.

"This is the kitten food I recommend for the first year. After that, switch him to the adult formula. Take it with you. Keep him quiet while he recovers. I've called Poppy Gold to pick you up, so we should check to see if they've arrived. I'll show you out."

"What do I do about the bill?"

"Call the office with a credit card." Through the waiting room window, Gideon saw a Poppy Gold Inns vehicle pull up in front of the clinic. He escorted Nicole to the exterior door and unlocked it. "You'll need cat litter and a litter box. Give him fresh water each day, but separate his food and water bowls. That's what felines prefer."

"How far?"

"Several feet, at the very least. Let us know if the kitten's condition changes in any way for the worse, including fever, lethargy and any flu-like symptoms," he explained rapidly. "I can't stay to talk. I need to check on my surgical patient. Have a good afternoon."

When she was safely gone, Gideon strode back to the surgical area. His veterinary assistant looked at him inquiringly. Sandra was sitting with the ancient English bulldog who'd had an abscessed tooth removed. Bogey had a heart murmur and required special monitoring.

"Go to lunch," he said. "I'll take over."

Sandra smiled. "I don't mind staying. He's a wonderful old dog. A real gentleman."

"Nah, go ahead. I've got it."

Soon the only sound was Bogey's sonorous breathing. He was awake, but not particularly alert, partly because of the pain medication. Occasionally he rolled his eyes back as if to ask what the heck had happened to him, but he didn't try to move.

Gideon stroked the bulldog's neck, unable to get Nicole Forrester out of his mind. *We'll return in my brother's private jet.* A private jet? She made his ex-wife look like a piker in the pampered princess department.

Why was he so stupidly drawn to women like that? Either he was a glutton for punishment or needed his head examined.

CHAPTER SIX

LUKE WAITED FOR a while to see if Nicole would return in time for lunch, and then walked with the girls to a pizza place he'd seen near the brick-paved pedestrian shopping street.

He wasn't overly impressed with the restaurants in Glimmer Creek so far. The offerings seemed limited to things like steak houses and glorified hamburger stands.

Figuring the vegetables would be canned or pre-packaged, he ordered an olive-and-pepperoni pizza, only to notice mushrooms and other toppings being prepared fresh in the open kitchen.

"I'd like to change my order," he said to the cashier, who had given him a credit-card slip to sign.

"Oh." The kid, who was probably barely out of high school, looked down at the cash register, non-plussed. He fiddled with the keys for a moment before turning his head. "Boss, how do you cancel a charge? Someone wants to change their order."

A faint ripple of groans went through the line of people who'd come in behind them.

A woman with a no-nonsense air came over and reversed the transaction.

"What will you have, sir?" she asked crisply.

Luke checked the menu. "A medium vegetarian pizza with artichoke hearts to go. And to eat here, a medium special pizza with extra mushrooms and..." He focused on Beth and Annie, realizing he should have asked their preferences first. "What would you like, girls?"

They whispered in each other's ears for a minute. "Pineapple," Beth finally pronounced.

"You mean Hawaiian, with Canadian bacon."

Beth shook her head. "Just pineapple."

The growing crowd behind them was getting restless and Luke gave them a cool glance. There were two cash registers and it wasn't his fault that the restaurant had only opened one.

He focused on the woman taking his order. "In addition to the pizza to go, we'll have a medium pizza to eat here, half the special with extra mushrooms, the other half with just pineapple. We'd also like a pitcher of lemonade and an order of cheese bread sticks with marinara sauce."

The woman rang up the charge and handed him a new slip. "Please sign here, Mr. Forrester."

Luke signed and took the girls to a table. The restaurant was similar to some of the dives he'd eaten at while in college. A trust fund from his paternal grandparents had been available to help with his education expenses, but he'd used most of it to start buying and selling real estate and investing in stocks. It hadn't left money for high living.

The teenager had returned to the cash register and was taking orders. Luke heard him apologize for the delay, saying their second cash register was broken and they were waiting for repairs. So that was the explanation.

The pitcher of lemonade arrived and he poured three glasses, wishing he could have the coffee supplied at Poppy Gold instead. The food they served was excellent, as well.

When the pizzas and bread sticks were brought to the table, he handed the server a twenty-dollar bill, though tips left on the table hadn't been customary at the pizza parlors he'd gone to in college. "Thanks. Can you tell me if the Poppy Gold caterer runs a restaurant in town?"

"Not a restaurant, but a bakery called Sarah's Sweet Treats. It's just down the street. Did you need change, sir?" she asked, gesturing with the bill he'd given her.

"No, that's for you. I just wanted to be sure you got it." She looked surprised, then smiled her thanks before hurrying away. He served slices to Beth and Annie. "Let the food cool down," he warned, and they obediently kept their hands in their laps until he told them it was all right.

The food was tasty, but Luke was distracted

watching his daughters. Pineapple? He liked Hawaiian pizza with Canadian bacon *and* pineapple, just not by itself. He'd half expected the twins to wrinkle their noses and refuse to eat after taking a bite, or else to scrape off the fruit, but they seemed to enjoy their choice.

The sky had cleared by the time they came out of the pizza parlor and the girls' moods brightened. On the walk back to Poppy Gold, Annie cried, "Carlie!" and took off running, with Beth not far behind.

Luke caught up with them and Carlie gestured to the pizza box he carried. "I see you've discovered Valentino's."

"It reminds me of the pizza I ate in college."

"I also like Giancarlo's Little Italy. They deliver, too, which is nice. I particularly enjoy their pasta primavera and salads."

He knew he'd annoyed her on Saturday night with his comment about an interview, though she'd tried to conceal her reaction. Since then she'd been coolly pleasant to him, but with the girls she was warm and approachable and they'd continued asking her to attend various activities with them. At a choral performance in the concert hall late Sunday afternoon, Annie had actually sat on Carlie's lap, while Beth leaned against her shoulder.

"By the way," Luke said, "what did you want

to talk to me about on Saturday? We never got back to it."

"Maybe Annie and Beth would like to check out our DVD library while we chat," she suggested.

"Sure."

Apparently Carlie wanted a private discussion. They returned to Old City Hall and she took them into one of the rooms they hadn't seen before, behind the reception area. It was paneled in mahogany, with an ornate fireplace and chandelier. Bookshelves matching the paneling covered most of the wall space.

"Nice," Luke murmured.

"This used to be the mayor's office. According to the stories, he paid to finish the interior of city hall, thinking it would guarantee his reelection, only to get booted out midterm when the citizenry discovered..." Carlie's voice trailed off and she looked at the girls. "Annie, Beth, kids' books and DVDs are over there." She pointed to the opposite end of the room and the twins began exploring.

"Discovered what?" Luke asked in a low tone, suspecting it was one of two things.

"That Mayor Colonel Stafford owned a string of brothels from Coloma to San Diego. He was also invested in shipping and patent medicines, but most of his wealth came from old-fashioned sex."

Owning brothels wasn't one of the options Luke had considered. "Really?"

"Definitely. Glimmer Creek started out as a rough-and-ready gold mining camp, but when Victorian civility took over, the town got prudish. For years a number of women refused to even *enter* Old City Hall because the services of 'good-time' girls had paid for the decorating."

Shaking his head, Luke set the pizza he'd gotten for Nicole on one of the side tables, only to have Carlie scoop it up with a faintly alarmed expression.

"That's an antique, original to the office," she advised hastily. "Let me have this delivered to the John Muir Cottage for you."

"I'll handle it," volunteered the young woman who'd stepped in from the reception area.

"Thanks, Christine."

Luke was rarely embarrassed, but discomfort went through him. The pizza box was warm and damp. Grease also stained the lid and presumably the bottom, so placing it on an antique table hadn't been the best move.

"That won't be necessary," he said. "I'll pick it up at the front desk."

"Very well, Mr. Forrester."

Christine exchanged a look with Carlie and left.

"What burning topic do you want to discuss?" Luke asked.

"Hardly burning," Carlie returned. "I wondered if Annie and Beth would each like to decorate a Christmas tree for their bedroom. They have such different styles, I thought it would be nice if they could explore them in a personal tree."

Though Luke recognized the differences between his identical twin daughters, it surprised him that a virtual stranger had seen the same thing. But then, Carlie was unusual. She'd been able to tell Beth and Annie apart from the beginning, something few people could do, even after knowing them for years.

"I'm sure they'd love it."

Carlie smiled. "In that case, I've already selected two high-quality artificial trees and boxes of ornaments for the project. I'll bring them over tomorrow and leave everything on the porch if you aren't there. I thought the trees could be Annie's and Beth's own individual works of art."

"I suppose, though they'll probably look similar when they're done."

Carlie hiked one eyebrow. "If that's what you think, then I suggest you watch which ornaments they pick and distract Beth from convincing Annie to make different choices." She checked the grandfather clock ticking in one corner. "Um, I have to go. If you want any books or DVDs, they can be checked out with the front desk. Don't forget your pizza in Guest Reception."

CARLIE HURRIED OUT.

She didn't know if she'd crossed the line with

her remark about Beth, but Luke didn't seem to realize how often Beth overrode her sister's wishes. In the few days they'd been at Poppy Gold, Carlie had already seen it happen several times.

Annie wasn't weak-willed; she just seemed more concerned about keeping the peace than her sister, sending worried glances at her father whenever Beth pushed for something to be done her way.

Kids squabbled. It was part of growing up. But why was Annie so concerned about not making a fuss? Perhaps it was losing her mother or a natural shyness that made her recoil from creating a scene.

Carlie wondered how much time Luke was actually spending with his daughters if he wasn't aware of the odd push-pull dynamic between the girls. She had a head start on understanding twin behavior after watching her brothers grow up, but Luke was obviously intelligent enough to see what was going on. Of course, he was ambitious and assertive himself, so he might approve of Beth's behavior.

Vaguely depressed, Carlie headed over to the Douglas House, where high tea was being served soon. There were two sittings, the first at 1:30 p.m. and the second at 4:00 p.m. It was presented as living history, with the "hostess" wearing a Victorian costume and greeting guests as if they were entering her home in 1897.

During the holiday season, high tea was available at the Douglas House seven days a week, except on Christmas Eve and Christmas Day. Carlie had loved going to the tea parties when she was a little girl, but now they were largely adult affairs.

Inside the living room, one of her aunts, Mattie Pennington, was doing a final check on the food and making sure the tables were set to her satisfaction. "Hi, Carlie. Are you staying for tea?"

"Wish I could. I just wanted a word with Jamie. Is she back from doing her spiel at the train depot?"

"No—sorry. I'll have her call when she's free, but the guests will be arriving shortly. What do you have in mind?"

Jamie Fullerton was another cousin who worked at Poppy Gold. She did a living-history performance at the train depot before coming to help serve tea to guests with Aunt Mattie. Jamie was a talented kid. Hardworking, too. She and her boyfriend, Lance Beckley, were taking college classes together at night and on their days off.

"I thought it would be nice to have a few morning tea parties for the under-twelve crowd," Carlie said, trying to snitch a cucumber sandwich from a plate and getting her fingers slapped by the "maid," who happened to be *another* cousin. They grinned at each other and Katie slipped it to her, anyway. "If Jamie is interested, I thought she could handle the hostess duties."

"I'll mention it. She's always thrilled to try something new. Oh, did you hear? Lance has decided against going in the navy. He'll keep working with Poppy Gold's antique vehicles while he gets a degree in civil engineering."

"That's terrific. Uncle Liam says he's very mechanically minded."

Carlie left, munching her tiny sandwich. She'd missed lunch again, but had wanted to get everything together for Annie and Beth's Christmas trees.

WHEN LUKE STEPPED through the front door of the Yosemite suite, a strange sight captured his attention. A scrawny kitten was scratching a piece of fabric on the stone hearth in front of the fireplace, trying to cover evidence of a puddle. A blue cone-type thing around its neck was impeding its progress and it seemed genuinely embarrassed being caught in such an ignominious position.

"Omigod." Nicole ran out of the kitchen wearing a different outfit than the one she'd been wearing at breakfast. She dropped a towel over the puddle before picking up the cat and cuddling it in her arms. "Sorry, Luke. This is the kitten I told you about."

"Told me about?"

"In my voice-mail message."

Damn.

He'd forgotten to turn his phone back on after

he finished working earlier. "I'm afraid my cell has been off. What happened?"

"I found him near a road outside of town while I was out walking. He's seen a veterinarian and I want to take him back to Austin with me. I already have food, but I have to call Housekeeping for other supplies. Poppy Gold has cats residing at the Victorian Cat mansion, so I thought they might have an extra litter box and stuff he could use," she said in a nervous rush.

Luke nearly grinned. Whatever it took, he'd make sure his sister kept the kitten to which she'd plainly given her heart.

"You haven't even been at Poppy Gold for twenty-four hours. How do you know about the Victorian Cat?"

"I explored the website, of course. Didn't you?"

He shrugged. The cursory glance he'd given the site didn't count. He would have learned a number of important pieces of information if he'd done a better job checking everything for himself. Not that their visit wasn't working out now that he'd adjusted his expectations.

"I'll take care of contacting the housekeeper," he said. "Watch to be sure your new friend doesn't do anything else that's socially unacceptable. Carlie just reminded me there are a lot of antiques here at Poppy Gold."

"Can we see him, Aunt Nicole?" asked Beth, hopping from one foot to the other.

The kitten shrank against Nicole as she sat on the couch and answered their questions about why he was wearing the cone around his neck. "He's still a baby and healing from an injury. You need to be gentle," she warned.

Luke took the pizza box into the kitchen and leafed through the information packet. Gloria Mendoza was the head of Housekeeping, so he dialed her number and explained their needs. "Naturally I'll pay extra. Also for any supplies."

"Don't be concerned, Mr. Forrester. The John Muir Cottage is one of the few buildings where we allow small pets, though we ask you to monitor their behavior. I'll have a litter box delivered immediately." She went on, saying something about the circumstances of their visit and that she didn't see the need to add a charge for supplies during their complimentary period, since the cost was minimal.

Luke was distracted by the sight of his daughters' excitement over the kitten, so the gist of her comments didn't sink in until after he'd disconnected.

Complimentary period?

It seemed odd, but he put it out of his mind as they waited for Housekeeping.

"There's a pizza in the kitchen for you," he told Nicole, "but it's cold by now."

"I'll have some later. Weren't microwave ovens invented to heat pizza and make popcorn?"

"Got me. In college, I'd stick a leftover pepperoni pizza under my bed and eat it cold until I ran out and needed to get more."

Nicole shuddered. "Yuck. You're lucky you didn't poison yourself."

Luke didn't remember it being that bad, but he'd been chronically short on sleep as a working student and eating cold pizza had been the least of his concerns. One thing was certain, though—it had made him determined that his sister wouldn't have to go through the same thing.

A short time later, a knock sounded and he opened the door to two Poppy Gold employees.

"Hello, sir. We understand you need a litter box for a rescued kitten," said one of the women. "Because your suite is two-story, Mrs. Mendoza thought it would be best to have a box on each floor. Would you like us to set them up?"

"Can you put one in the tower bedroom?" Nicole asked.

"Of course."

The job was handled quickly and Nicole decided to shut the kitten into her room to help keep him quieter while they went out to see a puppet show in the park.

Luke was surprised his sister was willing to leave her new baby alone. She reminded him of one of his senior executives when she'd first become a mother—fiercely protective and prone to separation anxiety.

CARLIE OBJECTED WHEN the Glimmer Creek High School drama class wanted to change the scheduled puppet program to a Punch-and-Judy show when they arrived, declaring it didn't fit the Christmas spirit. Perhaps that hadn't occurred to the young puppeteers, because they looked startled and agreed.

The budding thespians were doing the show as a class project and they'd probably decided their original story of a lost toy searching for its child was too tame. However, while "Punch and Judy" might provide comic relief, Carlie didn't care for its violent premise.

Carlie was glad the weather had cleared enough for an open-air show. While they'd been prepared to move the event into the concert hall, it was more fun this way.

She snagged a cup of cocoa and a mandarin orange from the treat table and waved at the Forrester family approaching down the block. She'd told the twins about the performance the day before and they had, as had already become their habit, begged her to watch with them.

For the next several weeks, some type of Christmas performance would take place every afternoon in the Poppy Gold town square park. In most cases it would be the local theater group, class projects, the glee and drama clubs from the junior and senior high schools or a choir from one of the churches.

"Carlie," called Beth, rushing over to her. "Guess what? Aunt Nicole found a lost kitty."

"It got hurt," Annie said in a much quieter voice.

"That's too bad."

"Uh-huh. He's got four white paws and—"

"They aren't white," Beth interrupted. "They're all dirty. He's got tiger stripes and long fur and has to wear this blue thing around his neck to stop him from licking the cut on his leg."

Annie's face scrunched up, but it wasn't clear whether it was from anger or hurt. Carlie didn't think it was her place to say something, but Luke didn't appear to have noticed, so she crouched in front of Beth. "White feet are white, kiddo, even when they're dirty. Okay?"

Beth nodded and Annie appeared happier. Kids were kids and they sometimes interrupted each other the way adults did; it just always seemed to be *Beth* doing it to Annie.

"Papa, may we have hot chocolate?" Annie asked.

"Sure. Let's go get it."

Carlie turned to Nicole Forrester when they were alone. They'd met the previous afternoon, but Nicole had been pale and withdrawn; she looked much more rested now. "How is the kitten?"

"Dr. Cartwright says he should be all right. The wound is already healing, but he's really thin. Apparently somebody dumped him outside of town."

"People like that make me crazy."

"Me, too. And he's such a darling little guy. You'll have to see him once he's settled down and feeling better."

Carlie could tell she was going to like Nicole Forrester, which was ironic considering her brother was such a royal pain in the behind. But she didn't have time to say anything before Luke and the girls returned with their cups and one for Nicole.

The puppeteers brought everyone to attention and began their performance, which, judging by the audience participation and applause, was still a success without the heightened action of a Punch-and-Judy show.

"Carlie, I wanted to ask about something," Luke said afterward. "When I spoke to Mrs. Mendoza about supplies for the kitten, she mentioned a complimentary period. What did that mean?"

It didn't surprise Carlie in the least that Luke Forrester was unaware of the circumstances of his visit. He probably had employees who took care of mundane details like making reservations and travel arrangements.

"The owners of Poppy Gold try to assist military families and service members who are, uh, going through rough patches." Carlie looked at the twins, hoping they weren't paying attention and that nobody *else* could hear what was being said. "We get referrals from a variety of sources. The first week is a gift. If there's a need to stay longer, an at-cost rate is given for the remaining time."

Luke stiffened. "That's unacceptable. I insist we move to a noncharity suite."

Carlie blinked. As the activities director, room rates weren't a subject she'd ever discussed with guests.

"It isn't charity," she said in a low, firm voice. "Besides, what's wrong with the John Muir Cottage? The Yosemite is the largest suite at Poppy Gold and one of the nicest. We don't provide substandard accommodations to our military guests. My cousin and uncle simply want to do something for service people and families going through a difficult time."

"Nevertheless, I want to be moved."

Considering Luke's belief that his money could buy everything, she shouldn't be shocked by his reaction. "I doubt anything is available. We have a long waiting list during the holidays. But you could speak to the front desk."

"I'll do that. Nicole, will you stay with the girls?"

His sister nodded and Carlie shrugged as he marched toward Old City Hall. The guy was impossible, but that didn't change the fact that his wife had died a hero and his daughters were adorable.

The front desk wouldn't have an easy time with him. They'd probably end up calling Tessa to ask about the emergency reserve rooms, but it would be more of a courtesy than anything. The Yosemite suite was the *only* suite with three or more bedrooms.

As a result, Luke might even decide to leave Poppy Gold, which would be a shame since Annie and Beth seemed to be opening up.

"I'M SO SORRY," Nicole apologized when Luke was out of earshot. It was almost amusing that Carlie didn't seem awed by her brother's wealth and good looks. Over the years, *dozens* of women had chased Luke and now he was dealing with one who apparently didn't care much for him.

"That's all right," Carlie assured her. "I'm sure everything will get straightened out. Honestly, this is just Poppy Gold's way of saying thank you to veterans and service members and their families. There's no charity involved."

"Aunt Nicole, what's charity?" asked Beth.

"It's something your papa has worked very hard to be sure we don't need," she said quickly. "Put your cups in the trash if you're finished with them."

"Okay."

After tossing their hot-chocolate cups, her nieces went over to see the puppeteers, who were now doing impromptu performances for children and adults alike. They'd probably be occupied for a few minutes.

Nicole turned back to Carlie. "Be sure to tell Poppy Gold's owners how much I appreciate them wanting to help my brother and the girls. The suite is absolutely lovely. Luke should have reacted better, but he's proud and…well, nothing has been the same since Erika was killed."

"You've all been through a lot."

"I feel helpless sometimes," Nicole confessed. "I don't know how to help the girls *or* Luke. But I *should* know what to do. I'm his sister."

"Some people—" Carlie's phone chimed, interrupting her. She pulled it out and read something on the screen. "Oops, I have to go. Maybe we could get together sometime for coffee or lunch."

"That would be great."

Nicole was interested to see the activities director head the same direction Luke had gone, but hoped it didn't mean anything.

LUKE TRIED TO restrain his impatience as the front desk staff called the manager and then explained that there weren't any other suites available at Poppy Gold. They were polite, but they couldn't understand how it galled him to think that he and his family were staying free of charge in a charitable outreach to military families.

He saw a movement from the corner of his eye; it was Carlie stepping through the double doors of the reception area.

"In that case, I want to be charged the full rate for our accommodations," he insisted, "as well as for any special services we've received. I don't see how anyone could have gotten the impression we'd anticipated staying for free. I *don't* accept charity."

"Carlie?" asked the young man at the desk.

"Do as Mr. Forrester asks. I'll clear it with Tessa."

"But we don't have a regular rate schedule for the John Muir Cottage."

"Ask Aunt Polly to work one up and send it to Tessa for approval. Is that satisfactory, Mr. Forrester?"

"I… Yes."

"Then have a nice rest of the afternoon." Carlie immediately turned and went through the ornate doors.

Luke cast one look at the registration desk employee and followed her. "Carlie, wait," he said, catching up on the sidewalk.

She turned with a chilly expression. "Yes?"

"You're upset."

"What was your first clue?"

"Several things, including calling me Mr. Forrester. Speak your mind. I prefer it."

"All right. Don't *ever* call what Poppy Gold does at the John Muir Cottage charity. Of all people, you know the sacrifices our military and their families make. Is it inconceivable that somebody would want to acknowledge those sacrifices and say thank you?"

"Of course not, but—"

"No buts," she interrupted furiously, her cheeks bright with indignation. "What if someone else staying there heard you call it charity? How do you think it would make them feel? They're going through enough—the last thing they need is for someone to judge them for accepting a few days of rest and relaxation."

An unaccustomed shame went through Luke. He hadn't considered how anyone else might take his ill-chosen words.

He checked to see if other guests were within earshot. "Let me explain why I reacted that way."

Carlie's eyes narrowed and she crossed her arms over her stomach. "Okay, explain."

"I, well, my parents are trust-fund kids. They're nice people, but irresponsible. When I was growing up they spent their money wildly, doing whatever captured their fancy. So every year they'd run out of funds by September or October and expect friends to put us up until January. If there were children in the household, they'd taunt us as charity cases. They made life miserable for Nicole and me."

"It isn't necessarily how their parents felt."

"They had to hear it from somewhere. Most of our hosts were friends of my parents from boarding school or college, so maybe they were amused by Mom and Dad. Nicole and I could have been the ones who weren't welcome."

"I understand how difficult it must have been," Carlie said slowly. "But that was a long time ago. Everybody knows how successful you are today."

"My gut reaction is still the same."

She nodded, still looking troubled. "All right. Just don't say anything else in front of our other guests. Poppy Gold doesn't advertise its policy at the John Muir Cottage. We receive referrals from various commanding officers and make the arrangements that way. In your case, the referral would have been from General Pierson's office. Other guests shouldn't know anything about it."

Luke released a harsh breath as he watched Carlie walk away, energy seeming to swirl around her. While he'd already noticed she was attractive, this time her appeal was striking a primal chord.

There was nothing indifferent about Carlie. She

was passionate, vital and far more beautiful than he'd recognized at first. She reminded him of the desert after a spring thunderstorm, where everything has been dry and desolate, only to awaken with a roar after a dose of life-giving rain.

A wry smile curved Luke's mouth—flash floods through an arroyo weren't uncommon after a spring storm, either, and they could be lethal. Besides, he wasn't a desert. He was a man who'd lost his wife.

But if nothing else, his response to her was proof that his body wasn't dead. After Erika's death he'd never expected to look at another woman that way again.

CHAPTER SEVEN

THAT EVENING, THERE was a Christmas cookie party being sponsored by the firemen's auxiliary at Poppy Gold's historic fire station, but Carlie decided to forgo it to get an early night. So for the first time since Thanksgiving, she left Poppy Gold by 7:00 p.m. She ran in to check on her dad when she got home. He seemed thinner and more tired than ever.

"I'm fine," he insisted when she mentioned it. "I had a long day, that's all. You look tired, too."

Her mom just shook her head. "Are you hungry, dear?"

"Starved," Carlie admitted, mostly because she knew it would make Leah feel better to feed her.

"I'll make you something."

After a hearty salad and sandwich, Carlie climbed the steps to the apartment over her parents' garage, eager to crawl into bed. But she'd barely closed her eyes when the phone rang.

Groaning, she pressed the button. "Hello?"

"Sorry, it's Greg on the front desk. We have a call from the Forresters."

She checked the time. At least it wasn't 2:00 a.m. "Don't tell me—they want a cup of tea."

"Excuse me?"

"Never mind, Greg. What's the problem?"

"Nicole Forrester is on the other line. She's quite apologetic and says she doesn't know your work hours, but hoped you were still at Poppy Gold because of the firehouse party. One of her nieces woke up with a nightmare and keeps crying for you. She told me not to call if you'd left, but I thought…"

"It's okay. Tell Nicole I'll be there in a few minutes."

"The girl will probably be asleep again by the time you arrive."

True enough, but Carlie wouldn't be able to sleep herself under the circumstances. Maybe it was because of the horrible dreams she'd had when her father was in intensive care and the doctors didn't know if he'd pull through. It was awful to think of Annie or Beth going through anything similar.

She swiftly prepared her mother's special sleep concoction in the microwave and poured it into a thermos before driving to the parking area closest to the John Muir Cottage.

Nicole answered the door, her face stressed. "Thank you for coming, Carlie. Luke told me Beth's nightmares were bad, but I didn't realize they were like this. I panicked when she kept screaming."

Carlie followed her up the stairs and saw Beth pushing her father away as she and Nicole went into the girls' bedroom.

"Hey," Carlie soothed, sitting on the bed. "What's up?"

Beth promptly scrambled onto her lap. "Somebody was chasing us."

Carlie tucked Beth close and gave Annie an encouraging smile. "It's okay. Nobody is here."

"But he wanted to hurt Papa," Beth wailed.

The air seemed to catch in Carlie's chest. Beth had already lost her mother; now she must be terrified she'd lose her father. But why wouldn't she want Luke's reassurance after a nightmare like that?

Lord, *nothing* about the Forrester family made much sense.

"Your papa isn't going anywhere. Nobody is trying to hurt him."

"Are you sure? Promise?"

"I'm sure."

Yet Carlie winced as the words left her mouth, understanding why her mom had once said that promises were the pitfall of parenting. You wanted to promise your children the world, but you knew that sooner or later one of your heartfelt vows would get broken. Not that Carlie had any reason to think anyone was going to hurt Luke…unless one of the Poppy Gold employees decided they'd had enough of his Grinchy behavior and bashed him with a Christmas wreath.

Annie wiggled closer and leaned against Carlie, as well. "It's okay, Bethie," she whispered. She looked worried but composed, and Carlie's tired brain rambled with the thought that Annie might be more resilient than her outgoing twin.

"Did your papa tell you about the Christmas trees?" Carlie asked.

Beth lifted her head an inch. "Christmas trees?"

"That's right. You're each going to have a Christmas tree to decorate right here in your bedroom."

"Can we keep the lights on when we go to sleep?"

Carlie glanced at Luke and he shrugged. "Of course you can. We can set up a timer to turn them off once you're asleep. I used to sleep on the couch when I was a little girl, just to be near our Christmas tree. The angel on top was like my guardian angel and I felt warm and safe when she was gazing down at me."

"Remember, Bethie, Nanny Dacia says Momma is our guardian angel now," Annie whispered, so softly it was unlikely her father or aunt could hear.

Carlie kissed both girls. "I'm sure she is," she whispered in return. It was one thing she wasn't worried about promising.

Beth sniffed. "We didn't get to go to the cookie party 'cause we fell asleep."

"There will be other parties. You can also bake cookies right here in the kitchen."

"Aunt Nicole and Papa don't know how."

"Will you make them with us, Carlie?" Annie begged.

"Oh, *yes*," Beth agreed, sitting up straight. "That would be splendiferous."

Carlie laughed. "Where did you learn that word?"

"From the gardener. He has splendiferous roses, but we can't touch them because they have thorns and we might get poked."

"Oh. Well, if it's okay with your papa, I'll bake cookies with you sometime next week. But right now you both need to sleep. We're having a Christmas scavenger hunt tomorrow afternoon and you don't want to be sleepy during it."

"Is there a prize, Carlie?" Beth wanted to know, which probably meant she was getting back to normal. She seemed much more competitive than Annie, who appeared to enjoy doing things at her own pace without worrying about what anyone else was doing.

"Yes, there are prizes. So it's time to settle down for a long winter's nap."

Beth hesitated. "Maybe me and Annie can sleep together like when we were little."

"How about moving your beds together?" Carlie

suggested. "Then you'd be close, but still have enough room to stretch your legs."

"Okay."

Luke was quiet as the three adults rearranged the furniture so the twin beds were pushed against each other.

Beth still looked tearful and Carlie reached for the small thermos she'd brought. "I made something for you to drink that my mother used to give me when I was a little girl. It's very special and would help me sleep soundly, all night long."

She filled two cups and the girls drank the warm milk, smacking their lips at the faintly sweet flavor. They were asleep by the time the blankets were tucked around them. Luke stayed behind while Carlie tiptoed from the bedroom with Nicole.

They walked downstairs and Nicole collapsed onto the couch. "I didn't think warm milk worked," she muttered.

"It always did for me."

"That's nice. I'm sorry about the 'baking cookies' thing. I never learned how to cook. I've looked into taking a class, but they're too advanced. I need to learn the basics first."

"You'll be here for over a month. My great-aunt Vera used to teach home economics at the high school and she might be able to give you a few lessons."

Nicole's face lit up. "I'd love that. But I'd insist on paying for her time."

"She's out of town for a few days, but I'll give her a call when she gets back." Carlie pulled out her smartphone and entered a reminder. It had been a weird evening and she didn't want to forget.

"Is Great-Aunt Vera the originator of your mother's magic sleep elixir?" Nicole asked.

"I don't know, but it isn't complicated—just heat milk and real maple syrup together."

"That sounds delicious."

"There's a little left. I'll pour you a cup," Carlie offered, taking out the thermos again.

"I'll gratefully accept, though I should give it to Luke. I don't think he slept more than two or three hours last night. He was at the computer working, dealing with emails and contracts or whatever. Not that it's new—back home I get messages from him at all hours."

Nicole was sipping the fragrant concoction when Luke appeared. He looked grim and a stab of sympathy went through Carlie. Much as she longed for a family of her own, parenting had its challenges.

"I'll walk you back to your office," he said.

"Don't worry about it. I'm headed home and my car isn't that far away." There wasn't any need to explain she'd been in bed when his sister called and was going straight back—he probably wouldn't care and Nicole would feel bad.

"It's getting late. I insist."

The small storm had passed and the stars were bright in the moonless sky. The grass crunched beneath their feet and Carlie figured the maintenance crew already had the snowmakers back at work, laying down new snow. Someone would stay out there all night, keeping watch and making sure everything was ready for early-morning fun.

The Christmas lights on the houses were dark. They went off at 10:00 p.m., while the ones in the park and low bushes in the gardens stayed on all night.

"I take it my sister is responsible for calling you," Luke said.

"Nicole called the front desk, who called me."

"Usually Beth wants her nanny, but Dacia has been wanting to visit her family in Ireland, so I gave her a plane ticket and travel funds for Christmas. I guess it was a mistake not to have her come with us."

At the lighted parking area, Carlie fumbled in her pocket for her keys. She'd forgotten her purse and hoped she wouldn't get stopped on the way home. Ever since her great-uncle Milt had retired as police chief and his grandson had taken over, the police force was more diligent about giving tickets, rather than issuing verbal warnings.

"Um, if Beth is afraid for your safety, why

doesn't she cry for you when she's had one of her nightmares?" Carlie couldn't resist asking.

"I have no idea. The girls don't even know the details of how their mother died. I didn't think it was fair to burden them with it."

"Maybe their imagination is conjuring something worse."

"What could be worse than knowing she was shot in the back by a sniper while trying to rescue another soldier?" Luke said harshly. "There's so much crap on the internet about us, I dread the day they start looking things up about their mother. Have you ever lost someone to senseless violence?"

"No," Carlie admitted. "Though I've seen senseless death. It isn't the same as what you've gone through, but one of my aunts died of pneumonia a few years ago. She wasn't elderly or chronically sick—she was vital and healthy. And when I was a kid, my uncle Tate was killed in a navy jet crash. He left a wife and two sons. They weren't much older than Annie and Beth at the time."

IN THE BACK of his mind, Luke noted Carlie wasn't wearing the same coat as earlier and that her long hair was loosely contained in a French braid. Most likely it meant she'd already gone home, only to be called back to Poppy Gold. He regretted that she'd been inconvenienced, but was too exhausted to deal with anything else at the moment.

"All death is senseless," he muttered.

"I can't argue with that." Carlie stuck her key into the lock of a small white sedan and Luke frowned. "*This* is your car?"

"Yup." She patted the roof as if patting a loyal dog. "I need new batteries for the electronic keys, but other than that, everything works well."

He was astonished. Judging from the styling, the vehicle was at least a decade old and couldn't have been top-of-the-line when it was new. "I thought everyone in small towns drove trucks and SUVs."

"Not quite. Anyhow, while I grew up in Glimmer Creek, I only moved back a year ago in August. Before that, I lived in the San Francisco area. Small cars are best there."

"What brought you home?"

Her expression closed. "Several things, including getting a job with Poppy Gold. It's late. I'd better go, and I'm sure you want to check on the girls."

Her face was softly illuminated by the old-style streetlights and he put his hands in his pockets, fighting the urge to kiss her, which was both insane and inappropriate. "Thank you for coming."

"Of course. I hope you can all get some sleep now."

She slid behind the steering wheel and Luke stepped back, watching as she closed the door and drove away.

It was understandable why the twins found

Carlie so appealing; she represented the fun things Poppy Gold had to offer. He was drawn to her, too, for purely masculine reasons. Yet acting on that wouldn't be right. Erika's loss was too fresh and raw and nobody could ever take her place—for him or his daughters.

THE NEXT MORNING, Luke went back to work on his computer while the girls were studying with their tutor, but for the first time in ages, he found it hard to focus on his business concerns. Maybe the holiday atmosphere was affecting him. Stock quotes and contracts and evaluating prospective acquisitions were dull compared to Christmas caroling and other things to do.

Nicole had returned from taking a walk and he told her he was going out to stretch his own legs.

There was energy in the air at Poppy Gold, a suppressed excitement related to all the lights and decorations and activities. Austin was nice at Christmas, but it couldn't compete with a place that threw itself into the holidays with the passion of Santa's elves.

From what Luke had been able to tell, the whole community of Glimmer Creek participated. Some of the activities were in other parts of town, such as the memorial hall and large community church, but a good many were at Poppy Gold, with locals invited to participate along with guests.

To Luke's surprise, his restless feet took him

to Old City Hall and through the rotunda toward Carlie's office. It wasn't a good idea considering his impulse to kiss her the night before, but he also wasn't an adolescent boy, confused by surging hormones. While they were unlikely to become friends, they could probably manage to have a cup of coffee together.

"How about a break?" he inquired at Carlie's door. "The girls are studying with their tutor and I needed to get away from the computer. You could introduce me to Sarah's bakery, or whatever it's called. My treat."

"I'm pretty busy."

"Surely you're entitled to a coffee break. We can go as acquaintances, not activities director and Poppy Gold guest."

She regarded him warily. "What does that mean?"

"It's an invitation to speak your mind. I appreciate people being honest with me, without worrying about good public relations."

Carlie regarded him for a long moment. "How can I turn *that* down?"

They went up the pedestrian shopping street and around the corner into an attractive building from which emanated the enticing scents of chocolate, spices and baking bread.

"I hope they serve Poppy Gold coffee," Luke said. He'd quickly become addicted to the blend and had discovered it was carried at the town's general store on the pedestrian shopping street. When he'd learned they took mail orders, he'd promptly arranged for monthly shipments to Texas.

"I'm sure they do. Hey, Aurelia," Carlie greeted the girl behind the counter. "This is Luke. He's a guest at Poppy Gold and wanted to see the source of his breakfasts."

The young woman smiled. "What can I get for you, Luke?"

"A tall cup of Poppy Gold coffee to start. Carlie?"

"The same. Also an apricot-banana muffin."

The bakery cases were filled with creations that looked delicious. Luke didn't want his daughters eating too many sweets, but it was Christmas, so he ordered a pound of cranberry-chocolate fudge, two boxes of assorted cookies and a second muffin.

At a café table in the corner, he pushed one of the cookie boxes toward Carlie. "These are for your staff."

"I'll put it in the Old City Hall employee break room. We keep a coffeepot going there 24/7." She poured cream into her cup and absently stirred the mixture.

Luke ate a bite of muffin and was pleasantly surprised; it was moist and chunks of dried apricot provided a tangy contrast to the banana flavor. "This isn't bad."

"Sarah is a whiz in the kitchen."

"You know her well?"

"She's one of my cousins. Same as Aurelia at the front counter. A lot of the people around Glimmer Creek are related in one way or another."

"I can't imagine having that much family."

"You don't have any cousins or aunts and uncles?"

"No, and I barely remember any of my grandparents. I believe they're still living, but they cut ties with my mother and father before Nicole came along."

"For heaven's sake, *why*?"

"All four of my grandparents are nose-to-the-grindstone type of people and didn't approve of Mom and Dad's frivolous lifestyle."

Carlie looked confused. "If that's how they felt, why were trust funds set up?"

"Those were established when they were born." Luke shifted his feet under the café table. He wasn't accustomed to confiding in anyone. Even with Erika it had been difficult since she was gone so much. Nicole would have been a logical person, but she was younger and he wanted to protect her.

Carlie was silent as she fiddled with her cup. Luke knew he should be grateful she hadn't asked another question, yet a part of him wanted to know what she was thinking.

"Do you know *your* grandparents?" he prompted.

"Sure. On my mother's side, Grandpa is the senior pastor at the Glimmer Creek Community Church and Grandma is a retired town mayor. My dad's parents own the small hardware store in town. I grew up with Sunday lunch alternating between the two families. And there would be these huge cousin sleepovers during the summer where we'd make ice cream and s'mores or have picnics down by the creek. We're more like siblings than cousins."

Luke had never experienced the kind of family closeness Carlie had known growing up. He couldn't even envision what it would be like.

Probably oppressive.

He cleared his throat. "By the way, you seemed stressed when I stopped by your office. Is something up?"

Carlie shrugged. "I'm just a little concerned about my father. How was Beth this morning?" she asked, clearly eager to change the subject, which made him want to pursue it even more.

"Fine. You'd never know anything had happened. I hope she didn't disturb anyone else."

"I doubt it." Carlie fished a pen from her pocket and began sketching on a paper napkin. "This is the layout of your suite. The house was enlarged several times and the section where you're staying is almost a separate wing. There must be four walls between the twins' room and one of the other suites' bedrooms."

"That's good to know. So, what's going on with your father?"

Irritation flashed through Carlie's blue eyes. "If you must know, Dad is a highway worker. A year ago this last summer, a guy in a pricey car decided he was too busy and important to obey the law. He took a shortcut through a construction zone to get around slow-moving traffic. Dad was hit and spent two weeks in intensive care. The damage was considerable and he's still in pain most of the time."

"Is that why you moved back here from San Francisco?"

CARLIE BLINKED.

Though it might be a shot in the dark, Luke's question hinted at a perceptiveness she hadn't expected. She'd chosen to come back to Glimmer Creek to help her parents, but she also hadn't wanted to stay at her old job, running into her ex-fiancé constantly.

"Partly," she said carefully. "Dad is stiff-necked, but I try to take care of things around the house that he has trouble with now—mowing, weeding, cutting back brush, that type of thing."

"You don't have a brother to take care of it?"

She rolled her eyes. "That's a chauvinistic question. I have two younger brothers who are away at graduate school, but I'm just as capable of assisting my folks as Quinn and Russ. *More* capable. I used to help with the yard as a kid, but *they* wouldn't do it unless they got paid. When this all happened, their suggestion was to hire a gardening service, which would have galled Dad."

Luke frowned. "What about the rest of your family? Don't they help out?"

Carlie made a scoffing sound. "You mean, isn't there a big strong guy who's willing to come over and do a man's work? You sound like a Neanderthal, masquerading as a twenty-first-century guy."

Luke choked on his coffee.

Okay, she should have been more tactful, but he *had* invited her to be honest and his old-fashioned attitude didn't make sense. He'd married a soldier, so she would have expected him to be modern in his views about women. Of course, maybe losing his wife had made him regress to caveman attitudes.

"The family would love to help with whatever needs doing," she said when Luke had stopped coughing, "but it's better to handle it my own way. I just told Dad that working on the yard was therapy for me after…"

"After what?"

Her cheeks heated. "Some of my plans for the future changed, that's all."

Having her wedding canceled just hours before

it was supposed to take place wasn't a secret, but she didn't want Luke Forrester to know those kinds of details about her. It might be hypocritical since *his* life was splashed all over the internet, but she wasn't a high-profile businessperson and wanted her privacy.

Derek was a sore point, anyhow.

Her mom had tried to get her to open up about it a few times, but what could be said? *I made a terrible error in judgment and wish I'd never met him*? Or how about, *I trusted the wrong man and now I'm paying for my mistake*?

Even if she didn't love Derek any longer, she was still angry at him. Dozens of her family members had come to a Sonoma Valley vineyard for her wedding, only to be told it wasn't going to take place. She'd insisted they turn the reception into a party and not let a single morsel of food or drop of champagne and punch go to waste, but inside she'd been mortified.

Taking a deep breath, Carlie focused on Luke. "How often does Beth have nightmares?"

"It's unpredictable. It sounds illogical, but they're more frequent lately," he admitted. "You'd think they would taper off with time. That's partly why I made a last-minute decision to go away for Christmas, hoping the change would do the girls some good."

Carlie broke off a piece of muffin and rolled it

around her plate. "I had terrible dreams when my dad was in the hospital," she said slowly. "I know it isn't the same as what Annie and Beth have been through, but I understand what it's like to feel the world is falling apart. And I'm an adult, not a six-year-old child."

Luke's mouth twisted as if there was something he wanted to say, but couldn't.

"At least you're doing what you can to help your daughters," Carlie murmured. "You aren't ignoring their problems."

"It doesn't seem like enough."

"Probably because you can't fix the unfixable."

"I guess. My wife had a favorite quote, 'Life isn't fair, it's just fairer than death.' I don't think I truly understood it until she was gone."

"That's from *The Princess Bride* novel by William Goldman. Right at the end."

"Erika didn't read many novels, so she must have heard it from someone."

Carlie finished her coffee, unsure how to respond. She wasn't sure she agreed with William Goldman, who'd ended his novel in a different way from the movie. Life often wasn't fair, but neither was death, and they couldn't be compared. You just had to do your best.

She glanced at her watch. Her team members took the lead on various activities, but they had staggered days off during the week and Tim Mahoney had called in sick. Because of that, she still had things to finish for the scavenger hunt he'd planned for that afternoon.

"I'm really sorry, but I have to go," she said finally. "Thanks for the cookies. I'll put a note on the box, saying they're from you. For future reference, Sarah has a few lunch items available here at the bakery, not just sweets. Her sandwiches and quiche are delicious."

She hurried away before Luke could suggest walking with her. She didn't know what he'd had in mind by inviting her for coffee, but it was better to keep things professional for everybody's sake.

CHAPTER EIGHT

GIDEON HAD ARRANGED to return to Poppy Gold on
Saturday to give the quarterly health exams to the
four-footed residents of the Victorian Cat mansion.

It would probably sound odd to guests, but the
cats were treated like working animals…feline
ambassadors. They were part of the distinctive
quality that Poppy Gold tried to give each of the
bed-and-breakfast homes. The VC cats even had
a private room for their supplies and veterinary
treatment, fitted out with a table, scale and other
basic equipment.

Gideon reviewed each cat's medical records before tucking their files in his medical bag. He arrived at the Poppy Gold front desk a few minutes
later.

"Good morning, Dr. Cartwright," said Bill
Blalock. "They aren't expecting you at the Victorian Cat for another forty minutes, but I'll see if
anyone can assist with the exams immediately."

"That won't be necessary. One of my patients
is staying here and I thought I'd drop by to check

on his progress. If the guest is in, of course. It's the kitten that Nicole Forrester found."

Bill's expression shifted subtly. "Oh, yes, the Forresters. They're at the Yosemite suite in the John Muir Cottage. It's right here." Bill pulled out a facility map and indicated the location. "I can have a shuttle driver take you over."

"No need to bother with that. I prefer walking."

Following Bill's instructions, Gideon took the garden path around to the back of the John Muir Cottage. He knocked, feeling both annoyed and foolish. His affluent clients in Beverly Hills had often expected him to make house calls, but these days most of his visits were to farm animals.

The door opened and Gideon saw Nicole Forrester, considerably less disheveled than she had been at his office. This time instead of silk and diamonds, she wore cashmere and pearls and looked as if she'd stepped off a fashion runway.

"Is there something I can do for you, Dr. Cartwright?"

"I'm sorry I didn't call first, but I came to check on my patient."

"Oh. All right."

She opened the door wider and Gideon stepped inside.

"I'll get him." Nicole crossed to the stairs on the far end of the room, her hips swaying gently.

Curious, Gideon gazed around. He'd seen a few of the suites at Poppy Gold, but this was more like a home than a bed-and-breakfast inn. A fire was crackling in the fireplace, brightening the large room, while Christmas music played in the background. Across from the staircase was an arched entry into a well-lit kitchen.

A couple of minutes later, Nicole descended the steps carrying the kitten, accompanied by two small girls who were mirror images of each other.

Gideon grinned at them. "Hello. Have you been helping to take care of the baby kitty?"

They both nodded, though one immediately ducked her face in apparent shyness.

"Yes. But he sleeps with Aunt Nicole," announced the one who seemed bolder. "He's going to live with her in Austin. I'm Beth and this is my sister, Annie. We're six."

"I'm pleased to meet you. My name is Gideon."

Annie was chewing her lip and looking at him seriously. "Are you going to hurt Chico?"

"No, Annie," Nicole said quickly. "The doctor is just going to make sure he's doing okay."

"That's right," Gideon agreed. "Is there a good place for me to do the exam, Ms. Forrester?"

"It's Nicole and there's a table in the laundry room." She handed him the kitten reluctantly and gestured toward the kitchen.

NICOLE WASN'T SURPRISED when Chico instantly began hissing. He was strong-willed and nearly impossible to keep quiet the way that Dr. Cartwright had instructed. How did you keep a kitten quiet, anyhow? It wasn't as if they listened to reason. Mostly she'd kept him in her bedroom so he wouldn't race all over the house.

She'd hoped having Chico would help her connect better with her nieces, but so far it hadn't happened. Instead, they still wanted to do everything with Carlie Benton.

Nicole shivered when she remembered Beth's screams during her nightmare. Luke hadn't been thrilled about Carlie coming over, but her presence had helped and that was what mattered.

"Maaaarroow," squalled Chico, grabbing Nicole's attention. He was doing his best to get away from Gideon.

"Is he okay?" asked Beth.

"He's terrific. I don't have a scale, but I can tell he's already gained weight. And his leg is much better."

The veterinarian almost sounded perplexed at Chico's progress and Nicole felt smug. Gideon Cartwright had acted as if she wasn't capable of handling an animal.

She might not be the bravest person in the world, but she could certainly give love and care to a kitten.

"A cat's skin heals quickly, so germs can get trapped underneath," Gideon explained to the girls. "I know it seems mean, but that's why I need to check where he got hurt and make sure it isn't getting infected."

Nicole's mouth tightened. Why couldn't Gideon have explained that to *her* back at the clinic? The way he'd examined Chico's wound had seemed cavalier.

"Can we take the cone thing off him?" she asked. "He really hates it."

"Sure. Do you want me to do it, or do you think you can manage?"

"It's a Velcro fastening, hardly a brain teaser," she retorted, narrowing her eyes at his superior tone.

It wasn't the first time he'd implied she was an idiot. His attitude toward her had *not* improved in the past few days, though by his own admission she'd done a good job with Chico. She hoped Beth and Annie were too young to understand, because her relationship with them was challenging enough already.

Nicole unfastened the blue cone and tossed it aside, then lifted Chico and cuddled him in her arms. He glared balefully at the veterinarian.

"I'd better get going," Gideon said. "I need to examine the cats at the Victorian Cat mansion."

"Can we go, too, Gideon? Pleeeeeze," Beth begged. "Carlie told us about the kitties."

"I think that would be all right."

Nicole's heart sank. The twins couldn't go alone with Gideon, which meant she'd have to go with them. The last thing she wanted was to spend time around a man who seemed so disapproving of her. "Beth, I thought you wanted to make Christmas ornaments at the concert hall."

"That's what Annie wanted. But you'd rather visit the kitties, wouldn't you, Annie?"

Annie looked torn. "I guess."

"I'm meeting someone at the VC in a few minutes, so get your coats on and we'll go over," Gideon urged.

"Goody." Beth ran out, followed by her sister.

Nicole leaned forward. "Could you refrain from treating me like an idiot in front of my own nieces?" she hissed. "At the very least, be the professional you're supposed to be."

For good measure, Chico spit and swatted his paw so fast that Gideon barely had time to get out of striking range.

"I may not have your lofty experience with animals," she continued, "but I have a degree in information technology. I bet I could program circles around you on the computer, but I wouldn't put *you* down because of it."

GIDEON GRITTED HIS TEETH, realizing he'd unconsciously revealed his feelings. Although he hadn't meant to, it was unprofessional and a stupid move. He owed her an apology, but there wasn't time for one, because Beth and Annie had reappeared.

Nicole put the kitten down and went to help them, but she was plainly inexperienced at helping someone else zip their jackets—especially children, who had little patience and antsy feet.

"Do you know Carlie?" Beth asked as they walked toward the VC.

"Sure do. I'm helping with the living nativity over at the church. Did you see it last week?"

"Uh-huh."

"How about you, Annie?" he said to the quieter twin.

"I liked the donkey best. Carlie is baking Christmas cookies with us next week, 'cause Aunt Nicole and Papa don't know how. Carlie is fantabulous."

"Oh, I see. Where's your daddy this morning?" he asked the girls.

"Papa is on a conference call with Japan," Beth explained matter-of-factly. "He's awful busy making money."

Gideon kept his expression neutral. It was Saturday morning, which meant it was probably around 3:00 a.m. in Japan. Not exactly a convenient time for the people on the *other* end of the call. He wondered if inconveniencing people was a pattern with the Forresters. Nicole certainly hadn't seemed to think twice about bringing a kitten into a historic home that didn't belong to her.

Inside the foyer of the Victorian Cat, they were met by Tessa McKinley. She would bring the cats for their exams one at a time.

"I see you have assistants today," she said, smiling at the twins.

"Yes, this is Beth, Annie and their aunt, Nicole Forrester. I stopped to check on the kitten that Ms. Forrester rescued a few days ago. The girls wanted to meet the VC cats. Is that all right?"

Tessa winked at the six-year-olds. "You bet. Our cats love people. I'll be right back with the first one."

"Where's little Meredith?" Gideon inquired when Tessa returned carrying a white feline known as Moby Dick.

"With her daddy. Gabe keeps complaining he doesn't get enough time with her."

Both Beth and Annie seemed fascinated by the huge white cat, but Gideon noticed that Nicole's eyes had widened and she'd taken a quick step backward. Granted, Moby Dick was twice the size of an average cat, but hardly dangerous. His favorite trick was coaxing treats from the people staying in his suite, employing a range of "poor me" and "I'm starving" techniques.

"Moby seems to be doing well on the weight-management food," Gideon told Tessa. "He's lost nine ounces."

"Kitties have to go on diets?" asked Annie.

"They do if they gain too much weight. It's better for them."

The exams continued and Gideon found himself watching Nicole's reaction each time one of the larger felines was brought into the room for examination. She couldn't be terrified of cats in general if she'd rescued Chico, but plainly the larger ones made her nervous. He had news for her—Chico was going to be a *very* large cat when he was grown. He had enormous paws and, despite his malnourished state, was sizable for his age.

How would she feel when he grew into a cat the size of Moby Dick?

Gideon frowned and focused on his examination. Nicole would probably adjust, though aside from his responsibility as Chico's veterinarian, it wasn't any of his concern.

"THAT SEEMS TOTALLY out of character for Gideon," Carlie told Nicole on Sunday afternoon as they sat on hay bales and watched Annie and Beth sledding. "I can't imagine him talking down to anyone and he's been really helpful with the living nativity."

"Maybe he just dislikes me."

"I don't see why. But aside from annoying veterinarians, how are you settling in?"

"Pretty well. Luke still is working most of the night. Mornings, too, while the girls are studying. I keep searching the area where I found Chico in case his littermates were dumped out there, as well. I haven't seen any sign of another kitten, though I've left food and bowls of water in different spots, just in case. It's disappearing, but that could be other animals enjoying a free lunch."

"True." Carlie shivered. She hated to think of a kitten being in such dire straits.

"By the way, I didn't thank you properly for coming over when Beth had her nightmare," Nicole said hesitantly. "Or when they asked you to be there when they decorated their Christmas trees. And, well, all the other time you've spent with them. I really appreciate it."

Carlie hid a smile, thinking about Luke's confusion at the sharp contrast between the trees his daughters had decorated. She'd deflected Beth when she started saying Annie's choices were boring and urging her to hurry up. As a result, Beth's tree was bold and brilliantly colored, while Annie's shimmered in shades of white, ice blue and silver. Lavish praise had been given to both, so with any luck, Beth wouldn't try to convince Annie to make changes. To be certain, Carlie had taken the remaining ornaments back to her office.

"Has Beth had any more nightmares?" she asked.

"No, thank goodness. From what Luke says, I don't think she's ever told anyone else what happens in them—at least, he's never heard the part about being chased and that someone was after him, too."

"I'm sure that any child who's lost her mother could be afraid of losing her father."

"Yeah." Nicole fidgeted and finally sighed. "Do you think I'm a terrible aunt because Beth wanted you, instead of me?"

"Of course not. Kids are unpredictable and I'm the one who represents doing fun things. Basically, I'm sledding, cookies, cake and hot chocolate. What child wouldn't ask for me? I positively reek of Christmas."

Nicole smiled uncertainly. She was a curious contrast to her brother, rather diffident and quiet, with none of Luke's arrogance. "Annie mentioned that Christmas is your favorite time of the year."

"It is. Oh, before I forget, there are two things… I spoke to my great-aunt and she'd love to give you cooking lessons if you're still interested."

"Absolutely."

"Okay." Carlie handed her a business card. "Great-Aunt Vera's phone number is on the back. She's expecting your call. The second thing I wanted to ask is that since you're going to be here all month, would you like to borrow one of my Victorian costumes to wear at Poppy Gold's two holiday dress balls? We're about the same size, so it should fit you. A lot of the guests come in costume."

Nicole pocketed the card. "I'd love it, if I attend. But somebody needs to take care of Beth and Annie."

Carlie grinned. "Babysitting is covered. Poppy Gold is hosting a children's party at the same time in the concert hall. There will be plenty of adults to entertain the kids and keep them out of trouble."

Nicole shook her head. "How do you do it?"

"Do what?"

"Put all of this together."

"Don't give me too much credit," Carlie warned. "The basic schedule was established when I was a kid. Having an activities director is new to Poppy Gold—this is only my second Christmas on the job and I'm still figuring it out."

"I never would have guessed."

"It helps that I practically grew up at Poppy Gold since my aunt and uncle owned the place. I always had ideas about things they could do here, so it seemed perfect when my cousin offered me the position. She's the manager now."

Carlie knew she'd skipped some of the highlights, such as being jilted by her cheating fiancé a few hours before their wedding, but Nicole didn't need to hear *that*. After all, someone who had lousy judgment in one area could be totally responsible in other ways.

"Still, you're so comfortable with people," Nicole said, sounding wistful. "Especially kids. Ever since Erika died, I'm always afraid I'll say the wrong thing and make them cry or miss their mother more. Though to be honest, I wasn't so great with them before that, either."

Carlie rubbed her hands together, wishing she'd remembered her gloves when Annie had asked if she'd come out to the sledding hill with them. "Don't be hard on yourself. I think it's harder communicating with twins. I've got identical twin brothers and they spoke their own language for years. It used to make me crazy when they'd point my direction, whisper to each other and giggle."

"They didn't."

"Oh, yes, they did. Quinn and Russ had their own private world when they were little. And they could get into ten times as much trouble *together* as they could apart. It's a twin thing."

NICOLE LAUGHED, LOVING how normal Carlie's family sounded.

Beth and Annie came down the snowy hill on their sleds. While it was a gentle slope, she still watched carefully to be sure they got to the bottom safely. She wasn't the only one; Luke would wait in line with them at the top, help his daughters onto their sleds and then hurry to meet them at the bottom.

Curiously, Carlie's story about her brothers was making Nicole worry about her nieces even more. Getting in occasional trouble was normal for children, but Beth and Annie seemed almost *too* well behaved.

"What sort of things did your brothers do?" she asked.

"Let's see. In kindergarten they let all the air out of Dad's truck tires to see how far down to the ground the undercarriage would go. They were smart little devils and didn't puncture the tires—just figured out how to do it with the valve."

"I'll bet your father was upset."

"A little. He had to take Mom's yellow Volkswagen to work that morning. I'm sure he didn't feel it fit his masculine image, though it would have taken a team of horses to drag it out of him—my mother really loved that VW."

Nicole bit her lip to keep from laughing again. "What else?"

"All sorts of stuff, like cutting up my prom dress to make a parachute—*before* the prom, I might add. I think the worst was when they ran hoses into the basement to turn it into an indoor pool. You should have heard Dad yelling when he discovered it the next morning."

"Omigod. How deep did the water get?"

"Deep enough to swim laps. Luckily it only fried one electrical circuit, but we had to call the volunteer fire department to suction it out with their equipment."

Okay, Nicole didn't think Beth and Annie needed to get into *that* much trouble, but surely a little innocent mischief wouldn't hurt.

AFTER TWO HOURS at the sledding hill, Luke told the girls it was time to leave. Beth stuck her lip out a fraction of an inch, while Annie looked longingly at the snowy slope.

He still wondered if coming to California had been a good idea, but his daughters' bright eyes and red cheeks were reassuring.

"Papa, can we go *one* more time?" Beth asked as they walked to where Carlie was talking to his sister.

Carlie had spent most of the afternoon chatting with Nicole and other guests, while the twins went over several times to ask if she and their aunt had seen them on their sleds.

"You need some quiet time," Luke said firmly. "If you're too tired you won't be able to ride in the lighted parade and go on the caroling hayride afterward."

Nicole looked confused. "Ride *in* the parade?"

"Yes. All four of us are going on the flatbed trailer used for the hayride. Carlie set it up."

"You're going, too, aren't you, Carlie?" Annie asked anxiously.

Carlie tugged her pigtail. "I'll be there before you leave, but I'm riding in one of the carriages tonight, all dressed up in a costume."

"Can I go with you?"

"Me, too," Beth cried.

Luke was frustrated by the girls' reaction. How was he supposed to reach his own daughters when they preferred spending time with someone who wasn't even family?

"Maybe another night," Carlie told them gently. "The hayride starts as soon as the parade is over and you don't want to miss going. It's really fun. You sing carols as you drive around and see the lights in town. Then on the way back, you stop at the old fire station for warm gingerbread with lemon sauce."

"Yummers," Beth said, though her sister seemed less enthused. She still didn't want to get involved in Poppy Gold activities unless Carlie was there.

"It's *very* yummy," Carlie assured her. "So go have your quiet time and I'll see you before the parade."

Beth started off happily, but Annie hung back. "Will you be at the fire station?" she asked. "Pleeeeze?"

There was a brief hesitation before Carlie nodded. "All right."

THAT EVENING, LUKE and Nicole bundled the girls in warm clothing and mittens and walked toward the area where the nightly parade was staged.

The caroling hayride wasn't new, but apparently it was the first time that guests would be part of the parade. A Poppy Gold employee was gathering the participants together and handing out blankets to use during the ride.

"Hey there," Carlie said behind them, but when Luke turned, she didn't look anything like herself.

The dark green velvet costume could have come right out of a historic painting. The jacket she wore was formfitting with lace accents at the throat and wrists, while her hair was piled high and topped by a frothy hat. She smiled at the twins.

"Whoa," Nicole exclaimed. "You must be wearing a corset."

"Not a chance," Carlie denied. "One of my aunts is a doctor and she doesn't approve of corsets. Since she's also the president of the historical society and they make most of the costumes, none of us wear them."

"Then I won't fit into one of your gowns. I'll have to find something else to wear to the dances."

"Dances?" Luke interjected.

Nicole turned. "Didn't you see them on the December activities schedule? There are two dress balls before Christmas. Carlie offered to loan me a costume, but my waist isn't *that* small."

"Optical illusion," Carlie declared. "I've got a pink velvet number that will look terrific on you. It'll be perfect with your dark hair."

"I think you're being optimistic."

"Trust me."

"Carlie?" called a voice from across the parade staging area. "Your carriage awaits."

"Be right there, Uncle Liam." She nodded at the girls. "I'll see you later at the fire station. Have a good time on your ride."

Luke suppressed the renewed stab of awareness that had gone through him at seeing Carlie in her Victorian garb. Even though her costume wasn't intentionally provocative, it showcased her figure very nicely.

Not that his response mattered. He wasn't looking for anything permanent and he suspected she wasn't the type for brief affairs—even if she liked him, which she didn't. Even more critical, he was only staying in Glimmer Creek for a few weeks and the girls needed stability. They certainly didn't need to start imagining that Carlie would be a permanent part of their lives. They were already getting too fond of her. His daughters' needs had to be his only priority.

CHAPTER NINE

ON MONDAY MORNING, as soon as Luisa Cabrera arrived to work with the girls, Luke found his feet taking him toward Old City Hall instead of back to his computer. After his first success in coaxing Carlie into a coffee break with him, he hoped he could do it again.

She had a connection with his daughters and he needed to understand it—though needing anything made him uncomfortable. It would be different if he were paying Carlie for all the extra time she was spending with his children, but he wasn't.

Perhaps he could do something to show his appreciation. Handing her a check would be crass, but back in Austin he sometimes gave vehicles to his employees as bonuses, a choice that seemed quite popular. Carlie's car was ancient and couldn't last much longer. Surely now that she was living up in the foothills, it would be good for her to have something larger—maybe a truck or SUV.

A quiet exchange would be best. He preferred keeping a low profile when he provided a bonus. After all, he was supposed to be thanking someone else, not the other way around. In Austin, he'd just have the keys and paperwork delivered to the person's office, but he didn't know how private things were at Poppy Gold, so he might have to come up with a different plan.

Meanwhile, he'd go online and see what arrangements could be made. It was unlikely there was a suitable car dealership in Glimmer Creek, but Stockton wasn't that far away and it was large enough to provide what he needed.

He could also make another gesture to the staff in Old City Hall. The number for Giancarlo's Little Italy was on his phone, so while crossing the park, he called in an order for lunch to be delivered at noon.

"That's a lot of food," said the restaurant employee doubtfully.

"I want to be sure there's plenty. Please don't put my name on the order. This is an anonymous thank-you to the staff."

"Yes, sir."

Pleased with his decisions, Luke ran up the steps of the Old City Hall and headed for Carlie's office.

"No," she said when he appeared at her door.

"I didn't say anything."

"You didn't have to."

"I'm bored and you're the activities director."

Her expression tightened and she stood up. "Fine, I have an activity for you. Come with me."

She led him to the Poppy Gold library. Unlike the first time he'd seen it, boxes were stacked on most of the available surfaces.

"We just got a shipment of new books and movies. You're going to have fun unpacking them," she announced, handing him a pair of tiny scissors. "When that's done, you may help me tag and catalog everything. Be careful not to cut yourself."

She disappeared before Luke could protest, yet the corner of his mouth twitched. It wasn't quite what he'd had in mind, but he shrugged and looked at the scissors.

They were useless.

The rounded ends identified them as safety scissors for children; he'd have to try hard to get bruised with them, much less draw blood. Was Carlie sending him a message or just making a joke? He finally pulled out his keys and used the serrated edges to rip through the packaging tape on the first box.

An hour and a half later, he'd sorted the books and DVDs and had flattened the shipping cartons into a neat stack.

"You're efficient," Carlie commented, carrying a tray into the library. "You like your brew black, right?"

Luke nodded and accepted the cup she held out. "Thanks. I'm continually impressed with the coffee here."

"What a compliment. You're a difficult man to impress." Her tone was cool and he suspected she was thinking about the day he'd arrived at Poppy Gold and had made a nuisance of himself.

He didn't enjoy thinking about it, either, especially in light of what Carlie had revealed about her father's accident. What had she said…that a guy in a pricey car had decided he was too busy and important to obey the law?

It explained a good deal about the underlying distrust he kept sensing from her. While he hadn't broken the law or nearly killed someone, he couldn't deny that he hadn't been a model guest.

Carlie left the library again, only to return immediately with a laptop and folder. "All right," she said briskly, "let's start by cataloging the movies. Then we'll do the books."

Luke took the top film from one of the stacks. "*A Christmas Carol*, with George C. Scott," he read aloud.

She entered the information on the computer and put a bar-code sticker on the back of the case. "Next?"

Luke smiled wryly. She plainly didn't want to talk and he was going to respect her wishes. *This time.*

CARLIE WAS ASTONISHED that Luke had actually proved helpful in getting the new purchases for the library unpacked and on the shelves. But then, he wouldn't be such a hugely successful businessman if he dragged his feet.

Her own tasks were stacking up. A nasty cold bug was going around her staff, so she kept falling further behind. *'Tis the season* ran through her head whenever one of them called, coughing and sniffling. She just hoped it was the same cold she'd gotten a month before, because that way she might be immune. Meanwhile, she needed to handle all of her division's responsibilities.

After Luke left to check on Annie and Beth's progress with their tutor, she wondered if he'd be back. Putting him to work had been rather brazen, but he was treating her as his family's personal activities director, and with so much of her staff out, she didn't have the time.

If Luke *did* come back…? Carlie grinned. She had an important project that needed doing. And if he didn't, that was okay, too. A few more nights working late wouldn't matter, though her mother had suggested she just sleep in her office for all the good her bed was doing her.

An hour later Carlie's phone rang and she picked it up. "Carlie Benton."

"It's Christine. Somebody ordered a truckload of food for the Old City Hall staff. We put everything in the lunch room, so come and get lunch while it's hot."

Curious, Carlie went to the employee break area and saw four enormous stacks of pizza boxes, along with various large sacks holding entrée and salad containers from Giancarlo's Little Italy.

"Who's this from?" she asked Christine, who was getting a slice of sausage-and-olive pizza.

"Got me. I called Giancarlo's and they said it was an anonymous thank-you. We're sending a bunch over to Housekeeping and Maintenance."

"Sounds good."

In one of the large bags Carlie found several containers of pasta primavera and recalled mentioning to Luke that it was her favorite dish. But it didn't seem likely that he was responsible. On the other hand, there was an excessive amount of food—probably enough to feed every Poppy Gold employee—and making a grandiose, over-the-top gesture might fit his persona.

"My staff will be sorry they were out sick today," Carlie said, snagging a container each of pasta primavera and Greek salad. "There's nothing like a free lunch to perk someone up."

Christine chuckled. "You sneeze, you lose. Take enough to have leftovers the rest of the week. Bring dinner home to your parents, too."

"Nah, cooking relaxes Mom. It's better than therapy."

"I wish I could say the same. I *hate* cooking. Fortunately, Jerry handles most of it, along with his share of the diapering. I swear, he's a better parent than I am."

The familiar, wistful twinge went through Carlie. Christine was the proud mother of an adorable toddler. After Sean was born, she and her husband had begun alternating day and night shifts at Poppy Gold to save on child-care expenses, though they tried to keep the same days off for family time. Carlie tried not to envy them.

She snagged another container of pasta primavera and a combination pizza, thinking it would be nice for her employees to have lunch available if they were well enough to come in tomorrow.

"I'll see you later," Carlie said, deciding to eat at her desk.

Another scavenger hunt had been scheduled for Friday and she couldn't make any sense of Tim Mahoney's notes; he must have been getting ill when he was making them. Finally she scrapped everything and started over.

Shortly after 1:00 p.m., she got up and headed for the park. The Forty-Niners barbershop quartet was scheduled to perform in the bandstand, and no matter how busy she was, she couldn't resist listening to part of the concert.

The mellow tones of "It's Beginning to Look a Lot Like Christmas" greeted Carlie as she crossed the street, sending warm waves of nostalgia through her. The Forty-Niners sang for most events in town and she could barely recall a time when they weren't part of life in Glimmer Creek.

Next came the "Carol of the Bells," "Silent Night" and "Deck the Halls," and then a string of songs popular with children, such as "Frosty the Snowman" and "Jingle Bells."

When they began singing "Let It Snow," Carlie thought it was a shame the snowmakers weren't there, showering everyone with white. Perhaps they could bring a couple of the machines to the park on Christmas Eve if it was cold enough. She added it to her mental list of things to talk over with Uncle Liam.

"What are you thinking so intently about?" She jumped at the sound of Luke's deep voice.

"Cold weather actually."

"It's certainly chilly in Glimmer Creek. Is this normal?"

"We're at a higher elevation than some of the other former gold camps, which means we get colder winters. But we've had more freezes than usual for this time of year. It's perfect for the snowmakers."

"I was glad to learn Poppy Gold doesn't use chemicals to make their snow."

"Perish the thought. We use good ole H2O." Carlie was still mellow from the music and cascade of memories it had generated...memories from childhood when things had been simpler.

Yet sadness quickly intruded; with their mother gone, Annie and Beth wouldn't have the same kind of uncomplicated recollections about growing up.

She almost asked if Luke had ordered the mountain of food for the staff and decided he would tell her if he was responsible and wanted them to know.

"Where are Nicole and the girls?" she queried instead.

"By the skating rink. They want to spend the afternoon with Nicole teaching them how to twirl. At least, that's what Beth wants. Annie didn't say much either way."

Carlie recalled Nicole's angst over her relationship with her nieces and hoped the lesson would be successful...and that Annie wasn't simply going along with her sister when there was something she wanted to do more.

"Don't you skate, Luke?"

"Not a chance. Why don't we go over and watch?"

"Sorry, I have to get back to work. But have a nice afternoon."

LUKE WAS AMUSED at having been more or less dismissed by Carlie. It was an unusual experience; ordinarily *he* was the one who decided when a meeting ended, rather than the other way around. Not that he had a professional relationship with her, but it also wasn't social.

Buying Carlie a decent vehicle as a bonus would help better define the relationship.

He glanced around at the crowd listening to the concert. While he didn't have much experience with barbershop quartets, the music was pleasant and melded with the historic atmosphere of Poppy Gold.

Erika would have hated it.

The errant thought made him frown, though it hadn't been a criticism. His wife had liked jazz and rock, with a little Bessie Smith thrown into the mix. They'd been her father's musical choices and Erika had wanted to emulate him in every way. Over the past year, Luke had sometimes wondered if she'd wanted to die in the line of duty like her father, too. Yet he also felt terrible for thinking it.

Erika had been a dedicated soldier, not fanatical. She'd believed in the tradition of service. That was all.

It was Luke's nagging guilt that was making him second-guess everything. The hard truth was, Erika had seriously considered resigning her commission and he could have easily influenced her decision. Instead, he'd stayed silent.

Wanting to shake off his grim mood, he headed for the skating rink as the barbershop quartet began singing "We Wish You a Merry Christmas." Beth and Annie were watching Nicole demonstrate how to start a spin. He sat on one of the benches next to the rink and watched, wishing he could see his daughters smile that way more often. Once they'd come tearing down the stairs when he'd arrived home, with excited hugs and descriptions of their day. Now the house was quiet, with no childish laughter. They stayed in their playroom.

The girls' counselors kept talking about the grief process and the need to move on. What did that mean, anyway? How did they move on from losing their mother?

Erika had been one of a kind. Now Luke had to try to put their shattered lives back together and nobody seemed to agree on how to do it. At the urging of one grief counselor, he'd even gone on a few dates, only to have Beth and Annie ask if someone was going to take their mommy's place.

Hell, no hadn't seemed like the best answer, so he'd simply told them it was way too early to think about that and not to worry.

CARLIE QUICKLY FINISHED the plan for the Friday scavenger hunt; it helped that she knew Poppy Gold inside and out. They didn't have the kind of scavenger hunt where people collected specific items—instead, participants had to look for something like a unique architectural feature or a certain kind of birdbath and be able to say where it was located.

Yet as she printed the pages on holiday paper,

she wasn't thinking about prizes or upcoming events...she was thinking about Luke Forrester. Maybe she *should* have gone and watched Annie and Beth skate. For all she knew, the girls had asked him to invite her.

Sighing, Carlie collected two cups of coffee and went back outside. She could afford a short break. The Forty-Niners had finished their performance and the crowd had dispersed, but there was the usual activity over by the ice rink.

Nicole and her nieces were still skating and Carlie spotted Luke on one of the bleachers. Christmas music floated through the air from speakers; the sound system had been turned on now that the live performance was over.

"Here," she said, sitting down and handing him the cup.

"You must have read my mind," he murmured. "These days I live on coffee."

"No wonder you don't sleep."

Luke's eyebrows shot upward. "How do you know that?"

"Nicole mentioned you work most nights. You look pretty grim just now. Don't you know that isn't allowed at Poppy Gold? Disneyland may be the 'Happiest Place on Earth' but I like to think we're the Christmasiest."

A corner of his mouth kicked up. "Christmasiest? Is that a real word?"

"Why not? I'm sure it's somewhere on the internet. Maybe even in a dictionary. So why are you so serious?"

"I was mulling on life and reality."

"Oh." Luke Forrester might be a pain, but he'd had a serious dose of reality when his wife died. "Sometimes reality sucks."

He let out a humorless laugh. "Yeah."

"Since you understand, would you like to help out people with too much reality and not enough Christmas?" she asked lightly. She figured doing something for others might help distract him from his troubles.

His eyebrows rose again. "Excuse me?"

"My staff volunteered to sort donations and fill Christmas baskets for the Glimmer Creek Rehabilitation Center. Also to wrap gifts for some of the seniors who live in the area. Unfortunately, my employees have all managed to get sick at the same time and I don't want to wait until the last minute to get things ready. Everything is in a huge pile in the ballroom at Old City Hall, begging for a pair of strong shoulders."

"SURE. WHY NOT?" Luke said. "It's been a long time since I did more than donate money to chari—"

"They're *gifts*," Carlie interrupted quickly. "Not charity. Some of the recipients are lower income, so we want to share with them, but others don't have much family and need to know they're remembered. Christmas is a lousy time to feel alone."

Luke was exasperated with himself. "You're right." He stood up. "Let me tell Nicole where I'll be."

At the edge of the rink, he gestured to his sister, who skated over gracefully. "What's up, Luke?"

"I'm going to do something with Carlie over at Old City Hall, unless you need me."

"We're fine. If the girls get tired, we'll go back to the suite. Say, I just heard there's a madrigal feast at the high school on Friday and Saturday. Kids are welcome and it would be fun to attend."

"I'm not sure what a madrigal feast *is*, but I'll check into getting tickets. No doubt Carlie will know where to find them."

"No doubt."

She skated back to Beth and Annie, and Luke watched for another moment before returning to Carlie's side.

"Lead the way," he told her.

Luke hadn't seen the second floor of Old City Hall. If he'd thought about it, he would have assumed it was more offices; instead, the open gallery above the staircase opened into a large ballroom with elaborate crystal chandeliers and numerous windows. Tables were set up on one end, covered with goods of various types.

"Looks like a big project," he commented.

"The employees donate part of it and Uncle Liam and Tessa and her husband give the rest. The churches collect toys and books for kids and fill food baskets for younger families, so Poppy Gold focuses on seniors."

Carlie explained the items needed to be sorted first. Then they'd be distributed into baskets, which the volunteer fire department would deliver, along with the wrapped gifts. At first they worked in a comfortable silence, but after a while Luke cleared his throat.

"Nicole wants to attend one of the madrigal feasts being held this weekend, but I've never heard of them."

"They're a lot of fun. It's a form of dinner theater. The high school has hosted madrigal feasts for almost forty years to raise money for their choral and drama program. The setting is the Middle Ages. You attend as if you're guests at a high feast of the king and queen, who sit at the head table in costume with lords and ladies on either side. Jesters and other entertainers rove around the hall and each course of the meal is heralded with a traditional Christmas song."

It wasn't something that normally appealed to Luke, but he could see Nicole and the girls enjoying the event.

"Is there any difference between the two days?"

"The menu varies, not the entertainment. On

Friday evening they serve *poulet du cloister*, which is chicken and ham with small onions and mushrooms in a cream sauce. On Saturday, it's roast beef with Yorkshire pudding."

"Which is your favorite menu?"

"Both," Carlie said promptly. "My mother has been in charge of the meal for years."

Luke hesitated. "What about your father? Is being left alone for that long a problem?"

Carlie cut another length of wrapping paper. "Mom took early retirement to be available when Dad needed her, but he's gone back to work now. He can't do his old job, so he's a flagger at construction sites. He hates it and has a hard time standing so long, but he doesn't need nursing care…though it could be argued that he needs a dose of good sense." Her tone betrayed both loving exasperation and worry.

"Surely he received a settlement from the guilty driver—an insurance payout, at the very least."

"Yes, but he refuses to live off it. 'A real man works,'" she intoned, obviously mimicking her father.

Luke felt a wry familiarity. "Sounds like what I remember of my grandparents."

Carlie grinned, and for the first time since they'd met, he didn't see any reserve in her eyes. "I suppose your mother and father would argue that if someone has money, they shouldn't take a job from somebody else who doesn't."

"I doubt they've bothered to think it through. They simply want to enjoy life without the daily grind of a job."

"Well, in defense of my work as an activities director, I think the ability to 'play' part of the time is a good thing. I just wish my father agreed." Carlie stirred restlessly. "I understand his wanting to be useful and do something satisfying, but he's important to our family, and when he's in pain, we hurt, too."

"Surely there's another job or volunteer project that would be easier physically."

"Probably, but he genuinely likes to build roads. He says it connects him to an ancient tradition that goes back to the Macedonians and Romans. At least as a flagger he has a small role. Mostly he wants everything to seem normal again, which is why Mom keeps doing the madrigal feasts."

Luke understood wanting life to be normal. It wouldn't ever be that way again, but it didn't stop him from wanting the impossible.

"I'm not good at playing, either," he admitted. "I'm not saying it's a bad thing—it just isn't something I ever learned to do. To be honest, I was too critical of my parents to really join in with their adventures and I've been focused on school or my business ever since."

"I'm sorry." Carlie looked sad and he wished he hadn't brought it up. He didn't feel sorry for himself and didn't need anyone else to, either.

"I was wondering if it would be outrageous if I bought tickets for both the meals," Luke said, needing to lighten the mood. "We have to eat somewhere and the menus are interesting. On the other hand, I don't want to exclude anyone from attending if the tickets are limited."

CARLIE BLINKED. FROM what she'd observed, sensitivity wasn't Luke's strong suit.

"It's hard to say, but they sometimes end up with unsold tickets. You can buy tickets when the drama class is here. The Madrigal Feast Choir and Players are coming Wednesday through Friday to do short performances. It helps promote the dinner for Poppy Gold guests and they sell tickets at the same time."

"Sounds good."

"But if you go to the dinner on Saturday, be sure to visit the pedestrian shopping street when you get back. It's hospitality night. There will be Victorian street entertainers, treats and all sorts of stuff."

"All right."

They continued working and Carlie was impressed that Luke was being such a good sport about the whole thing. Yet she also had the strangest conviction he wanted to say something and was taking a long time getting around to it.

"Is something on your mind?" she asked finally.

"Uh, Beth and Annie might not want to go to the dinner without you. Will you be our guest?"

"I have a ticket for Friday, so you can tell them I'll be there. Anything else?" she prompted.

"Not exactly. Well, I've been thinking about something that happened the day we drove up to Glimmer Creek. Annie got sick in the limousine. She wouldn't let me help her, either then or afterward. She pushed me away. I'm her father and she pushed me away. It's the same with Beth and her nightmares."

The anguish on his face and in his voice was heartrending.

Carlie finished another package and put it on the growing pile of wrapped gifts.

She sneaked a glance at Luke, still convinced he wasn't telling her the whole story, and equally convinced he wasn't going to. It was strange to feel bad for the guy. He'd been a thorn in her side since his arrival, however fond she'd grown of Annie and Beth. He was also extraordinarily attractive, a fact her body kept taking notice of, much to the disgust of her brain.

"I can't speak for Annie," she said slowly, "but I drove my mother crazy when I got sick as a kid. She wanted to do the hovering-mother thing and I just wanted to be left alone. My brothers loved being waited on, but I didn't. Mom still complains about it."

Luke shook his head. "I hope that's all it is with Annie. I worry because she's so much quieter than Beth."

"They're individuals. Being quieter isn't necessarily something to be concerned about."

"Hey, it's easier to worry about everything. It really takes the pressure off deciding what is and isn't a problem."

The sly wit made Carlie grin. Who would have guessed that Luke Forrester could crack a joke?

CHAPTER TEN

GIDEON SMILED AT the little girl standing next to her mother by the examination table.

"Pedro is a very healthy bunny rabbit," he pronounced solemnly. Technically it was an American fuzzy lop, but Maria wasn't in the 4-H club and didn't care which breed her new pet bunny might be.

Maria shyly put her hand out so Pedro could sniff it.

The Alvarez family was one of Gideon's favorites. The older children each had a pet and were faithfully taught how to care for them. They asked thoughtful questions at the annual health exams and plainly loved them. The youngest, Maria, was four and had just been deemed old enough to handle some of the basics of animal husbandry.

"But I'll tell you a secret," Gideon whispered, leaning closer. Maria stretched up on her toes to listen. "Pedro is going to have babies."

"Goody," Maria exclaimed.

Her mother began laughing. "They said it was a male."

"Someone doesn't know their Y chromosomes from their X's."

"And then they let the rooster loose in the henhouse. Or vice versa, as the case may be."

Gideon chuckled appreciatively. Gloria Alvarez was an attractive woman with a warm sense of humor. She and her husband owned one of the local animal feed stores. Like many small towns, Glimmer Creek had a number of nurseries, animal feed stores and beauty salons, but no computer services, and medical care was limited to a single clinic. It didn't bother Gideon, though having a few more organic products available would be nice.

Gideon returned Pedro to the carrier. "You should call the breeder and let them know there was an error. Where did you get her?"

"At a place in the valley. At least they were right about Pedro being trained to use the litter box. We brought him—that is, *her*—home yesterday and she's used the box faithfully."

"Maybe she'll train her babies to use it, too."

Mrs. Alvarez let out a good-natured groan as she left with the carrier and her daughter.

Gideon was adding a couple of notes to the electronic file when his veterinary assistant stuck her head around the door. "Urgent case in B."

"Thanks, Sandra."

A curious sense of foreboding struck him as he strode into the room next door. It was Nicole

Forrester. *Déjà vu all over again* flitted through his brain. But while he'd expected to see Chico in dire straits, it was a different kitten huddled on the table. Black-and-white and so listless from malnutrition it didn't have the energy to spit, though its fear was unmistakable.

"I found him in the same area as Chico," Nicole explained tearfully. "I've been putting food out and searching every day, but I didn't find him until this morning. That is, I think it's a 'him.'"

"It is," Gideon said, examining the painfully thin kitten. "Did he bite you?"

"No, not even a scratch."

Sandra returned with a warming pad, which they slid underneath to help maintain the kitten's body heat, then handed him a syringe with glucose. He rubbed some on the cat's gums and continued with the exam. There was an abscess on its shoulder, grossly swollen.

Gideon glanced at Nicole. Judging from her tear-streaked face, she knew the kitten was in bad shape.

"We'll have to keep him here. He needs IV fluids, antibiotics and monitoring for the best chance of survival."

"W-will he make it?"

"No promises, but we'll try."

"I just don't want him to…to suffer. If only I'd found him sooner." More tears spilled down Nicole's cheeks and he could tell she felt responsible, though God knew, it wasn't her fault.

"You did everything you could."

"It wasn't enough."

NICOLE WATCHED AS Gideon and his assistant worked with the kitten, doing some things she understood and others she didn't. But what struck her was Gideon's gentleness with the terrified animal.

She hadn't seen it with Chico, but now he coaxed and soothed and seemed to do everything possible to alleviate the kitten's discomfort as blood was drawn and the infected lump treated.

Best chance of survival...

The phrase kept running through Nicole's head. The kitten could die.

The results of the blood tests were reviewed and she heard a reassuring "good, kidney function normal," along with more esoteric remarks.

Either they didn't notice or decided not to protest when she followed them to the rear of the clinic and watched them put the kitten in a sort of incubator. A faint meow of protest sounded when an intravenous needle was inserted and his mouth opened for the first time in a faint hiss.

"Getting some feisty back, eh?" Gideon said, sounding pleased. "You're a tough little guy. That's good."

The veterinary assistant wrote "no name" on the ID card, but Nicole shook her head. "Put Bandit."

The other woman looked at her sympathetically. "You might want to wait before choosing a name. It could make it even harder if…"

If they lost him.

Nicole understood, but this tiny scrap of a feline deserved a name. A name represented belonging and home. If there was any chance Bandit could sense the difference, it might help.

"His name is Bandit," she insisted as she brushed away more tears.

She'd never had pets or been around animals that often, and now she was turning into a waterfall because of an abandoned kitten.

The assistant smiled sympathetically and filled out another card. "Okay, *Bandit* it is. What made you choose that?"

"The black and white markings on his face remind me of a mask and I was thinking about Joaquin Murrieta when I was out walking. I'd read that he might be just a legend, not a real outlaw."

"Then why not call him Joaquin or Murrieta?" Gideon asked in a low voice.

Nicole jumped. She was entirely *too* nervous around Gideon Cartwright. "I want something easy for Beth and Annie to pronounce, but please don't mention him if you see them. It would be too upsetting if he doesn't make it. They…they lost their mother last year, so they're especially vulnerable."

She rarely mentioned her sister-in-law's death to anyone in case they knew about the family's history. It seemed all right with Carlie, but some people looked for any opening to ask questions about Erika and Luke. It was horrible. What was left to ask? The media had covered every aspect of the terrible story, leaping light-years beyond anyone's "need to know." What remained was intimate and personal and nobody else's business.

"I won't say anything," Gideon promised quietly.

He listened to Bandit's chest with his stethoscope again.

"We've done what we can for now," he said, straightening. "Try not to worry. An attendant is here around the clock."

"How do I visit him after the clinic is closed?"

GIDEON BRIEFLY CLOSED his eyes, praying for patience.

"Be reasonable, Nicole. We aren't set up for after-hours visitation. Few veterinary clinics are."

"But what's the problem if someone is always here? I'll be happy to pay a fee if that's the issue. I'm sure Bandit already recognizes me and I can't let him feel abandoned again."

"He's weak and barely aware of what's going on."

Nicole defiantly reached out and rubbed behind the kitten's ear, murmuring softly. An uneven purr rose.

"See?" she demanded. "He hissed at you, but he purrs for me."

Gideon was torn between frustration and amusement. However prejudiced he might be against Nicole, she'd gone to considerable lengths to help a distressed animal. And despite her tears, she hadn't distracted them from working with the kitten. As a rule he wouldn't have allowed a client to stay during the treatment, but it had worked out all right.

"Very well—you can visit," he conceded reluctantly. "I'll let the after-hours staff know I've authorized it. There's a side door with a bell and intercom. Explain who you are and they'll let you in for a short time. A *short* time," he emphasized. "The kitten needs quiet and rest in his condition."

"I realize that. I just want him to feel loved."

"I'm sure he'd still feel that way from a distance, but I'm not going to argue. I'll show you to the waiting room."

Gideon led the way to the front of the clinic. He held the door open and Nicole stepped into the reception area, only to shrink against him as a resounding "woof" echoed through the air.

"No, Godzilla!" Rita Jenkins yelled, hanging on to the German shepherd's leash.

Gideon let out a sharp, authoritative "Down, boy."

The dog sank back with a wounded expression. He was a large, rambunctious puppy with a habit of getting into trouble. But he was also thoroughly good-natured.

"I'm surprised you don't carry pepper spray if you're *that* afraid of animals," he murmured to Nicole.

She didn't answer, just edged along the wall and out the door to where a cab from the local taxi service was waiting.

Still burning with the imprint of her body against his, Gideon let out a breath and turned his attention to his patient, who'd probably eaten something he shouldn't have. The German shepherd's tongue lolled to one side and his tail was wagging so hard that his entire butt moved on the floor.

"All right, Godzilla, what have you gotten into now?"

CARLIE WAS RETURNING from judging a snow-person-making contest when she saw Nicole Forrester.

"Hey, what's wrong?" she asked, alarmed by the tearstains on the other woman's face.

"I found a second kitten, but it may not survive. He has to stay at the clinic for treatment, so now

I'm going out to search again to see if there are any others."

"I'll go with you," Carlie offered instantly.

They headed for the wild area south of Poppy Gold and began hunting around every bush and rock, calling, "Kitty, kitty," and other entreaties.

"Dr. Cartwright was relatively pleasant part of the time today," Nicole muttered breathlessly as they climbed a steep slope. "But he didn't want to let me see Bandit during off-hours, even though someone is always there on duty. He told me to 'be reasonable' in such a patronizing tone of voice I wanted to scream."

"That's so strange. He's always friendly whenever I've seen him."

"Strange or not, I insisted on being able to visit and he finally agreed. I was proud of myself, thinking I'd shown him I was strong and independent."

"You *are* strong and independent."

Nicole looked embarrassed. "Actually, I'm a terrible coward. And my bravado didn't hold up when a giant dog barked at me in the waiting room. I almost freaked and Gideon saw, so now he knows it was just an act."

"I'm not crazy about big dogs, either," Carlie said firmly. "And you can't be a coward when you're such a good skater. You do things on the ice I'd never try."

Nicole's expression became more thoughtful.

"I never thought of it that way. I feel so free when I'm skating, I don't think about falling or if I look ridiculous."

"Well, you're amazing. Oh, by the way, if it's convenient for you, I'll come over tomorrow evening to make cookies with Annie and Beth. I sent your brother out for the supplies this morning."

Nicole blinked. "You sent Luke grocery shopping?"

"Why not? It's for Annie and Beth's benefit and I wasn't sure I could get away when the market was open. Besides, I was under the impression he'd planned to spend all his free hours taking care of his business concerns, but he's come to my office several times when the girls are with Mrs. Cabrera."

"I can explain that—he's outside the company firewall on the computer here, so he can't do as much. But he still works at night and a lot of other times, too. I'm not sure when he sleeps. Luke has always been driven, but since Erika died, he's had a compulsive need to stay busy."

That's depressing, Carlie thought, though she didn't have any illusions that Luke was coming around because he'd developed a romantic interest in her.

"Um, he told me about your parents and how you grew up."

Nicole pursed her mouth. "That's unusual. He usually doesn't talk about that stuff."

"He was trying to explain why he'd acted like a—" Carlie stopped abruptly, deciding she probably shouldn't call Luke a jackass to his sister.

"Jerk?" Nicole contributed sweetly. "While I love my brother dearly, he *can* be a challenge. Did you know the media used to called Luke and Erika 'the Beauty and the Autocrat'?"

"That's harsh."

"Yes. And while I hate to admit it, he *can* be high-handed. It's gotten worse since losing Erika. But he means well and it's only from believing he knows what's best."

Carlie got even more depressed, though it was unreasonable. She already knew that Luke was autocratic. Who wanted to be with a man who acted that way, even from good intentions? If she ever fell in love again, she wanted it to be with someone who was looking for a real partner.

Pushing the thought away, Carlie peered into a drainage pipe by the road, wishing she had the small flashlight on her key chain. Unfortunately, she'd loaned her car to Luke, which meant he had both the keys *and* the flashlight.

"Kitty, kitty," she called and then listened intently. "Nicole, where did you find the second kitten?"

"Down the hill. I'd looked there before, so he must have been moving around."

They continued searching, covering every inch

of the area, chatting about both the charms and drawbacks of living in a small community like Glimmer Creek.

"The stores *are* limited," Carlie admitted when Nicole mentioned needing more casual clothes. "That's why online shopping is so popular here. It's that or driving down to the valley. I can loan you jeans and sweats while you're waiting for an order to arrive. Nothing fancy, just knock-around clothes."

"That would be great. I really feel out of place in the stuff I brought." Nicole tugged at her linen slacks. "Yesterday I found sweatshirts and tops in the gift shops for me and the girls, but I want to wash them first."

Carlie brushed her hands off. "I have an idea. I'll talk to Uncle Liam about putting live traps out to catch any other cats. He uses them to relocate wild critters that get overly friendly at Poppy Gold. I should have thought of it when you first found Chico."

"That would be great. Thanks."

"No problem. Now let's go have tea or coffee in the Poppy Gold library and get warm," Carlie suggested. "Unless you need to go back and watch the girls…?"

Nicole shook her head. "Luke has arranged with Mrs. Cabrera to stay if we aren't there and I don't want Beth and Annie to see me before I can get cleaned up. They might be upset and start asking questions. Bandit is strictly a secret until we know he's going to recover."

We?

Though it was probably just an innocent comment, Carlie kept thinking about it as they walked toward Old City Hall. Nicole had talked a fair amount about Gideon Cartwright and obviously wasn't the least bit neutral about the town veterinarian.

Was it possible she was attracted to him?

NICOLE CHOSE TEA along with Carlie and they settled down in front of the crackling fire in the library, kicking off their shoes.

"This is wonderful," Nicole moaned, instantly growing sleepy.

The stress of getting Bandit to the clinic had taken its toll. Not to mention dealing with Gideon Cartwright again. At least he hadn't seemed disgusted by the way she'd cried the entire time, though why that mattered was beyond her.

She glanced at Carlie, still envying her ability to be comfortable with children and adults alike; she was probably great with animals, as well. But envy aside, it would be nice to be friends.

"You should visit me in Austin," she said, trying to sound nonchalant. "I have an extra bedroom in my condo and I'd love to show you around the city."

"For some reason, I never think of Austin as a big city," Carlie murmured. "I have this image of a picturesque Western town where gorgeous Texas Rangers hang out wearing badges and cowboy boots."

Nicole laughed. "The Texas Rangers are based in Austin, but you don't see them on every corner." She squirmed as she recalled telling Gideon about Austin being the eleventh-largest city area in the US. "I just thought of something... Does Dr. Cartwright have an issue with city people?"

Carlie swirled the tea bag in her cup. "It doesn't seem likely, since he moved here from the Los Angeles area. But you should know that he's in the middle of a divorce. While he hasn't said anything to me, you can't keep secrets in Glimmer Creek."

"I'm not interested in the guy," Nicole protested, her cheeks warming. "I just want to understand why he doesn't like me. It isn't as if I insulted him or refused to pay the bill."

Carlie just smiled.

"Okay, he's delicious," Nicole admitted. "But he also makes me nuts with his superior attitude. He even acted that way in front of Beth and Annie when he came to check on Chico."

"All men are impossible... There's no way around it."

"Unfortunate, but true."

Nicole fingered her cup, thinking about Carlie's

warning that Gideon was getting divorced, with the implication that he might not be in the best frame of mind for romance. Should she suggest caution in return about Luke? Women fell for him right and left, but he wasn't likely to ever get over Erika.

"Luke mentioned that he may have been too demanding the day he got here," she said slowly.

"I have to admit, he made it clear Poppy Gold wasn't what he'd expected."

Nicole winced. "He's gotten spoiled when he travels. Erika was rarely stationed near Austin after they were married, so when she could get away, he'd go to the extreme, such as renting a fully staffed Italian villa or a French château to make the most of their time together. Servants took care of their slightest whim so they could simply enjoy themselves. He'd do some work when Erika and the twins were asleep, that's all. They might attend a party or two, but mostly it was just them and the girls."

"Sounds idyllic." Carlie's eyes had become watchful; she was smart enough to catch the subtle warning Nicole was sending.

"It was. Basically his marriage was a series of perfect interludes."

"It must have been difficult getting to know your sister-in-law if you didn't see her often."

"I didn't mind. I just wanted my brother to be

happy. But as far as his trip to California is concerned, he probably assumed his executive assistant had made a similar arrangement here at Poppy Gold."

"Uh, this is a bed-and-breakfast facility in a historic Gold Rush community. We provide conference center services, but none of the suites have a business center or private staff."

Nicole wrinkled her nose. "Yeah, but I doubt he bothered to check it out for himself. Tilly probably decided it would be a good lesson for him."

"Doesn't she worry about job security?"

"Not in the least. She's the first employee that Luke ever hired and it would be like cutting off an arm to lose her. For her part, Tilly is fiercely loyal because he hired her when no one else would—it's rough for a fortysomething, inexperienced divorcée entering the workforce."

Wishing she could stay longer, Nicole finished her tea and pulled on the canvas loafers she'd found at a local store. They looked absurd with the rest of her outfit, but were more practical than Louis Vuitton pumps for walking in rough country terrain. Aside from ski clothes, she didn't have much outdoor gear in her wardrobe.

She should have gone shopping when Luke had first suggested the trip, but a Victorian village wasn't the sort of place she'd expected to need anything special. Lord knew she had more than enough clothes with all the gift cards her brother kept giving her. He'd tried to set up charge accounts, but that was one thing she'd managed to put both her feet down about and keep down.

"I'll see you later," she said to Carlie, who'd also gotten up. "Thanks for the help."

"Not at all. I'm just glad you cared enough to keep going out to search."

WHEN SHE WAS ALONE, Carlie phoned her uncle and explained about the two strays and the possibility of more. He immediately said he'd send someone from Maintenance to set out live traps and to comb the area again.

"I have some canned sardines to use as bait— nice and fragrant. If there are any more cats out there, we'll find them," he promised. "I'll adopt one myself."

"Thanks, Uncle Liam, but you might have to fight me for it. Or Nicole Forrester. She has a proprietary interest in any cat that's found."

He chuckled and got off.

Carlie tidied the library, then went out to Guest Reception. "Any messages for me?" she asked.

"No," Bill said. "But Mr. Forrester returned your keys. I put them in your left desk drawer."

"Thanks." Carlie looked at the time and yelped. "Yikes, I've got to go."

The Madrigal Feast Players were expected to arrive any moment. She raced over to the park and a minute later a shuttle of students from the high school pulled up.

"You look terrific," Carlie declared as they got out. "New costumes?"

"Aren't they *awesome*?" Kerri Laughton, one of Carlie's younger second cousins, adjusted her crown and struck a regal pose. She was playing the queen and wore a sapphire-blue gown trimmed with gold.

"Yes, but where is everyone else, Kerri? Normally it's a much larger group."

"They're coming. They decided to walk from the parking area and do extra promotion on the way."

Carlie saw what Kerri was talking about when a merry group of "lords and ladies" came singing down the street, with jugglers, jesters and acrobats cavorting around them. They arrived and scattered across the grass, entertaining the guests who'd followed them like the children of Hamelin following the Pied Piper. Two of the students sat at a table to sell tickets, while others handed out old-style handbills, calling, "Hear ye, hear ye, enjoy the Madrigal Feast Players," to attract attention.

It was another few minutes before Luke, Nicole and the girls came walking across the green.

She waved, and Annie, followed by Beth, took off running toward her.

"Papa says you're coming tomorrow to make cookies with us," Annie said, the words tumbling out quickly. Beth let out an exasperated sigh, possibly because she'd wanted to speak first.

"That's right. I'm bringing my special stand mixer and extra cookie sheets and stuff, so we can make several different kinds."

"Yippee!" both girls cried together.

"You need a mixer?" Luke asked, frowning. "It wasn't on the shopping list."

Carlie laughed. "You can't get the one I use in Glimmer Creek. Mine is a professional model. But it isn't a big deal to bring it. I'll just load it in my trunk along with everything else and park in the lot nearest the John Muir Cottage."

Luke nodded, an odd expression in his eyes. "Okay. Let me know when you arrive and I'll help carry everything for you. To save time," he added.

"Whatever. If you still need to buy tickets for the madrigal feast, they're selling them over there." Carlie gestured and he walked over to the table.

"What kind of cookies are we making?" asked Beth.

"All sorts, including gingerbread, chocolate chip and snickerdoodles. Also sugar cookies we can cut in shapes and decorate with frosting and sprinkles."

"Yummers!"

One of the jugglers came by at that moment, distracting the girls, and Nicole moved closer. "After I got back to the suite I realized you wouldn't have time to eat lunch. I'm awfully sorry."

Carlie shrugged. "No biggie. I'll get something later." Pizza boxes still crowded the employee refrigerators and it wouldn't take long to heat up a slice. "You should get seats for the performance. Near the front, so Annie and Beth can see well," she urged.

"Oh, right." Nicole collected her nieces and they sat in the first row.

Carlie stood to one side and watched, loving the colorful display and energy from the students. She'd often thought it would be fun for Poppy Gold to host a renaissance fair and they were partway there with the madrigal feast, which mixed both medieval and renaissance music and costuming.

Number 6,537 on my idea list, she thought. The list just kept getting longer. It might not be the same as saving lives, building roads or teaching impressionable children, but it was satisfying to help people relax and enjoy themselves. Everybody needed downtime.

IT WAS AFTER 7:00 p.m. when Carlie finished a rough plan to host a renaissance fair at Poppy Gold. She knew it was ridiculous to work on it when there were other tasks that needed doing, but she'd had several thoughts and had wanted to get them down. Offering something new was part of what kept Poppy Gold fresh and popular for their regular guests, as well as being a draw for various conferences.

She fished her key ring from the desk drawer, but it didn't feel right. Frowning, she looked down and saw an unfamiliar key…and a second key ring with a very expensive logo.

Carlie hurried to the employee parking lot. Her car was nowhere to be seen. She pressed a button on the new key and the lights on a shiny white SUV flashed. She marched up and opened the door. A manila envelope was sitting on the driver's seat—inside were documents from a Stockton dealership with her name on it and two additional keys. Also an envelope with a brief, unsigned note about transferring ownership of her old car. That was all, but she knew the damn thing had to be from Luke Forrester. Who else would do something so high-handed?

She slammed the door and sped across Poppy Gold toward the John Muir Cottage.

LUKE WAS SITTING in the family room with Chico draped over his leg, watching the opening scene of *Rudolph, the Red-Nosed Reindeer* with Nicole and the girls, when he heard a sharp knock on the front door of the suite.

"Don't stop the show," he told his sister as he got up and handed her the kitten. Beth and Annie were on the floor, gazes riveted to the television, though they'd seen the classic program a dozen times. He'd borrowed a stack of DVDs and Blu-rays from the Poppy Gold library for them, but *Rudolph* was the one they'd chosen for the third evening in a row.

Luke threaded his way out to the living room. He opened the door and saw Carlie on the porch. She shook her keys in his face.

"What were you thinking?" she demanded.

He stepped outside and closed the door for privacy. "Your car is old and small and can't be that reliable. I thought it was time you had something new."

"New isn't always better. I *like* my sedan and it gets great mileage. What's more, I paid for it myself and I don't want to spend a fortune on insurance for an oversize SUV I don't need. You can't have one rule for yourself and a different rule for everyone else. If you're so opposed to charity, why don't you understand that other people might feel the same?"

Luke was appalled. If that was how she'd perceived the gift, he could see why she was upset. "It isn't charity. I give Nicole a new car every year."

"I'm not your sister."

She certainly wasn't. If Carlie was his sister, he wouldn't be having so much trouble keeping his hands to himself. The flush of anger and outrage had brought a flush to her skin and a sparkle to her eyes that was nearly irresistible.

"For Pete's sake, Carlie, it's just an SUV, not the crown jewels. I wanted to say thanks for everything you're doing for my kids. And to—"

"I'm not your employee and I don't take gratuities," she interrupted sharply. "But that's the problem, isn't it? You're too proud to accept anything from people, even a little extra attention for your daughters. So you want to pay me exorbitantly for the time I'm spending with them, because *God knows* you can't be a regular human being. But don't worry—you aren't under any obligation. I'm doing it for Annie and Beth, not you."

"Can't you accept a gesture of appreciation?" he countered, though Carlie's accusation was a little too close to the truth for comfort.

She rolled her eyes. "A gesture is a poinsettia, not a ridiculously expensive SUV. Are you *really* so blindly arrogant that you can't understand that? And by the way, it isn't your place to decide my car isn't safe or reliable. I'm perfectly capable of taking care of myself."

Luke's brain was starting to spin. "I wasn't implying that you weren't capable."

Carlie let out a derisive hoot. "Where did you get my home address, anyway?" she demanded, shuffling the items she carried and holding up the paperwork for the SUV.

"The registration was clipped to your sun visor. Look, it really isn't a big deal. I give cars away all the time."

"It's a big deal to me. I'll drive the SUV home tonight, but you'd better have my sedan back by tomorrow night if you don't want me to report it stolen. Here are the extra keys to the SUV. I *won't* be needing them." She slapped them into his hand.

Still visibly outraged, she stepped backward and stumbled on the top step. Luke lunged to grab her and they stood toe to toe for a moment.

Without thinking, he bent and kissed her.

CARLIE GULPED, HER senses filled with Luke's clean, masculine scent.

Don't be an idiot, one part of her mind whispered. Unfortunately, the voice of wisdom was swamped by the sensation of his hard length against hers and angry adrenaline turning swiftly to passion.

He really knew how to kiss and it was like

throwing gasoline on a fire. Every cell in Carlie's body was screaming for more.

Then Luke slid a hand under her jacket and cupped her breast, bringing reality crashing down.

CHAPTER ELEVEN

CARLIE PUSHED LUKE away and they stood staring at each other for an awkward moment.

"I have to go," she muttered.

"I'll get my shoes and walk with you to the parking lot."

She nodded, but took off the minute he stepped back inside the suite, furious with her lack of restraint. Even as a teenager, she'd never gotten involved with a Poppy Gold guest. Vacation flirtations rarely worked out, at least for the one being left behind. Even so, over the years, a few of her girlfriends had believed they'd found true love with a visitor, only to get their hearts broken.

Now here she was—old enough to know better— and she was getting her emotions twisted around by a wealthy businessman who couldn't possibly have any serious interest in her.

She didn't *want* him to be interested. Even Luke's sister had admitted he was controlling—not that Nicole had been so explicit, but that was what it boiled down to. He thought he knew best and steamrollered ahead to do it. And according to Nicole, his behavior had gotten worse since his wife's death. Carlie wondered if that was possible, or just his sister's impression. Her original internet research suggested Luke already possessed a master-of-the-universe complex.

Carlie reluctantly got into the white SUV, knowing she'd have to use it until Luke straightened everything out. It was a nice vehicle with luxurious features she'd never dreamed of having, but the gas mileage would be appalling compared to her little sedan. The whole thing offended her environmentalist's soul.

She drove out cautiously, feeling as if she was behind the wheel of a tank. In the rearview mirror she saw Luke appear on the walkway leading to the lot, but didn't stop. He clearly had no clue how outrageous it had been to replace her car with another.

Too many wealthy people seemed to think money could fix anything. The man who'd hurt her father had acted the same way. He'd been at the hospital after the accident because of a mild concussion. She shouldn't have confronted him, because he'd just shrugged and taken out his checkbook, asking how much it would take for her family to leave him alone.

The familiar anger rose.

Her father had been in surgery, barely hanging on, and the man who'd put him there had offered her *money*. The only consolation was when a law-enforcement officer stepped up and told the guy to remember he was under arrest…and to start praying that he didn't get charged with manslaughter. The implied threat had instantly wiped the patronizing expression from the creep's face.

Carlie parked across the street from her parents' house, hoping they wouldn't see the SUV and wonder about it. The hour was early enough that she went in to say hello.

"Mom, you should have seen the kids doing their show today," she said, walking into the den. "They have new costumes this year and it was wonderful. I bet they sold eighty tickets to the madrigal feast. Did you know Kerri is playing the queen?"

Leah put her crocheting aside and smiled. "Yes. I remember the year you played the queen. You were lovely."

"They only made me queen because she doesn't sing as much," Carlie retorted. Her singing voice was fine in a choir or for group caroling, but not for solo performances.

She sank onto the couch and saw the worry lines around her mother's mouth that never seemed to go away these days.

"Don't put yourself down," Leah scolded. "Can I get you something to eat?"

"Thanks, but I had something earlier." Carlie

had munched on pizza and leftover Greek salad, but her mom didn't need to know the details.

"It must be chilly. Your cheeks are nice and rosy," observed Carlie's father.

Carlie was certain her face was flushed from arguing with Luke Forrester, but she shrugged. "Yeah, it's another freezing night. Say, did I tell you we have identical twins staying at Poppy Gold right now?"

"I hope it's still standing next week," Mike said in a dry tone.

She laughed. "I think these kids are less inventive than Quinn and Russ."

Her father scratched his whiskers. "I'll never forget the time they decided to keep the woodpile dry by bringing it into the house in the middle of the night."

Carlie wouldn't forget, either. She disliked bugs and had encountered far too many creepy crawlies after the woodpile incident. Not that she'd shown Quinn and Russ that it bothered her; letting younger brothers learn your weaknesses was an invitation to torment.

"Yeah, but my favorite story is the one about the basement swimming pool."

"Lord, *yes*," Leah affirmed. "They were a handful."

"They still are." Carlie rose to her feet. "On that cheerful note, I'm going to have an early night.

Mom, do you have a roll of parchment paper I can use? I'm making cookies with some guests tomorrow night and baking them on parchment is much easier. I'll order more for you."

"Don't worry about that—I always have plenty. There are several rolls in the pantry, on the second shelf to your right."

"Thanks." Carlie kissed them good-night and went to fetch one of the rolls. Yet as she walked out to her apartment steps, she scowled, thinking it was best to load everything into the SUV tonight. There might be fewer people around to see and ask questions.

She already had her mixer and other supplies packed in boxes ready to go, so she hauled those out and put them on the floor of the SUV's passenger seat.

Slamming the door, she glowered at the shiny paint. Maybe if she lived in snow country it would be good to have four-wheel drive, but snow was rare in Glimmer Creek.

"New car?" called someone from behind her.

Carlie fixed a smile on her face and turned. She'd forgotten Dr. Suehiro walked his dog each evening. "Good evening, Dr. Suehiro. Hey, Pancho." She gave the beagle a pat. "It's a temporary loan from a guest."

"I hope your car hasn't broken down."

"No, there was a misunderstanding, that's all. Everything will be sorted out quickly."

She hoped.

"Excellent. Insurance and registration on such a vehicle would be quite high. And gas mileage?" He shook his head gravely. "I prefer my hybrid. Very economical at the pump."

Yes, Carlie thought triumphantly.

Dr. Suehiro was an ophthalmologist who saw patients one day a week in Glimmer Creek and commuted to the city the rest of the time. The town was fortunate—few specialists were available in such a small community. And with his profession he could afford a luxury car; instead, he preferred trendy practicality.

"I agree completely," she said. "You and Pancho have a nice walk."

They continued on, the beagle as dignified and serious as his master.

Though tempted to kick the tires of the SUV to vent her frustration, Carlie went up to her apartment again. After a hot shower, she crawled under the blankets, her brain still churning. But instead of thinking about an unwanted luxury vehicle, she was recalling the way Nicole had described her brother's marriage.

A series of perfect interludes.

Exasperated, Carlie turned on her back and stared at the dark ceiling.

It was hard enough competing with a memory, never mind with perfection. Of course, no one could compete with Erika Forrester, regardless—with her flawless beauty and heroism, she was practically mythical. And as a military officer, Erika had probably been one of the few women who could challenge Luke's autocratic behavior.

As for Luke? Carlie was quite sure he didn't want to feel obligated to anybody, and the SUV was his way of discharging a perceived debt. She was even willing to believe he'd tried to be nice in his extremely inept way.

Finally Carlie got up and fixed her mom's sleep remedy. She poured the mixture into a china teacup and curled up on the couch, the scent of maple wafting through the air. Her mother had always served warm milk to her in a special cup decorated with tiny roses, making the drink particularly special. If she ever had a daughter, she'd do the same.

Pushing the thought away, she clicked on the television and checked the channel guide, pleased to see that *I'll Be Home for Christmas* was starting in a few minutes. There were at least three films with the same title, but this one was set during the last days of World War II and starred actors like Hal Holbrook, Eva Marie Saint and Peter Gallagher.

Quickly she set the DVR to record it so she wouldn't need to stay awake for another two hours.

Carlie finished her warm milk and slid down on the cushions, letting the film murmur softly in the background. With any luck, it would distract her enough to keep her from thinking about SUVs and Luke Forrester.

And kisses.

LUKE FURIOUSLY TYPED out a string of emails.

Nicole and the girls were in bed and he was trying to figure out what to do about Carlie. He was appalled that he'd lost control with her, however briefly.

What if Beth and Annie had seen them kissing? They could have gotten bored with the movie and come looking for him, or just gone to the kitchen for milk and spotted them through the window.

The girls liked Carlie, but he'd already dealt with their questions about a new mommy. They weren't ready for a new mother figure in their lives, even casually.

Hell, *he* wasn't ready. First he needed to come up with answers that would make sense to them. Maybe Beth and Annie were too young to have thought things through, but sooner or later they'd start to wonder why their mommy hadn't stayed with them instead of going half a world away to be a soldier. He worried they'd blame him, but he also didn't want them to think Erika hadn't loved them enough. Somehow he'd have to help them understand…which was going to be difficult since *he* didn't understand that well himself.

All he could do was try to keep things under control so nothing *else* could happen to his family.

Luke's phone rang and he saw the call was from William Gunderson, the salesman who'd delivered Carlie's SUV to Glimmer Creek. Earlier he'd left a message saying he needed her sedan back and asking him to return the call, no matter how late.

"Hello," he answered.

"Mr. Forrester, I'm sorry for not calling earlier," the man sputtered. "My phone was—"

"That's all right. But as I mentioned in my voice mail, I need that sedan back here by morning."

"You want to return the SUV?" William sounded dismayed, probably because he'd received two generous commissions, one for the sports utility vehicle and the second for immediately driving it to Glimmer Creek.

"No, but the ownership will need to be registered in my name, not Ms. Benton's. She'd, uh, prefer to choose her own vehicle."

The SUV could be donated to a worthy cause when they left for Texas and would be useful in the interim.

"If you return the sedan to Glimmer Creek by four o'clock this morning, I'll double the commissions you've already received," Luke added. "You'll need to pick me up and we'll take it over to her home."

"Of course, sir. I can leave within the hour. I just need to arrange for a ride back to Stockton."

"Excellent. Call when you get into town. I'll be awake."

Luke disconnected, glad *one* problem was getting resolved. Carlie's outrage was another issue. She was a talented woman who was helping his daughters enjoy the holidays, and she was spending extra time at Poppy Gold because of his family's needs. Didn't she deserve the kind of bonuses he gave to people for hard work?

Still, she wasn't his employee. If she *had* been in his employ, he never would have kissed her.

So he was a hypocrite. No wonder she was upset.

Much as he hated to admit it, Carlie was right that he had one rule for himself and a different one for other people. He'd refused to accept the use of the Yosemite suite as a gift and wouldn't listen to what anyone had to say about it, yet he'd expected her to be all right with being given an SUV?

His best intentions aside, maybe he should have stopped at the anonymous lunch he'd sent to Old City Hall.

THE NEXT MORNING, Carlie stared blearily into her bathroom mirror. She was supposed to be perky and cheerful like Julie McCoy, the cruise director on the old *Love Boat* television series. Instead, she looked pale and sleep deprived.

Obviously her mother's warm milk concoction had worked better when she was eight and worried about an upcoming math test. It had less effect on a grown woman whose body was at war with her mind.

It wasn't that Carlie thought Luke was a skunk like her ex-fiancé, but she couldn't understand why she was drawn to him. He wasn't the kind of man she normally found appealing. It had to be sex and a ticking biological clock. A broken heart, moody good looks and unquestioned authority might entice some women, but not her.

She splashed cold water on her face and padded into the bedroom to get dressed. The apartment was cute and functional. Her dad had built it years before as a rental, only to discover he hated being a landlord. She'd insisted on paying rent herself, however, claiming she would find somewhere else to live if he didn't agree.

I have my pride, too, she'd announced.

With her keys and a bag of clothes to loan Nicole in hand, Carlie went outside and saw her silver sedan in the spot where she'd left the SUV. She felt a rush of relief. Dealing with the fallout would have been ugly. She couldn't even imagine how much the gift tax, insurance and registration would have cost—probably more than a new car of her choosing.

There was just one problem… She hurried across

the street and saw her baking equipment had been loaded into the backseat. It would have been so typical to have her lovely KitchenAid mixer and AirBake cookie sheets disappear when the vehicles were exchanged, provoking yet *another* confrontation. She wouldn't put it past Luke to overlook something like that. He was a big-picture guy, oblivious to the nitty-gritty of everyday life.

Carlie fished her spare key from her purse and unlocked the door. There was a manila envelope on the passenger seat and she tipped the contents out to find the spare key to the sedan, a VISA gift card and a folded sheet of paper. Impatiently she shook the paper open and saw a note scrawled in strong, angular handwriting.

I couldn't fill your tank since there isn't a twenty-four-hour station in Glimmer Creek, so I got a gift card at the convenience store. It's only right to replace the gas that was used, so don't get all stiff-necked on me. We need to talk. L.

Carlie scowled. No, they *didn't* need to talk. She'd be happy if they never talked again.

She didn't know if he was just bored or wanted an affair, however unlikely that seemed. Boredom she could take care of as the Poppy Gold activities director. If it was an affair, he could forget it. She wasn't cut out for short-term relationships.

NICOLE COULD TELL that something was going on with Luke.

The night before, he'd come back after answering the door to say he'd be out for a while. But then he'd returned almost immediately, only to sit moodily as Beth and Annie finished watching Santa admit that he'd treated Rudolph badly.

Tension was still thick at breakfast and her brother wouldn't talk, so Nicole decided a trip to the Glimmer Creek Veterinary Clinic would be easier than trying to get him to open up. When Luke didn't want to talk, he was as impervious as a glacier.

"I need to run an errand this morning," she said casually. She hadn't found an opportunity to tell Luke about the second kitten she'd found. Further explanation was impossible with the girls sitting at the breakfast table, finishing their oatmeal. "I won't be gone long."

Luke handed her a key. "I've arranged for an SUV to use while we're here. You'll find it parked in the Mark Twain lot—the white SUV with no plates yet. Take all the time you want."

"Thanks."

It was odd that he hadn't said anything about them needing their own transportation, but she shrugged and headed out. While the clinic wasn't that far, visiting after dark would be easier with independent wheels. Taxis weren't always easy to get in Glimmer Creek. Poppy Gold often provided rides, but she couldn't impose on them to visit a sick animal.

Nicole parked at the clinic and got out, praying Bandit was all right.

"Hello," she said to the receptionist at the front desk. "Is, um, my kitten…that is…" She trailed off into silence.

The other woman smiled. "He's holding his own. Dr. Cartwright mentioned you might visit. He schedules routine surgeries on Thursday mornings, so he doesn't have regular office hours. I'll show you to the feline treatment ward."

Nicole smiled politely, though she knew the way. In the back she saw Bandit curled into a more normal position and reached in to pet him. "Hey there, little one."

He pressed against her finger and purred briefly, but he obviously wasn't much stronger. Nevertheless, knowing he was warm and being cared for made him *look* better. She pulled up a chair next to him, vaguely aware of the receptionist leaving. Her heart ached that she hadn't found him earlier.

"Sleep, baby. It's good for you," she whispered.

GIDEON DROPPED HIS surgical scrubs into the laundry bin and came down the hallway, not particularly surprised to see Nicole Forrester sitting with the kitten she'd rescued. But unlike some pet "mommies," she wasn't fussing at the cat, trying to get him to respond; she was just quietly watching him sleep.

He'd wondered if the little guy would survive the night and had gone down a couple of times to check, only to be scolded by the night attendant.

"Don't you trust me?" Peter Talua had asked, looking wounded. He was a certified EMT who'd discovered he'd rather treat animals than people. He liked the night shift because he was taking online classes, and Gideon didn't object to him doing course work on the clinic computer, provided his duties weren't neglected.

Gideon had reassured Peter, but he couldn't admit that it was his attraction to a client making him restless—a nervous-Nellie client who jumped when a dog barked.

Get a grip, Gideon thought now, staring at Nicole.

Despite her fears, she seemed to have more affinity for animals than his ex-wife, but that didn't make her safe. Nicole's casual comfort with wealth was another huge problem. Maybe it wasn't fair, but he'd never seen her wear anything except fine jewelry and clothes, though her current footwear...

Gideon raised his eyebrows at the inexpensive canvas shoes on her feet. He'd noticed them the previous day, as well, but only in the back of his mind.

"Good morning," he said, the words sounding inordinately loud in the quiet room.

Nicole jumped and put a hand to her chest. "I think you gave me a heart attack."

"Sorry." Gideon walked over and did a quick exam of his patient. "He's doing all right—that's the only thing I can tell you."

"Okay."

"It looks as if you've been shopping at the Argonaut Market," he commented, gesturing to the loafers she wore.

"Aren't they great?" Nicole said, lifting her right foot and wiggling it. "I got two pairs and they can go right in the washing machine. I didn't expect to do much outdoor stuff at Poppy Gold, so it was a relief to find them."

He'd anticipated embarrassment, not enthusiasm.

"Er, yeah. They carry a little bit of everything at the Argonaut since there are so few regular stores in Glimmer Creek. Aside from souvenir shops, of course."

"I noticed, but the Argonaut's sweat clothes and T-shirts are way too big for me." Nicole's gaze shifted to the kitten and she stood up. "I'm afraid we're disturbing Bandit. I'd better get going and I'm sure you have things to do."

"Yeah, I have another two surgeries this morning."

It was true, but he felt illogically out of sorts. Yet when Gideon went to check on the cat he'd just spayed, he decided it was mostly because he'd expected trouble getting Nicole out of the clinic. Instead, she'd done as promised, visiting Bandit and leaving without a fuss.

"Our patient is awake and feeling sorry for herself," Sandra observed in the postoperative area. She was entering information on the computer terminal.

The six-month-old feline growled grumpily when Gideon checked her over. It was the nature of his work. However much he liked cats, they didn't appreciate being vaccinated, prodded or operated upon. There was also something about the way a vet's office smelled that set them off—one whiff and they either got terrified or bared their teeth.

At least he had the satisfaction of knowing he was doing his part to give them a long, healthy life.

CHAPTER TWELVE

THE SECOND VISIT of the Madrigal Feast Players was just as successful as their first, but it was difficult for Carlie to enjoy the performance. She expected Luke to walk over any minute and bluster through an explanation that he hadn't meant anything by kissing her and not to make anything of it.

She wasn't going to make anything of it. She planned to pretend that kiss had never happened. A few problems *did* go away if you pretended they didn't exist.

Not many, but a few.

"Are you still baking cookies with us?" Annie asked her as the audience began to disperse.

"Yes. I'll be there at seven."

"Come early and eat dinner with us," Nicole urged. "We're getting Mexican and Luke always orders too much."

"Goody," Beth cried, clapping her hands.

Carlie didn't dare look at Luke. Plainly his sister was unaware of the previous day's events.

"I'll try," she said, "but don't wait for me. Things get hectic this time of year."

The twins looked disappointed, but they didn't understand adult problems and relationships.

Not a relationship, Carlie amended. The idea of having anything other than a professional association with Luke was absurd. She was the Poppy Gold activities director; he was a guest. She had to remember that.

"I'll see you later," she told the girls brightly.

Yet as Carlie stepped backward, Luke said, "I'll walk with you."

She didn't say anything until they were far enough away not to be heard. "Thank you for returning my car so promptly. That's all we have to discuss."

He regarded her narrowly. "Are you sure?"

"Absolutely."

With that, she hurried toward Old City Hall.

LUKE WAS BOTH amused and relieved that Carlie seemed determined to ignore their kiss. The real test would be how she acted toward him over the next few weeks. Of course, if the chill in her eyes was any indication, she wouldn't mind giving him a boot in the rear end.

A wicked impulse made him follow her. "Wait a minute, Carlie. Maybe I should take the mixer and your other baking equipment to the suite now, to save time later."

She froze, then turned around.

He smiled as innocently as possible, though he

hadn't been innocent since Ellen Kay Atkins had snuggled up to him when they were thirteen and playing spin the bottle. Come to think of it, he hadn't been all that innocent *then*, either.

"May I borrow your keys?" he asked.

A breath hissed through her teeth and Luke wondered if he'd gone too far.

"Fine. You need the SUV key back, anyhow." Carlie pulled her keys from her pocket and tossed it to him. "My car is in the employee lot. Please take the butter out of the refrigerator this afternoon so it'll be at room temperature."

Luke kept from smiling until she was inside Old City Hall. It wasn't nice of him, but she was fun to tease.

THAT EVENING, NICOLE watched carefully as Carlie efficiently mixed one batch of cookie dough after another with the girls. She explained that if they didn't get everything baked tonight, they could keep the remaining dough in the refrigerator for a few days, baking them fresh with their aunt's help.

The words made Nicole cringe. She'd had a couple of cooking lessons with Carlie's great-aunt, but was nowhere close being able to make cookies. According to Vera, they were easy for some cooks and impossible for others, no matter how good they might be in the kitchen. The elderly lady had winked and said it was all right, though…that most people who couldn't bake a decent cookie were unable to tell the difference, so they were happy and everyone else just quietly threw their offerings away.

Vera Fullerton McKay had a droll sense of humor and an opinion about everything. She insisted that cooking wasn't hard; it was just a question of paying attention. So far Nicole had turned out a decent baked chicken, scalloped potatoes and a peach cobbler. She was ecstatic with her successes and thought she might even try making dinner for the family one night.

"The sugar-cookie and gingerbread doughs need to chill longer before we can roll them out," Carlie told Beth and Annie. "But now that everything is mixed, we can start baking the drop cookies."

Nicole watched every step, scribbling notes, fascinated that the cookies were going to be baked on sheets of paper.

"It makes cleanup *much* easier," Carlie told her in an aside.

The first pan went into the oven and the timer was set while they spooned out another group. Yet Carlie seemed distracted and finally looked at the girls. "Annie, Beth, the first batch is almost ready to come out of the oven. Maybe you should invite your papa to taste the cookies while they're hot."

"I think Papa is working," Annie said doubtfully.

"I'll get him." Beth jumped down and raced out of the kitchen, followed by her sister.

Nicole got up. "And I'll make coffee. Decaf, unless you want regular…?"

"No, I'd rather sleep tonight."

"Luke prefers regular, so I'm not going to tell him it's decaffeinated. I don't think he went to bed once last night."

"That's too bad," Carlie murmured.

The timer went off for the oven, just as the twins returned, dragging their father by the hand. Nicole could tell that he was pleased his daughters had wanted him.

"Let me," Beth screamed, racing to the stove, but Carlie told her to stand back.

"It's very hot," she warned the girls. "So I'll put the cookies in and take them out."

Beth pouted, while Annie stepped farther away. But their eyes still widened in excitement as the baking pan came out covered with golden chocolate-chip cookies.

Luke stayed and watched as the various kinds of cookies were baked. Carlie had also brought wire racks to cool them more efficiently, and Nicole was astonished at how swiftly the pans went in and out of the oven.

Even though Beth and Annie were probably more hindrance than help, before the evening was over they were frosting sugar-cookie bells, stars and Christmas trees, along with gingerbread boys and girls.

Nicole wasn't sure how it happened, but she gradually began spooning dough onto the cookie sheets for baking and rolling it out to be cut into shapes. Nothing disastrous happened except one batch got too dark.

"That's okay," Carlie said carelessly. "Some people like them baked longer."

It was terrific fun and the cookies were delicious, but Nicole noticed that Carlie and Luke barely spoke to each other. Perhaps that was for the best, since her brother *did* have an incomparable talent for sticking his foot in his mouth.

ON FRIDAY EVENING, Carlie donned one of her medieval dresses, wishing she could enjoy the madrigal feast *without* having to deal with Luke Forrester.

Many of the local residents wore costumes to the feasts. Sometimes the most unlikely person would show up dressed as a court jester or member of the nobility. Often they'd discover it was someone who had participated in one of the first madrigal feasts, decades earlier.

Throwing a cloak over her shoulders, she walked

onto the staircase landing and saw her father waiting at the bottom.

"I was just coming to see if you were ready," he said, smiling up at her. "You're so beautiful, darling."

"You're pretty handsome, too."

It had long been a tradition for him to escort her to the feast since her mother was in charge of the kitchen. No matter how frantic things might have been in San Francisco, Carlie had made it a point to come home for the madrigal feast weekend. Of course, she'd come home almost *every* weekend during the Christmas season, much to Derek's annoyance once they'd started dating. There had been so many clues he was wrong for her, but she'd ignored them all. Love really *was* blind.

Holding up her long skirt with one hand, Carlie cautiously descended the steps and gave her dad a hug. Mike Benton wouldn't be caught dead in a costume, medieval or otherwise, but he wore his good suit and a tie. She tried not to see how loose it was on him; he'd lost too much weight since the accident.

At the high school, they parked in one of the side lots and made their way to the door, greeting friends and family arriving at the same moment.

The lighting inside was dim, with much of it provided by the hundreds of battery candles around the room. Carlie smiled. The scents and sounds and decorations weren't that different from when she'd been in school. Her father helped her out of her cloak and folded it over his arm as they walked around.

When Annie and Beth spotted them, they rushed over to say hello.

"You look like a princess," Annie declared.

"What a gorgeous dress," Nicole affirmed. "I didn't know people wore costumes here, too."

"We do it to support the Madrigal Feast Players," Carlie explained. "Everybody, this is my father, Mike Benton. Dad, this is Nicole, Annie, Beth and their father, Luke."

Luke put out his hand and the two men shook. "Delighted to meet you, Mr. Benton."

"It's Mike." He bent a few inches and looked into Annie's and Beth's faces. "My daughter told me identical twins were staying at Poppy Gold, but I didn't know they were such grown-up ladies."

Beth giggled. "We aren't grown-up—we're six."

"That's a good age to be. How do you like first grade?"

"It's okay. Why do you walk funny?" Beth asked in her artless way.

Carlie caught her breath, but her father didn't appear upset by the question.

"I was in an accident, Beth. The doctors did their best, but they couldn't fix my leg completely."

"That's too bad."

Annie shyly pressed her cheek against Carlie, clearly wanting to stay out of the discussion. Her reaction wasn't surprising; she was in a new place crowded with people she didn't know, so she wanted someone familiar. But it still seemed odd that she wasn't clinging to her father or aunt.

Carlie glanced at Luke and their gazes held. She hadn't wanted him in the kitchen while baking the cookies, but it was such a family activity that she'd broken down and suggested an invitation to sample their efforts. Then he hadn't left. He'd stayed, drinking coffee and munching on their various offerings.

"Beth, Annie, let's go visit the washroom," Nicole urged the girls after a few minutes.

Carlie's father had already gone to visit her mom in the kitchen, so once Annie reluctantly left with her aunt and sister, Carlie was alone with Luke.

"The girls really enjoyed last night," Luke said. "Nicole, too. I appreciate it."

Carlie wanted to ask if it was choking him to thank her instead of offering money, then decided that wouldn't be nice. She smiled resolutely. "Some people feel it isn't necessary to make cookies with Sarah's Sweet Treats in town, but nothing beats the fragrance of cinnamon, molasses and vanilla wafting through the house."

"True." Luke moved closer. "I like your father."

"He's good with kids."

"I suppose your parents are pushing for grand-children."

IF LUKE HADN'T been watching closely, he would have missed Carlie's subtle flinch.

"Did I say something wrong?" he asked.

"No. But much as I'd love to have a family, I can't think about it right now. Mom and Dad will have to wait for grandkids."

Luke tried not to focus on Carlie's slim figure, sweetly outlined in the medieval gown. The style was striking on her, even if it wasn't supposed to be deliberately provocative. Or maybe it was. People living in the medieval era hadn't been strangers to sex and seduction. But he was old-fashioned enough that it bothered him to ogle her when her father might see.

"I, uh…" He cleared his throat. "I only bought tickets for tonight's madrigal feast, not the one to-morrow. There was such a huge response to the performances at Poppy Gold, I decided it was best to leave openings for other guests."

"In that case, don't forget hospitality night on the shopping street. The Glimmer Creek General Store puts out wonderful cheesy biscuit sand-wiches and fruit. All sorts of things are offered.

There's no need to eat anywhere else, just munch your way down the street."

Carlie stopped and smiled at Beth and Annie as they returned with Nicole.

"I was telling your papa about something fun to do tomorrow night, after the lighted parade. It's like a big party on the pedestrian shopping street. Entertainers will be dressed in Victorian costumes, singing Christmas carols and doing skits. All the stores will be open and they'll have yummy things to snack on. We can go together, if you'd like."

Luke was grateful she didn't wait for Beth or Annie to beg her to come with them. It was difficult always hearing his daughters ask for someone else.

"More goodies? I'll have to start exercising at the fitness center," his sister complained. "This place is murder on the waistline."

At that moment, Mike Benton returned. He seemed like a nice guy, but he was obviously in pain, his face drawn. It wasn't any wonder that Carlie was worried.

Luke thought about the photo he'd seen in Carlie's office—her father tanned and muscular, with a broad smile. The contrast was dramatic and Luke was outraged on the other man's behalf. He had his faults, but he didn't believe his wealth entitled him to endanger other people. A financial settlement seemed too small a price to pay for destroying someone's health.

Just then a horn sounded, heralding the start of the feast, and Luke tried to put it out of his mind.

GIDEON HAD JUST returned from an unexpected trip to sew up a laceration on a cow's rump when the clinic bell rang. Allie Martinson was on duty and he automatically started down the stairs, knowing he was being overprotective and probably sexist by not letting her handle it on her own. But he'd gotten used to the crazies in the city, where it was risky to find out what someone wanted later in the evening.

He stopped on the second-to-last step, listening.

"Hello," Allie said into the intercom.

The old intercom crackled and he heard Nicole's voice asking if it was too late to visit Bandit.

"No, it's fine, Nicole." Allie opened the door. "Please come in. Mmm, what's that heavenly odor?"

There was a faintly rustling sound. "*Poulet du cloister.* I attended the madrigal feast tonight and one of the teachers was saying how sorry she was that Dr. Cartwright had to leave for an emergency before dinner. When I mentioned I was coming over here, they asked me to bring his meal to him."

The edge eased from Gideon's nerves, to be replaced by a different kind of tension.

Allie chuckled. "I meant your perfume."

"Oh, Shalimar. My brother gives it to me several times a year, which is nice of him, but not too perceptive. I don't bathe in the stuff. When I get back to Texas I'll send you a bottle. I've got a drawer full."

"That would be amazing."

"Good. I brought a meal for you, too, but is there a refrigerator for Dr. Cartwright's food?"

"No need—I'm here." Gideon descended the final step and rounded the corner.

Allie gave him a scolding look, knowing perfectly well why he'd come down.

"I'll take Ms. Forrester to see her kitten while you eat," he continued.

Nicole gave Allie one of the bags she carried.

Allie sniffed inside and groaned. "Awesome. My boyfriend is taking me to the madrigal feast tomorrow, but he always picks the night with roast beef. I've wanted to try the chicken dish, like, *forever*. Gideon, do you mind if I go up to my apartment to eat?"

"No problem."

Allie lived in the second apartment above the clinic. When Dr. Chevalier had originally designed the large building, he'd hoped to have a son or daughter who would live there and work with him, but he and his wife hadn't been able to have children. Instead, the Chevaliers had hosted a long string of veterinary students during the summer. None had chosen to return to Glimmer Creek once fully qualified, though apparently they'd written often and visited.

When they were alone, Nicole handed him the second bag she carried and took off her coat. She was stunning in a simple black velvet cocktail dress, with crystals sewn to the bodice, glittering and swaying along with her diamond drop earrings. Her long, dark hair was twisted high on her head, and despite the chilly weather, she wore open-heeled pumps, with straps that crisscrossed over her feet and around her ankles.

Which label? he wondered. The names of designers that his ex-wife had casually thrown out were starting to fade in his memory, but enough remained to know Nicole's wardrobe came with a hefty price tag.

Except the canvas loafers.

It still boggled his mind that she'd been pleased with the inexpensive shoes. Gideon knew she was employed at Forrester International, but unless she was getting an exorbitant salary, her brother *must* be footing the bills for her jewelry and designer outfits.

He led the way to the feline care ward and watched Nicole rub behind Bandit's ear, murmuring softly. After a brief time, she straightened.

"There are two desserts in the bag," she said. "I

saved mine in case you were here, so you wouldn't have to eat alone. Some people hate that. But I can always take it with me."

A jolt went through Gideon. It was a measure of thoughtfulness that he hadn't expected. Back in Los Angeles he'd gotten a burger on the way home whenever he was late, knowing Renee most likely would have already eaten or gone out with friends. It simply hadn't occurred to her that he might enjoy her company.

He took out the various containers and put them on the counter. "Do you want to eat here or in my office?"

"Here. I'd like to watch Bandit."

Whoever had filled the large take-out tray had been excessively generous and Gideon dug into the food with a healthy appetite. As the only veterinarian in the area, he missed a fair number of meals.

It would be easier once he'd hired a resident to work with him. The practice was growing rapidly. Dr. Chevalier had been revered by the large animal owners in the area, but aside from treating the cats at Poppy Gold, he'd been doing less and less with domestic pets. By the time he'd retired, the clinic facilities had largely gone unused. Clients were returning now that they had a vet who was consistently available.

"Bandit is improving," Gideon explained between bites. "But he'll have to stay a full ten days as a precaution."

"Why? Surely he'd do better at home with his brother."

Gideon resisted reminding her that the John Muir Cottage wasn't "home." Nicole's casual presumption that she could keep Chico in the suite still bothered him. Though they'd allowed it, the owners couldn't be thrilled at the idea of a rambunctious kitten clawing its way up the drapes or knocking over antiques.

"The wound on his shoulder appears to be from an animal bite," he explained. "I have to keep him in quarantine to be sure he hasn't been infected with anything contagious."

Nicole's eyes widened. "I hadn't thought of that."

"It's unlikely, but it's best to be cautious."

He shot a glance at Bandit, who was watching the container from the madrigal feast with a gleam in his eyes. Being interested in food was a good sign.

"Then we still shouldn't say anything about him to Beth and Annie. But you think he's going to be okay?" Nicole asked. "I mean, otherwise?"

"It's too early to be sure, but he's responding to the antibiotics and has a small appetite."

"Actually, I think he wants your chicken pretty badly."

Gideon chuckled. "You're probably right, but it's too rich for him."

She smiled in turn, but her nose wrinkled a little and he suddenly realized that the warmth of the clinic was intensifying the barnyard odor clinging to his jeans and boots.

"Sorry about the stink," he murmured. "I just got back from working with an injured farm animal."

"That's okay. We have cows in Texas, too. One of my coworkers grew up near a stockyard and calls it the smell of money. I told my nieces that when they visited a ranch on a school trip, but Beth promptly announced it just smelled like poop to her."

Another chuckle escaped Gideon. "How about Annie?"

"Annie prefers thinking about things before talking. After a few minutes she wanted to know why, if cows smelled like money, did cowboys ride horses instead of driving cars?"

"Smart kid."

"They're both smart. It simply shows in different ways."

NICOLE SLOWLY ATE her apple dessert, trying to stretch it through Gideon's meal, though why she cared was a mystery.

A dog barked nearby and she jumped so hard she nearly dropped her spoon.

"S-sorry," she muttered nervously.

"It's just Pandowdy. We board him when his family is out of town. Don't worry—he's gentle."

"That's what everybody says." Nicole wiped her mouth with a napkin.

"Everybody?"

"Dog lovers. When I was seven, we stayed with friends of my parents who owned a large Doberman pinscher. I'd never been around animals and was nervous. Maybe he sensed my fear, because he starting nipping me. The owners just laughed, saying how cute it was that he wanted to play, but it kept getting worse until this happened." She pointed to two rows of jagged scars that extended around her forearm. They'd faded over time, but the memories remained painfully clear.

"Hell." Gideon dropped his fork and looked closer. "That was a nasty bite."

"They claimed I must have provoked him. I've never seen my brother so angry."

Gideon's expression darkened. "With good reason. A properly trained dog doesn't nip *or* bite. And nobody provokes an animal that frightens them."

A tightness inside Nicole uncurled. She still remembered Luke shouting at everyone as he wrapped a towel around her arm and demanded a doctor. He'd even called the police from the emergency room to report what had happened.

Immediately afterward they'd gone to stay with a different family.

"Luke is the only one who gets why I'm so afraid of dogs and large animals," she said awkwardly.

GIDEON WAS ASHAMED that he'd been scornful of Nicole's fear. If nothing else, as a veterinarian, he ought to have been more understanding.

"You sound close to your brother."

"He's too protective, though I understand why. Our childhood was…" She seemed to shake herself. "Anyhow, I've tried to stop being so afraid of dogs, but I freeze inside when they start barking. I'm sure it seems ridiculous to someone who treats horses and cows."

"I grew up on my foster parents' farm in Nebraska, so I had a head start with animals. But if I'd gone through what you did, I'd probably feel the same."

Gideon was startled to see Nicole light up excitedly.

"A farm? How wonderful. Do you visit often?"

"I see Lars and Helga a couple times a year and we talk on the phone regularly. They're retired now and have sold the farm."

"They must miss you."

The simple statement wasn't what Gideon had expected. Most people seemed unconvinced that he was fond of his foster mother and father. His ex-wife had never understood his closeness to them. "But they aren't your real parents. They were paid to keep you," she'd declared. It was true that many foster relationships weren't good, but he'd been lucky. Lars and Helga were special and had given him a real home.

"I miss them, too. I'm hoping they'll move to Glimmer Creek."

Nicole started to say something, only to stop when Allie appeared around a corner.

"The food was amazing. Thanks again, Nicole."

"Yeah, thanks," Gideon echoed.

"I'm glad you enjoyed it." Nicole stood up. "I'd best go. My brother was worried about me coming over here this late, but he couldn't leave the girls alone to come with me."

"Do you need a ride?" Gideon asked as she said good-night to Bandit.

"No. Luke got an SUV for us to use while we're staying at Poppy Gold. It wasn't necessary, but it's easier to get around."

Gideon escorted her out, the cold air cutting through his shirt. His eyebrows lifted at the white SUV sitting near the side door. "Big."

"Very. Annie named it 'Moby Dick' after one of the cats she saw you examining at the VC."

Moby Dick was a darned good name. He looked down at Nicole's face, and in spite of the warnings shouting in his head, he stroked a silky strand of hair from her forehead.

She was so beautiful it took his breath away.

"Gideon?" she whispered.

"Thank you for sitting with me while I ate."

Her eyes widened. Then she smiled slowly and rose on her tiptoes. "You're welcome," she whispered against his lips.

His arms slid around her waist and pulled her flush against him. Nicole was far more complicated than he'd realized and it was difficult to resist temptation.

The faint scent of Shalimar filled his senses, along with the flavors of apple and butter from the dessert she'd eaten. Gideon tried to close his mind to memories of Helga sitting with Lars as he ate a late meal. It had surprised him when Nicole had done the same, but a single gesture didn't mean that much. She was more empathetic than Renee, that was all.

And a whole lot sweeter to hold.

Nicole arched against his body and he no longer felt the cold night air. He deepened the kiss, their tongues playing, his blood pumping hard, impossibly increasing the pressure against the zipper on his jeans. Yet slowly he became aware of her hand on his chest, pushing away ever so slightly.

He lifted his head and stared down at her, but he couldn't read her expression in the shadows. "What?"

"I have to go. My brother will be worried."

"Yes, of course."

Gideon helped her into the high seat of the SUV and closed the door, knowing he should be grateful that one of them had shown some restraint.

But he wasn't.

CHAPTER THIRTEEN

SATURDAY WAS HECTIC and it wasn't until midafternoon that Carlie got a chance to read her emails.

One was from a former coworker in San Francisco. Carlie hadn't kept in touch and felt a flash of remorse as she opened the message. Frances had been staunchly supportive after the disaster with Derek.

It was just a brief note.

Carlie, I just heard Derek's wife is planning to send a birth announcement the way she sent you an invitation to the wedding. She's a WSWAB, in triplicate. I don't want you to get blindsided again. FYI, they had a baby boy two days ago. Hope you're well. Miss you. Frances

WSWAB was their acronym for Witch-Spelled-with-A-B.

It was a surprise that she'd emailed rather than called since they'd both seen personal messages become unhappily public, but Frances probably trusted her to be careful.

Carlie sat for a long minute, sorting out the emotions cascading through her. The strangest part was realizing that thinking about her ex-fiancé with another woman no longer made her angry. But even if she didn't hate him, she still grieved for the baby she'd wanted.

Carlie sent a message thanking Frances, for some reason thinking about Luke. However blunt, inconsiderate and high-handed he might be, he was also generous, intelligent and adored his daughters. She alternated between being furious with him, admiring his fumbling attempts to connect with Annie and Beth…and wanting to rip his clothes off.

He wasn't a skunk, but she had excellent reasons to keep her distance from him, too. Trust being one of those reasons.

Carlie got up and walked restlessly around her office.

It wasn't that she distrusted men in general—her male relatives were an awfully nice group of guys and it wasn't as if Luke had ever broken his word to her—it was just hard to have faith that someone could love her as much as she loved him and wouldn't hurt her.

LATER THAT EVENING, Carlie sipped hot wassail as she wandered along the pedestrian shopping street with Luke and the girls, enjoying hospitality night. Nicole had stopped at the Days Gone By clothing shop, telling them to go on while she explored the costumes and vintage garments.

"I think your costumes are making my sister envious," Luke commented.

"It isn't intentional. My mother sews, and being the Poppy Gold activities director offers me plenty of excuses to enjoy her talents. It's nice being able to indulge in the charm of a bygone era, without having to live with some of its drawbacks."

Tonight she was wearing a dark red velvet skirt and jacket trimmed in black. The fitted waist of the jacket flared partway over her hips, like a second, very feminine overskirt. She told herself she'd worn it because she'd ridden in the lighted parade again, but that was just an excuse. At heart, she was still a little girl who'd never grown out of wanting to play dress-up.

She'd thought about offering Nicole the loan of a Victorian outfit for the evening, but she was already too involved with the Forresters. Baking cookies with them? Loaning out jeans and sweatpants from her personal wardrobe? Kissing Luke…?

Carlie swiftly directed her thoughts into a safer channel. "Annie, Beth, look at the juggler."

A man in a Victorian suit and top hat was juggling brightly colored balls, while another entertainer on stilts would try to catch one of them, eventually causing the rest to tumble to the ground. This prompted a mock argument before they laughed and started all over again. Annie and Beth were transfixed.

Carlie glanced at Luke and saw an odd expression on his face.

"What's up?" she asked.

"Just thinking. The Christmas celebrations here are beyond anything I anticipated."

"I'm glad. We love Glimmer Creek and want visitors to love it, too. Tonight is a good example of community spirit—the street entertainers are volunteers and the profits go to the fire department."

"That's nice."

"What do you think?" said Nicole from behind them.

They turned and Carlie saw Luke's sister in a rich emerald green Victorian dress and coat, her fingers in a mock fur muff and her hair piled high under a hat.

"You look fabulous," Carlie declared.

"Thank you." Nicole curtsied. "I'll have to visit Poppy Gold every year during the Christmas season, just to have a place to wear my new finery."

"I'll get you into the parade tomorrow, riding in one of the carriages. That will show it off."

"I'd love to… *Oh*," Nicole yelped as an old bicycle horn honked nearby.

"Excuse, ma'am, excuse. My penny farthing doesn't know where it's going," said a street performer wearing a Victorian-era police uniform.

"Papa, what's a penny farthing?" Annie asked, bringing both pleasure and confusion to Luke's face—the latter because he probably didn't have a clue what to tell her.

"*This* is a penny farthing, lovely lady," exclaimed the performer, patting his bicycle with a huge front wheel and a much smaller one in back. He dismounted and swept off his hat, bowing low to the twins. "Officer Bradigan at your service."

"Always flirting with the pretty girls and ignoring your sworn duties," scolded another costumed policeman as he bustled forward. "Though I must say, Bradigan, I can't entirely blame you. They *are* charming." He bowed low, as well, and pulled two peppermint sticks from his pocket.

The girls giggled and accepted the candy.

Officer Bradigan remounted his penny farthing and wobbled forward a foot, only to have his hat tumble to the ground. A third officer rushed forward to berate him for poor comportment, unworthy of his uniform.

They were members of the Poppy Police Beat, a group of players from the local theater group. They performed often through the year, improvising their comical skits. While Carlie had seen their act dozens of times, she loved every minute. Annie and Beth obviously felt the same; they laughed and clapped their hands in glee.

Guests were snapping pictures, including Nicole and Luke, and Carlie wondered if he'd ever allowed himself to just be a regular tourist.

After a while, the Poppy Police Beat continued down the street, Officer Bradigan leading the way on his penny farthing.

"Luke, I'm going to take Beth and Annie with me for a while," Nicole said after the girls had tugged at her skirt and whispered something in her ear.

"All right. Just find us when you're done."

Carlie would have preferred not to be left alone with Luke, though being in a mass of people was hardly *alone*.

"Annie and Beth seem to be having fun," she said, selecting one of the sandwiches at the Glimmer Creek General Store.

"YES." LUKE FROWNED DISTRACTEDLY.

He'd noticed that, unlike most people, Carlie generally spoke Annie's name before Beth's. He didn't know how they'd gotten into the habit of saying the names the opposite way—maybe it was just how they rolled off the tongue. After all, did anyone know why it was peanut butter and jelly, instead of jelly and peanut butter?

"Carlie, I've wanted to ask, why do you always put Annie's name first?"

She scrunched her nose. "I shouldn't say anything."

"For Pete's sake, would you forget about being the activities director?" he ordered, exasperated. "We've gone way past that."

Carlie looked into his eyes for a long moment, seeming to weigh his sincerity. "Okay. The thing is, I grew up with identical twin brothers, so I've seen how complicated the relationship can be."

Luke's attention sharpened. He didn't know anyone else who had experience with twins. When he and Erika had looked for a nanny, they hadn't thought it was an issue—their daughters were to be treated as individuals, and that was that. Yet lately he'd started to wonder if a little twin-expertise would be helpful.

"Quinn is quiet and introspective," Carlie continued, "while Russ is more outgoing and competitive."

"There's nothing wrong with competition," Luke interjected.

Carlie rolled her eyes. "*As I was saying*, when they were kids, Russ would badger or blackmail Quinn to get his way. A lot of the time, Quinn would finally do whatever Russ wanted, just to make him shut up. Ironically, Russ would then act as if it had been Quinn's idea all along. Maybe he even believed it. My folks knew they needed to break the pattern, so they began calling Russ out on his behavior."

"How does that relate to Beth and Annie?"

Carlie hesitated. "From what I've seen, Annie has her own approach to things and usually doesn't care that much about winning. It doesn't seem to bother her if Beth gets the prize or does something in a different way."

He nodded. "Okay, but how does this relate to their names?"

"Beth is much more competitive. She wants to win, particularly over her sister. She's a terrific kid, but I've seen her treat Annie the same way that Russ used to treat Quinn. That's why I say Annie's name first, so she won't feel that she's always second and might feel freer to stand up for herself."

"I see."

Luke had never thought having two little girls would be so complicated. He'd assumed he'd get ulcers when his daughters were sixteen, not six. Of course, Carlie wasn't necessarily right; she'd only known them for two weeks.

Yet he started thinking about the evening the girls had decorated the trees in their bedroom— Beth rushing around, grabbing ornaments and sticking them on the branches, and Annie methodically choosing the ones she wanted before starting. He also remembered how Carlie had intervened when Beth started telling Annie she was taking too long and that her choices were "booooorrrrring," so she should pick something else.

Beth *did* push Annie around. When something mattered deeply to Annie, she wouldn't budge an inch, but the rest of the time she acted as if it wasn't worth the trouble to argue. For both their sakes, he needed to be more observant and break the pattern.

"I wish I could say you were wrong," he said quietly, "but you aren't. Your brothers turned out okay, though, right?"

"Yes, they're both equally annoying to their big sister."

A laugh escaped Luke's throat. "How reassuring."

He looked at Carlie. She fit perfectly with the street entertainers in her period dress. He'd never thought a bustle would have much appeal, but it emphasized her figure; slim and shapely in front, with that saucy little bump in back.

Awareness shot through Luke before he could control it. He still hadn't resolved his feelings about being attracted to another woman besides Erika. It wasn't that he believed there was a time-line for grief, but he remained torn. So, all things considered, it wouldn't be fair to Carlie to get involved with her, even casually.

Assuming she was even interested.

"I wonder where Nicole and the girls went," he murmured as a distraction.

"They can't be far. Let's head back toward Old City Hall. They may have decided to use the washroom there."

They'd only walked about twenty feet when Luke saw his sister and daughters coming toward them. Beth and Annie wore long ruffled skirts and petticoats, along with coats and hats that were virtual duplicates of the ones worn by Nicole, except for the colors.

He lifted his camera and took several pictures, thinking he'd never seen his sister look so pleased. He knew she wanted to get closer to Beth and Annie, so maybe dressing up together would help.

"You're all gorgeous. Now I'm the only one left out," he complained.

Nicole gave him a saucy smile. "You know where the Days Gone By shop is and it's open late tonight. At the very least, you need something for the dress balls, so get cracking."

"Forget I said anything. I'm not a costume kind of guy."

"You never know unless you try. Come on, girls, let's eat more Christmas treats. I've heard that the Glimmer Creek Mercantile is serving *five* flavors of fudge and I want to try every single one of them."

"Yum!" Beth exclaimed.

Luke grinned as his sister took Beth and Annie into the store; the twins weren't the *only* ones blossoming in Glimmer Creek.

"Let's go make sure the girls eat some healthier choices, as well," he said to Carlie. "I think Nicole is enjoying being an aunt too much—she gets to spoil the girls, and I'm the one who has to say no."

It wasn't until later that he wondered about the odd expression on Carlie's face.

GIDEON WAS ENJOYING hospitality night. He'd come over after helping to set up the living nativity and the event was in full swing. Poppy Gold visitors weren't the only people enjoying the evening. Quite a few of his clients stopped him to say hello and he'd stayed busy shaking hands, chatting and trying to remember names while being introduced to still more people.

It was a reminder of why he liked small towns, though admittedly, they weren't *all* friendly. To see if this was the right place for him, he'd visited several times before deciding to relocate. If he ever had kids, he wanted to raise them in a place where he knew his neighbors and the schools were a manageable size. Glimmer Creek had seemed like a good place to do that. And though loans were tight at the local bank, he'd been assured he could get a mortgage when he chose to buy a house.

He was eating a cookie in the general store when

he looked out the window and saw Carlie and Nicole, both dressed to the hilt in Victorian finery, one in red and the other in green. He inhaled so sharply he choked on a crumb; they'd already moved on by the time he'd stopped coughing.

When Nicole had come by the clinic earlier that afternoon, he'd deliberately stayed in his apartment. It was Saturday and he wasn't obligated to see a client who'd insisted on visiting her cat even when the clinic was closed.

Kissing her had been foolish, if for no other reason than she was making him ask questions about his marriage that he preferred to avoid.

In the beginning, things had been good with Renee, but they'd pulled apart, bit by bit. And in the end, they'd each underestimated how strongly the other felt about city versus country life. He'd just been marking time until he could take up a rural practice, while she'd believed he wouldn't care about moving once he'd experienced success and the fast-paced life of Los Angeles.

Gideon went out and looked around the brick-paved street. The two women should be easy to spot in their vibrant costumes, but they might have gone into one of the stores or the fire station.

Why he wasn't attracted to Carlie Benton was beyond him. They had a huge amount in common and she was smart, beautiful and devoted to her hometown. Children gravitated toward her and she seemed open and honest. Yet it was Nicole making him lose sleep and he already lost plenty as a country vet who got called out at all hours to see his patients. In some ways it wasn't that different than Beverly Hills, except in the city he'd gone on house calls at three in the morning because little Fifi had cocked her head funny...two days ago.

Gideon pushed the thought away. The vast majority of his clients in the city had been nice people. He was just dwelling on the negatives because he didn't want to soften toward another city woman.

Yet a flash of humility made him shake his head.

He was behaving as if Nicole was chasing him, but she wasn't; she was learning how to be a responsible pet owner. Not that *owner* was the right word when it came to felines—cats were such arrogant, independent creatures, it was more like *they* were the owners.

Finally spotting Nicole near the old apothecary shop—now a candy store with a taffy puller in the front window—he strode down the street. Avoiding her had smacked of cowardice and it wasn't something that went down well.

"Hello, everyone," he said.

"Gideon," Beth cried. At least he thought it was Beth since she wasn't as shy as her sister.

"Hey there. How is Chico?" he asked, deciding it was safer not to call her by name. Children were so changeable that Annie might be the bold one today.

"He's splendiferous. He plays and plays and won't let Aunt Nicole sleep."

"Oh, yeah?" Gideon looked at Nicole, whose eyes seemed to be challenging him. "Sleep is important."

"Yes," she agreed, her eyes narrowing. "Gideon, you haven't met my brother, Luke Forrester. Luke, this is Dr. Cartwright, the veterinarian who treated Chico after I found him."

"Nice to meet you."

"Same here."

They were shaking hands as Carlie came out of the candy shop, the scent of fresh caramel corn wafting along with her.

She smiled. "Hi, Gideon. Sorry I didn't get over to the living nativity while they were setting up tonight."

"You can't be everywhere, but I miss the lunches we had while we were making plans for it."

He glanced again at Nicole and saw a strained expression on her face, then decided it had to be his imagination. She couldn't possibly be jealous.

LUKE WAS PLEASED when Beth and Annie went the whole day after hospitality night without insisting on Carlie's presence. They'd waved wildly at her while skating and sledding, but there hadn't been the usual pleading requests for her to stay and watch them.

As promised, Nicole had been invited to ride in the lighted parade. The invitation had included the twins, so they'd proudly dressed in their Victorian outfits and ridden in an open carriage with their aunt. He'd taken dozens of pictures and had already downloaded them to the computer.

It wasn't until later that Luke realized that, for the first time since his wife's death, he hadn't instinctively evaluated each photo for sending to Erika. He also hadn't questioned whether she'd approve of her daughters dressing as children from a period in history where women couldn't even vote.

Apparently life *did* march on, whether he wanted it to or not. He was a single father now; he had to make the best decisions for his kids. By himself. He'd go crazy if he tried to weigh his wife's silent voice into everything.

ON MONDAY MORNING Luke was going through financial reports, including the section on charitable donations, when he thought about the Christmas baskets and gifts he'd helped Carlie prepare for the seniors in Glimmer Creek. It *had* been satisfying. Impulsively, he called Carlie and offered to bring everything to the fire department for distribution.

"That's nice of you," she said, sounding surprised, "but two of the volunteer firefighters are coming tomorrow to pick them up."

"Let me save them a trip. I've got a big SUV with lots of cargo space. It should be used for *something*." He tried not to smile as he spoke, even though she couldn't see him.

"So I've heard," she returned crisply. "Fine. We've moved everything to a ground-floor storeroom. It'll take a few trips with one of the Poppy Gold shuttles to get everything loaded in your... *vehicle*."

"Sounds good. I'll be there in a few minutes."

CARLIE HUNG UP the phone, annoyed that Luke had mentioned the SUV. He'd seemed so grim and humorless when they'd first met, but now he was delighting in giving her a hard time.

It was frustrating the way he was creeping into her thoughts. She'd even had trouble getting to sleep Saturday night after the way he'd talked about the two of them making sure Annie and Beth ate something healthy.

Let's go make sure the girls eat...

It hadn't meant anything, but the words had instantly raised images of parental solidarity.

Disgusted with herself, Carlie headed toward the employee break room with her mug, needing coffee to deal with Luke. But as she reached for the pot, her cell rang.

Her breath caught when she saw her parents' home number on the caller ID. Dad was at his job site—there was a road farther up in the hills where a bridge was under repair—and her mother didn't call unless it was important.

"Mom, what is it?" she answered.

"Your father fell," Leah said, her voice shaking. "I've spoken to him and he insists he's all right, but they're taking him to the Glimmer Creek Medical Clinic to be checked."

"I'll meet you there."

"He'll be upset if we both show up. He hates a fuss and he knows you're busy."

"He'll just have to deal with it," Carlie said firmly.

"All right. I'll see you in a few minutes."

Carlie got off and ran to give her staff instructions on what to do about Luke in her absence, only to find him already waiting.

"Sorry, Luke, something's come up and I can't stay." She glanced around and saw Tracy Wade. "Tracy, would you help Mr. Forrester get the Christmas baskets loaded in his car and give him directions to the fire department? I've got an emergency."

"Of course. I hope it isn't serious."

"Me, too. My dad fell and they want to be sure he didn't break anything."

"Let me drive you," Luke urged. "I can take care of the baskets later."

"No, I'm fine."

She hurried to her car, worrying that her father might need another surgery on his leg. Or worse, that he'd get so despondent about never having a normal life again he'd simply give up. The second concern was instantly dispelled when she walked into the medical clinic and heard Mike Benton's voice coming from the rear of the building.

"I don't need X-rays. I'm going back to work." Her dad didn't use strong language when he was angry, but he made up for it in volume.

Carlie looked at the office manager behind the counter. "At least we know his voice still works."

"Yep." Rosemary grinned. "Go on back."

In the urgent-care area of the clinic, Carlie saw her mother and father and Aunt Emma, all wearing equally harassed expressions.

"What are you doing here?" her father demanded as the physician's assistant cleaned the deep abrasions on his hands. Aunt Emma was a doctor, but she didn't treat family members except in emergencies.

"I considered taking part of the morning off. Then I found out you'd tripped over your big feet," Carlie returned calmly. "So instead of getting a spa treatment, I came here instead."

"I'm perfectly all right and don't need to be poked and prodded."

She shook her head. "If I gave up a morning a

the spa, the least *you* can do is cooperate. Behave and I'll get you an ice-cream cone." It had been his old bribe to her as a child when she was getting vaccinations.

A smile threatened to break through Mike's grumpy expression. "Oh, very well. But it had better be a double scoop."

Carlie sat next to her mom as they waited for the results of the X-rays.

"Nothing is broken," Aunt Emma announced. She gazed sternly at her brother-in-law. "You were lucky, Mike, but you *have* to rest for a few days. Falling is hard on the body. The PA concurs. Come back next in three days and she'll decide whether to clear you for work."

"No."

"Yes," Carlie and her mother said in unison, with Aunt Emma not far behind.

He muttered something about there being too many hens in the henhouse, but he didn't have much choice. He was soundly overruled.

CHAPTER FOURTEEN

CARLIE GOT BACK to Poppy Gold shortly after the lunch hour. Her father was already restless and talking about sweeping the walkway, but she knew he'd just get more uptight if she stayed. It would be up to her mother to keep him quiet.

"Is everything okay with your dad?" Tracy asked.

"Seems to be. He's staying home for a few days as a precaution."

"Great. I hate to say it, but the Mitchells called. They want to know if you'd come by sometime and see their costumes for the ball."

"I just hope they aren't going as Lady Godiva and her horse."

"It could be worse—they could be going as Adam and Eve…before they ate the apple."

A choked laugh escaped Carlie. The Mitchells were nice, but they lacked discretion. They'd been coming to Poppy Gold for years and their costumes each Christmas were interesting, to say the least. But particularly the previous Christmas. While guests weren't required to attend in Victorian dress a scantily clad Tarzan and Jane didn't quite fit—particularly when Tarzan's loincloth wasn't that secure. Luckily the dance was one of the few fully adult events at Poppy Gold during the holiday season.

"I'll take a look and try to be diplomatic," she promised. "Any other news?"

"The fire chief called to thank us for having the gifts and baskets brought to the station. Plus, the first children's holiday tea party is on Wednesday at the Douglas House. Housekeeping will leave flyers in the rooms tomorrow with the details."

"Thanks."

Carlie went into her office to take some aspirin. She'd expected to work most days until after the New Year and normally it wouldn't be a problem, but the incident with her dad would complicate things. Heck, she hadn't even found time to have the battery in her electronic car key replaced. If Luke had really wanted to do something thoughtful, he could have taken care of *that*.

Carlie rubbed her forehead, knowing she wasn't just worried about her father. Luke was also bothering her, or more accurately, her reaction to him. She wanted to believe it was purely physical urges vying for attention, because falling for the guy was emotional suicide.

It wasn't just that he was grieving for his wife. She simply wasn't ready to put her heart out there to get stomped on by any man. But *especially* Luke. He had two major strikes against him—his memories of Erika Forrester and his domineering ways.

Men in general remained a question mark for Carlie, at least from a romantic standpoint. Perry Fisher had asked her out a number of times—his comments about her being his "dream girl" aside—but she kept deflecting his invitations with a joke. She'd enjoyed having lunches with Gideon Cartwright, but had limited their conversation to the living nativity and Glimmer Creek.

In the meantime, she had a job to do, so Carlie squared her shoulders and dialed the Yosemite suite. There wasn't an answer, so she reluctantly called Luke's cell number. At least at the suite there'd been a chance she would have gotten Nicole.

"Hi, Carlie. Is everything all right with your father?" Luke asked when he answered.

She kept forgetting about caller ID. "Yes, thanks. I wanted you to know the fire chief phoned to say thank you for bringing over the gifts and baskets."

"No problem. I'm at the ice rink, watching Nicole and the girls skate. Why don't we get together for coffee? It might help to have someone to talk to about your dad."

"I'll come over there," Carlie said. She didn't intend to vent, but Luke and her dad possessed th same stiff necks. Luke might have some insight that would help her understand better.

She got coffee from the break room and crossed the park to the skating rink. Luke was alone on a festive bleacher on the far side and she handed him one of the cups she carried.

"Thanks."

Annie and Beth waved from the ice but didn't come over. Carlie missed the way they'd shadowed her in the beginning, though it was best they wanted to be with their aunt and do things independently. She'd have to suggest to Nicole that the three of them dress up in their Victorian finery and attend the Christmas tea on Wednesday.

Yet Carlie felt a pang of conscience. Was she playing favorites? Poppy Gold tried to give top service to everyone, but they'd never had anyone stay as long as the Forresters. There was a tendency to provide extra attention to guests you knew well, if for no other reason than you got familiar with their likes and dislikes. So to be fair, she should also call a few other families about the tea party.

Luke gulped down some coffee. "I take it your father's injuries were minor."

"Bruises and scrapes on his hands. He refuses to wear gloves when he's working. On doctor's orders, he's spending a few days at home, which means we'll probably have to tie him to the couch by tomorrow morning. I may have to pull out the line 'pride goeth before a *fall*.'"

Luke groaned. "Spare him that. I understand where he's coming from."

"You *would*. You said yourself that you don't know how to play."

"Hey, I'm trying to do better. If only for Beth and Annie's sake."

Carlie curled both hands around her cup and gazed at the skaters. Christmas music played from speakers, lights were strung everywhere and decorated Christmas trees ringed the ice. Finally, she turned her head and looked at Luke's strong, handsome face, trying to see if there was any trace of the boy who'd lost his childhood. He had wealth beyond imagining, but he could never get that part of his life back.

It might explain some of his need for success and control.

"Have you ever seen river otters playing?" she asked. "Surviving in the wild is serious business, but they play whenever possible, throwing themselves into it with joyous abandon."

"I may be trying to expand my playful side, but I'm not going to cavort like a river otter."

"But you *could* get a costume for the dress ball," she suggested.

"I told you, that isn't my thing."

Carlie started to say something, then stopped

Luke had invited her to be open with him on more than one occasion, but it was still tricky.

He sighed. "How many times do I need to tell you? Say what you think, Carlie. I can see when you're holding something back."

"It's just that being a little silly and having fun wouldn't mean you're becoming like your parents."

Luke shrugged. "I'm spending Christmas here at Poppy Gold. Isn't that enough?"

"You tell me. You're on your computer all night, making Nicole worry that you aren't getting enough sleep. During the day, you mostly just watch your sister and the twins have fun, while you get by on coffee and adrenaline."

"I sleep after 3:00 or 4:00 a.m."

Carlie rolled her eyes. "Two or three hours, tops. Sleep deprivation is a major health risk." She shivered and wondered if the temperature was dropping earlier than usual, or if she was just anxious about her dad and what the future would bring them as a family.

"I'm healthy," Luke insisted.

Just then the haunting notes of a Celtic Christmas carol came over the speakers. Carlie loved Celtic music, with all the joy and sorrow it conveyed. But Luke had known too much sorrow. He needed more joy.

"Think how pleased Nicole and your daughters would be if you got a costume to go with theirs," she coaxed. "I'm not suggesting a fake mustache or sideburns, just an evening suit. Then you'd be having some fun yourself, instead of just watching other people."

LUKE FELT THE tug of what Carlie was saying. *Fun.* Silliness. Being able to just throw himself into the moment. It was seductive. But it had always felt as if he stood at the top of a slippery slope, with his parents at the bottom, beckoning him to join them.

He loved his mom and dad and no longer tried to change them. He even recognized that, as a kid, he'd missed dozens of opportunities to kick back and just enjoy things that most children never got to experience. Carlie was bringing that recognition home to him even stronger than before. Perhaps Beth and Annie responded so well to her because she possessed a sense of fun and joy that he'd never had.

It was something to think about.

He leaned toward Carlie. "All right. I'll get a costume, but you'll have to go shopping for it with me. For Beth and Annie's sake."

"That's blackmail."

"Whatever works. I'm not going into that costume shop alone."

"Okay, but we should go now. The closer we get to the ball, the less choice you'll have."

He agreed and gestured to his sister to say he was leaving. She waved back, smiling happily. Until Luke had seen the changes in Nicole over the past few days, he hadn't realized she might be having troubles, as well. He hated thinking he'd been so focused on his own he'd missed seeing something she needed.

At the costume shop, Carlie waited while he tried on her top choice, a black evening suit that wasn't all that different from a modern tuxedo. He fought with the high shirt collar, but finally got it fastened, then put a top hat on, trying not to feel ridiculous.

He stepped out of the small dressing room and both Carlie and the salesclerk's eyes widened.

The clerk let out a wolf whistle that resounded through the small building, crowded with shoppers. "If my husband looked that good in one of our suits, I'd never let him wear anything else."

No doubt it was a sales ploy, but Luke wasn't displeased when he saw his reflection in a long mirror. He was startled, in fact. The suit wasn't as tailored as the ones he always had made in London, but it had an elegance he hadn't anticipated.

"Not bad," he murmured when Carlie lifted an inquiring eyebrow.

"It may be more Edwardian than Victorian, but we won't split hairs," she said. "Do you want to try anything else on?"

"Maybe a less formal suit, too. In case it's needed."

"Right. Perhaps something you could wear riding in one of the lighted parades."

Luke thought he glimpsed a smile on Carlie's face, but she hid it quickly. She also didn't appear smug, which was a point in her favor.

"OMIGOD, THAT'S UNBELIEVABLE," Nicole whispered Monday evening as she stared up at the night sky ablaze with stars.

"It sure is," Gideon agreed, deciding not to point out that this kind of display wouldn't be visible in the city.

They'd just eaten a take-out meal on the tailgate of his truck and Nicole had lain back to stare upward. He didn't know how she'd convinced him to get food in the first place, but with his stomach comfortably full of enchiladas and rice, he wasn't complaining.

The day before, she'd appeared with three giant sacks of sandwiches from the Gilbraith Delicatessen and a box of cookies from Sarah's Sweet Treats, enough to feed the clinic's employees for a couple of days. Peter Talua had yet to meet her, but he'd sworn undying devotion while munching roast beef and Swiss on a sourdough roll.

Food was a great way to smooth the way with people, but it didn't have anything to do with the odd sort of peace that had fallen between them. Ever since they'd talked about her getting bitten by a dog as a child, things had been far more comfortable.

Well, not physically. Gideon's body was too aware of Nicole as a woman to be completely at ease. But other barriers seemed to have come down.

"Orion is my favorite constellation," she said, pointing to the distinct row of stars that made up Orion's belt. "You know why?"

"It's the easiest for you to recognize?" he guessed.

She laughed. "Yes. What was the sky like on the farm where you grew up?"

"Like this, I suppose. I didn't hang out at night to see it, at least during the winter. Eastern Nebraska is *cold* this time of year. I would have gone back after I qualified if it hadn't been for the weather."

Nicole shivered. "Glimmer Creek is cold compared to Texas."

"Do you miss the city when you're away?" Gideon tried not to wonder why the answer was so important to him.

"I hadn't thought about it." She turned her head. "There's always something to do and see in Austin, but I don't have anything against small towns. I've just never lived in one. I love how peaceful it is in Glimmer Creek."

"And we don't have traffic jams."

Nicole chuckled softly. "That part is especially nice."

Though he was reluctant to end the companionable interlude, Gideon straightened. "Sorry to break this up, but I have patients to examine and you probably want to see Bandit again before you leave."

NICOLE KNEW GIDEON might be hinting that she should quickly say hello to Bandit and leave, but it wasn't that easy. Instead, she cuddled the purring kitten and watched as Gideon carefully checked his various patients, adjusting the treatment as needed and recording information on the computer.

What she'd seen of the software he was using seemed cumbersome, but she hadn't said anything; she'd never worked on medical records systems. Maybe she'd ask to take a closer look before she left Glimmer Creek. Even if Gideon was offended, it was getting easier to confront him and she was only curious because she wanted to help.

Well, she was starting to want a whole lot more, but that was another matter.

Anyhow, while being assertive had always been difficult for her, she was seeing its benefits...such as being able to visit Bandit. Gideon was the last person she could have imagined challenging, but she'd been convinced that loving contact was just as important to the kitten's recovery as IVs and medicine.

"Yikes, what is a possum doing here?" she asked when a snarl greeted Gideon in a kennel at the end of the row.

"It was brought in after being hit by a car—broken jaw, but otherwise in okay shape. I devised a way to put the bone back together but he doesn't appreciate being messed with. We're going to transition him to the outdoor pens that we use for wildlife."

Nicole shuddered. Possums reminded her too much of large rats. "It must have taken a while to do the surgery," she said, unsure why he'd spent the time.

"My staff thought I was nuts, but a possum's jawbone isn't that different from a cat. Besides, his life is just as valuable to him as any other animal."

Suddenly, a heavyset dog appeared around a corner and Nicole sucked in a breath. Bandit tensed at the same moment and started spitting, though the possum was even more vociferous, making sounds that were downright bone-chilling.

"Hold on, Bogey," Gideon said, catching the dog's collar. "The lady isn't used to you."

"Bogey?" Nicole croaked.

"That's right. His full name is Humphrey Bogart—Bogey for short. Can't you see the resemblance?"

All she saw was teeth.

Bogey rubbed his huge head against Gideon's

leg before collapsing to the floor and rolling over. He grunted and his legs paddled in the air as Gideon rubbed his stomach.

"Okay, pal, time to go back to your kennel," Gideon said after a minute. "Allie must have let you out for a walk while she was cleaning."

The animal obediently stood up—albeit with difficulty—and went with Gideon.

Nicole released a shaky breath and focused on Bandit in her arms. She was curiously convinced that the kitten with his baby teeth and clipped claws was more of a danger than the massive, slobbering love bug who'd wandered out to say hello.

"Okay, you can stop growling, Bandit. You showed him who was boss." She put him back in his kennel and fastened the door.

Unsure if she was insane or merely unbalanced, she walked to the rear of the clinic where the animals were kept for regular boarding. Was Pandowdy still here, the dog with the deep bark that had reverberated through the clinic?

Nicole peeked around the corner. Gideon was examining Bogey's mouth with careless disregard for his teeth...though now that she had a better look, it appeared one of the large front ones was missing.

"Is, uh, he all right?" she asked, hoping the cracking in her voice wasn't too obvious. She'd become more at ease around animals in the past few days, but this was a really *big* dog.

Gideon glanced up, seeming surprised to see her. "He's fine. I removed an abscessed tooth the day you found Chico, but it's healed well. And unlike the possum, Bogey appears quite grateful for my services."

Gathering her courage, Nicole came closer. Bogey was so ugly that he was actually cute. She held out her hand, determined not to shake. The old bulldog sniffed and let out a small whine.

"Wh-what does that mean?"

"You have Bandit's scent on you," Gideon explained. "Bogey lives with three cats and they're his best friends. Not to worry, though—his family will be back in a couple of days. The cats stay at home with someone checking on them, but they feel Bogey is too sociable to be left alone like that."

The poor thing was homesick.

Though her hand shook, she rubbed the bulldog's neck and he rolled over, exactly the way he had for Gideon, snuffling and waving his legs. With her heart in her throat, she stroked the dog's tummy.

It was hard to know if she was trying to prove something to herself or to Gideon. But either way, it was progress.

"OKAY, OLD FELLOW," Gideon said after a couple of minutes. Bogey was a genuinely nice dog and a favorite patient at the clinic. "Time for bed."

Bogey accepted a last caress from Nicole before obediently going into the kennel and lying down on his bed.

Gideon closed the kennel door. He couldn't imagine how hard it must have been for Nicole to touch the bulldog. It didn't matter that Bogey was harmless; she'd shown a remarkable amount of resolve.

"Would you like something hot to drink?" he asked. "I have tea and coffee in my apartment upstairs."

His thinking had been shifting lately, from thoughts of why they were unsuited for each other, to the way she turned him inside out. And at the moment it was hard to consider *anything* except how much he wanted her.

Nicole seemed to be debating. "All right." Upstairs in his living room she crossed immediately to the patchwork quilt hanging over the couch. "How beautiful. Did your foster mother make this?"

"Yes. She says I should be using it because quilts are made to keep people warm. But I like it there."

"Beauty keeps people warm, too. Does she ever sell her work?"

"There isn't a market for it back home. The town is small and tourists don't go through that much. Do you want tea or something else?"

"Tea is good."

She was still gazing at the quilt when Gideon went into the kitchen. He'd updated everything, wanting it to be a comfortable home where Lars and Helga might consider living. Lars missed working with the animals on his farm, and being able to interact with the clinic's patients would be good for him.

"Your apartment has a nice open feel," Nicole said, coming in as he put the kettle on the burner and set out cups, teaspoons and tea bags.

"I like it, but I'm hunting for a house."

"Why? This is lovely."

"I'm hoping my foster parents will move to California and agree to live here. Besides, I'd like to have enough land for a few animals and space to better rehabilitate injured wildlife."

"And a family?" she asked lightly.

"Someday. My ex-wife didn't want children, but I don't feel the same."

"Is that why you broke up?"

"There were too many reasons to count. Renee hates the country and loves the city. I'm the opposite. She wanted a live-in cook and housekeeper, while I didn't like the loss of privacy. She's devoted to fashion and I just want clothes that are comfortable. I could go on and on. By the time we split, there just wasn't anything left between us."

"I'd heard you were in the middle of a divorce."

"No doubt from the Glimmer Creek rumor mill. Carlie claims there's an underground stream that runs from house to house, picking up information along the way. Anyhow, my divorce recently became final."

"You seem close to Carlie."

Interestingly, Gideon saw the same flash in Nicole's eyes that he'd seen when telling Carlie that he'd missed their lunches together.

"We've become friends and she's helped me learn some of the ways that Glimmer Creek works. Customs and expectations, that sort of thing. In the city, you can be anonymous, but sooner or later, everybody knows your business in a small town."

The kettle whistled and he filled their cups.

"Cream or sugar?" he asked.

"No, this is fine."

They went into the living room and sat on the couch next to Helga's quilt. Gideon was thinking about what Nicole had said…that beauty kept people warm, too. He'd never thought of it in those terms, but it wasn't just the beauty of design and workmanship of the patchwork quilt that warmed him. It was the love Helga had sewn into it.

"Beth and Annie were cute in their costumes," he said idly. "They really seem to be enjoying Poppy Gold."

"It would be hard for them *not* to enjoy Poppy

Gold. They study with their tutor in the morning, but they adore Mrs. Cabrera, and the rest of the time it's pure Christmas fun. I just hope they won't feel a letdown when we go home to Austin."

"A little letdown is inevitable, isn't it?"

"I suppose. Things have worked out so well with Mrs. Cabrera that Luke wants to look into home schooling for the rest of the year. I'm not sure it's for the best. Beth and Annie need friends, though I don't care for the private school they're attending, either. Way too snooty."

Gideon would have expected Nicole to prefer an exclusive, high-toned school. Yet as he watched her sipping tea from one of his mismatched mugs, it occurred to him that for all her designer clothes and her inordinately wealthy brother, she *didn't* put on airs. She had expensive tastes—today she sported a striking blue topaz necklace and matching earrings—but she was also wearing a plain yellow T-shirt printed with the Poppy Gold logo, jeans and the canvas loafers he'd seen before.

"Are those the jeans Carlie loaned you?" he asked, his voice unintentionally husky. The denim could have been painted onto Nicole's shapely thighs and hips.

"Yeah. I know they're snug—Carlie generously claims we're the same size, but I'm at least a half size larger. She wants to loan me one of her costumes for the dress ball, but I've worried about splitting the seams, so I got two ball gowns from the clothing shop to wear instead. Do you think she'll be offended?"

"I doubt it. She just wants guests to have a good time."

"I could never do what she does. She's *sooo* comfortable with people and has all these creative ideas."

"You don't think you're creative?"

Nicole shrugged. "I work on computer software, but that's a different kind of creativity."

"Sounds creative to me. As for Carlie, she comes up with new things for people to do, but she'd be the first to say that many of the activities at Poppy Gold are a long-standing tradition."

THE REMARK PLEASED NICOLE. She wasn't proud of envying Gideon's relationship with Carlie, but at least it seemed to be friendship, not romance.

What a tangle it would be if she liked Gideon, but he'd liked Carlie, while Carlie seemed attracted to Luke, who barely noticed women now that Erika was gone. It could be the plot of a soap opera or an Oscar Wilde play.

Of course, Luke *was* spending more time with Carlie than strictly necessary, but the girls were fond of her and he'd do anything for them. But what if Carlie fell for Luke? Nicole genuinely doubted he'd ever get over Erika; Carlie could get terribly hurt if her brother wasn't careful.

Nicole pressed a finger to her throbbing temple.

"Hey, what's wrong?" Gideon asked gently.

"Just thinking too much, I guess. It's been a hard year for us."

He nodded. "Your sister-in-law's death. I didn't connect the names right away, but I remember reading about what happened. It must have been awful."

"I'd never lost anyone I cared about before," Nicole murmured. "But the worst part has been seeing Luke and the girls grieve and not being able to help. People think he's cold, but he isn't. He's just learned to hide his feelings, and he'll never be the same without Erika."

"My foster mother once told me that when our hearts gets broken, it can make room for something else."

It was an uplifting thought, but Nicole shifted restlessly. Since they'd kissed the night of the madrigal feast, Gideon hadn't made a single move to suggest he was interested in her. Yet she was absolutely certain he'd wanted her during that embrace.

Of course, inviting her up to his apartment crossed the boundary between client and friend. It would be nice to make it *more* than friendship, but she suspected she'd have to make the first move, which wasn't her strong suit.

Still…

"So how much more to this apartment is there?" she asked lightly. "Is there a bedroom, or does the couch open up?"

Gideon's eyes were suddenly much more alert. "Bedroom, bath and small spare room. Want a tour?"

"I'd love one."

Seeing his king-size bed sent quivers through the base of Nicole's abdomen. Gideon was a tall man; he'd need something large.

"It looks comfortable." She stepped closer and touched his face. Tonight she didn't want to worry whether his heart still belonged to his ex-wife, despite the divorce, or about rebound affairs being a bad idea.

"Nicole?" Gideon whispered hoarsely.

"I don't know how to be coy," she breathed. "I just know what I want."

He slowly grinned. "Whatever you want, you can have."

"That's good to hear." Nicole stepped back and began shimmying the jeans she wore down her legs. Gideon's eyes seemed to glaze as he watched, so she added a little extra wiggle to her hips, pleased to discover she possessed a hint of exhibitionism.

After all, sex *ought* to be fun.

"I'm just saving time," she said innocently, while doing her best imitation of a striptease. "These things are as hard to get off as they are to get on."

Gideon chuckled. "You're forgetting that I used to be a teenage boy. I could get girls out of their jeans in nothing flat."

She tossed the soft denims to one side. "Big talker. You're still dressed."

Nicole got down to bare skin before he did, but only barely, and they tumbled to his mattress, laughing. His eyes darkened as he stroked her breasts, coaxing her nipples into hard points before leaning down and tasting them.

Heat swept through her and she arched toward him.

"You *do* have protection, don't you?" she gasped.

"Don't worry—no unwanted kids."

"They wouldn't…" She moaned as he teased her beyond rational thought.

"Wouldn't what?"

Nicole shook her head, trying to regain her focus. "Uh, they wouldn't be unwanted. But I'd rather decide when and with who. Er, whom?"

Gideon eased her legs apart. "Who cares about proper grammar?"

Nicole didn't care about anything at the moment

except her spiraling need. A second later, he thrust into her, setting up a rhythm that quickly made the world explode.

CHAPTER FIFTEEN

EVEN AFTER A couple of days, Luke still couldn't believe he'd gotten a costume for the dress balls or that he'd purchased a second one for less formal events.

The shop had his daughters' clothing sizes on record, so he'd also chosen another outfit each for Beth and Annie. They'd gotten so excited that they insisted on trying them on and getting their picture taken in every conceivable location at Poppy Gold.

His favorite photos were of them skating in ruffles and their Victorian coats and hats, looking like figures from an old painting. He wasn't the only one taking pictures—Nicole had dressed in her new costume and the three had charmed guests and employees alike.

He was still worried about his relationship with the girls, but he'd been encouraged when Annie had gotten up two nights after the madrigal feast and appeared in the room he was using as an office. She'd been very solemn and had said she was sad about Carlie's daddy having to limp because his leg got hurt. Luke had tried to explain that sometimes bad things happened, but that he'd always try to protect her.

"A bad person hurt Mommy," she'd said in a small voice.

His chest tight, he'd finally nodded. "Yes. But she'd never want us to forget that she was doing something important to help other people."

Annie had fallen asleep in his lap after that and he'd put her to bed, unsure if he'd said the right thing. The next morning, she hadn't seemed any different, but she was so much quieter than Beth it was difficult to tell what was going on in her solemn little head. Still, he felt awed that his six-year-old daughter had shown so much concern for a man she'd met only once.

Restless, Luke left the suite and walked to Sarah's Sweet Treats to get a cup of coffee.

Nicole had gotten back late on Monday. He knew she'd gone to visit the second kitten, who remained under observation at the veterinary clinic. Since he didn't think she'd sat cuddling the cat for several hours, the most likely explanation was Dr. Gideon Cartwright.

While Luke had liked the vet when they'd met at the hospitality night, that didn't mean he was right for Nicole.

Carlie might know more about Gideon, though she wouldn't necessarily be willing to say anything; she was friendly with Nicole and might feel it was disloyal to discuss another woman's love life. But maybe there was something he could do to assist Carlie with her professional duties, and in the process he could ask a few questions.

At Old City Hall he walked back to her office and heard her talking on the phone. He leaned against the doorjamb and watched.

"I understand, Mrs. Gunderson...many guests do, but costumes aren't required to attend the dress ball."

Carlie looked up and waved toward the couch. Luke sat and glanced through a box on the floor containing fanciful masks.

"The Days Gone By clothing shop rents and sells costumes," she continued. "Yes, definitely, the rentals are carefully cleaned after each use, but I don't know what they'll have available when you arrive on Friday... I'd be happy to give you their number." She recited it slowly and after another moment said goodbye.

Luke gestured to the box of masks. "You didn't mention the dress balls were also masquerade parties."

"They aren't, but our New Year's Eve celebration has a Mardi Gras flavor. It's similar to hospitality night and very kid friendly, which means no adult beverages," she warned. "The New Year is toasted with sparkling apple cider and hot chocolate."

"I probably won't even make it to ten that night

with the girls. And I'm definitely not wearing something like this, no matter how hard you try to make me." He held up a glittery concoction.

"I haven't 'made' you do anything. Those are just samples from the Days Gone By shop. We'll add them to our decorations when Christmas is over. It helps soften the after-holiday blues and advertises the New Year's Eve event."

"There's an after-holiday-blues period at Poppy Gold? I'm shocked. Does that mean everything vanishes on December 26, like the skating rink and sledding hill?"

"They'll both run until mid-January, but the multicolored lights shift to white and blue on New Year's Day. So, what brings you here this morning?" she asked.

"Just thought I'd offer my services. Is there anything I can do to help out?"

She regarded him suspiciously. "Well, a group of guests are having a snow-people-building contest. It's their annual family reunion and they've asked for an impartial judge. Joan Peters was going to do it, but I could send you instead. Can you be impartial?"

Judging a contest wasn't what he'd had in mind, particularly since it was clear that Carlie wouldn't be going with him, but he might still use it to his advantage.

"Sure. Will you have lunch with me afterward?

Nicole and the girls have gone to the Christmas tea in lieu of their lessons today. Then they're going skating."

"What happened to the obsessed businessman who wanted satellite communications in the Yosemite suite?"

"I'm still working at night and at free moments during the day, but I think this place is corrupting me. Besides, you need to eat and I want to hear how your dad is doing. Honestly," he assured her at her skeptical expression. "We met at the madrigal feast, remember? He's a nice guy."

Luke also thought Carlie could do with a good lunch. He would swear she'd lost weight since they'd arrived at Poppy Gold.

"Okay," she agreed finally. "I'll get prize ribbons for you to give out. The key is to make it fun for everybody, so throw some panache into your presentations."

She led the way to a large storeroom and he saw an interesting variety of supplies. From a stack on a shelf, she selected a plastic box. It turned out to contain first-, second- and third-place ribbons, along with a large quantity of white "honorable mentions."

"I take it all contestants get a ribbon of some type," he said.

"Yes. Does that offend your competitive soul?" Carlie asked in a dry tone.

"I'll survive."

He headed toward the area where the snowmakers were stationed. Competition was a fundamental part of the business world, but he was beginning to think there was something to be said for Carlie's philosophy that everyone should win in some way.

"THE CONTEST WENT OKAY," Luke told Carlie as they sat down with their food in Sarah's Sweet Treats bakery later that afternoon. "But I think the Rodneys were disappointed you weren't there."

"I'm sure they were fine with you as their judge."

Luke shrugged. He'd enjoyed evaluating the entries and handing out the ribbons, much to his amazement. "Tell me about your dad," he urged.

"There isn't much to tell. He's irritable and driving Mom crazy. Tomorrow he's going to ask the doctor for a release to return to work. That's all there is to report."

Luke glanced down, not wanting her to read anything in his eyes. He'd thought a great deal about Mike Benton's condition since the madrigal feast, debating an idea he'd had for helping both Carlie and her father, and questioning whether it was appropriate. Luke understood pride; he suffered from an excess of it himself. But the injustice of the way the other man had been injured rankled and he kept remembering the solemn, worried expression on

Annie's face when she'd talked about Mike Benton's leg.

Then Mike had fallen.

It had been too much.

So Luke had made two calls on Monday afternoon, one to Tessa McKinley, and the other to a top orthopedic specialist in San Francisco, who'd agreed to visit Glimmer Creek soon. Tessa had enthusiastically endorsed Luke's plan, explaining they kept a few rooms in reserve and she'd be happy to make one available whenever needed… anything to help her cousin and uncle.

With luck, they could make it appear that the specialist just happened to be visiting Poppy Gold and had agreed to evaluate Mike Benton's medical records.

But should Carlie be told?

She was making him think about the way he attacked problems—Tilly likened it to the Allies landing on D-day—but this was different than exchanging a car with a new SUV. And while he couldn't prove it, he knew he wasn't doing it as a gesture of appreciation. He'd begun to care about Carlie as a friend and wanted to help.

Still, maybe he'd better prepare for potentially explosive revelations.

"From what Nicole says, Dr. Cartwright appears to be a capable veterinarian," he said. "I understand he's new to Glimmer Creek."

Carlie blinked. "Gideon has been here for eight or nine months. What brought that up?"

"Chico is a mooch, probably from being a stray. He leaps into our plates if we aren't careful. I thought a veterinarian might have ideas for getting him to stop."

"You must be bored if you're thinking about training a kitten. That is, *attempting* to train one. I love cats, but they aren't that trainable."

"I'm not bored," Luke insisted, but she cocked her head at him in patent disbelief. "All right, I want to find out more about Dr. Cartwright. I think Nicole is getting involved with him."

Carlie rolled her eyes. "Gideon is a nice, law-abiding citizen and Nicole is a grown woman."

"He's a small-town vet who's probably still paying off student loans and in debt from buying the practice."

Carlie dropped her sandwich on her plate and leaned forward. "That's none of your business, Luke. Leave it alone. Now, would you all like to wear your costumes in the lighted parade tonight?" she asked in a blatant effort to change the subject.

Luke was accustomed to getting what he wanted, but he decided to let it go. *For now.*

"Sorry, we can't. I made reservations for the stargazing hayride tonight," he said. "I understand a visiting astronomer offered to talk about the visible constellations."

Carlie nodded. "Dr. Purcell is a retired professor from the University of Arizona. He comes every year at Christmas."

The conversation through the remainder of the meal stayed light and impersonal, but he continued thinking about it, especially after leaving Carlie at Old City Hall and crossing the park to the skating rink.

Despite what Carlie thought, he wasn't trying to make decisions for Nicole. He was just worried about her.

WHEN CARLIE RETURNED to her office, she found a white poinsettia had been delivered from one of the guests at Poppy Gold. She put the plant on the corner of her desk. Several had been sent to the activities staff and were in the common area, but maybe she'd keep this one in her office. Joan and Tracy didn't care for specialty poinsettias, preferring red the most, but Carlie liked the mix.

Edgy, she took a walk around Poppy Gold to see what was happening. The skating rink was busy as usual, but she didn't go over in case Luke and the girls were there. The line between guest and employee kept getting blurred with Luke, and she needed to reinforce those boundaries.

She checked the time and ran into the Douglas House. It was after the first high tea and her aunt was busy setting up for the second.

"Hey, Aunt Mattie. Did you hear how the kids' tea party went this morning?"

"Jamie says it was a full house and everybody had a good time. It's a great idea with so many children staying at Poppy Gold for the holidays. Not that we had any boys at the tea party, just girls."

"It might be different if boys that age were more interested in girls," Carlie said with a laugh.

"True. Your uncle still watches musicals with me because I love them, and you know how he feels about people spontaneously bursting into song."

"Uncle Henry would do anything to make you happy."

Aunt Mattie smiled and Carlie left as the second group of guests began arriving. Even among adults, high tea was mostly a feminine gathering. Men sometimes came with their wives or girlfriends, but rarely on their own.

Carlie continued her walk around the facility, greeting guests and considering what other activities could be planned. The main reason she'd thought of having a children's tea party was because of Annie and Beth and she wanted more new things for them to do. Yet even as she evaluated different ideas, she questioned whether always keeping busy was the answer to her dilemma with the Forresters, or how they were dealing with the loss in their lives.

Finally she headed back to Old City Hall and saw Luke sitting on one of the old wrought iron benches in front of the building. She sighed. It was difficult to keep her perspective about the guy when he was always around, mixing up her emotions.

Luke stood up. "How about some coffee?"

"*No.* Nicole hasn't confided in me and I wouldn't tell you anything, even if she had," Carlie said bluntly, certain that was why he wanted to talk.

"Why is it so wrong for me to be concerned?"

"There's nothing wrong with it, but frankly, I'm not sure you'd stop at just being concerned."

"If this is about the SUV, I apologized."

"Actually, you *didn't* apologize, but that isn't the point. I'm sure you have good intentions, but you can't run Nicole's life the way you run your company."

LUKE FROWNED.

"That isn't what I'm doing."

Just then, a shuttle from one of the parking areas arrived and dropped off passengers. They nodded pleasantly, but Luke was instantly on edge; he'd spent too many years guarding his privacy to enjoy having private conversations in public.

"Let's go to my office," Carlie suggested.

Luke hadn't looked closely at the architecture of the rotunda on his previous visits, but as they went inside now, he glanced around, appreciating the feeling of space and stateliness. The design in the parquet wood floor even came to a point under the center of the dome above, increasing the visual impact. He didn't have much imagination, but he could easily envision Victorian gentlemen disembarking from carriages and entering Old City Hall, escorting women in ball gowns.

"This is impressive, but surely it was much larger than the town needed at the time," he commented.

Carlie chuckled. "It's larger than what we'd need *now*, but Glimmer Creek once dreamed of becoming the California state capital."

"One of the books Nicole got at the general store says Columbia was once in the running for that, but it doesn't mention Glimmer Creek."

"I doubt we were ever actually considered, but town legend claims that underhanded tactics were employed by opponents. When the town fathers built our civic buildings, they allegedly wanted to show up Sacramento, because the capitol building was taking so long to complete. The O'Connor family donated enough money to buy the land and build both the concert hall and city hall, with the proviso that Glimmer Creek come up with the funds to do the interior finishing."

"O'Connor? That must be connected to Connor's Folly," Luke said before realizing that a group of guests had come into the rotunda and was listening to them.

"What's Connor's Folly?" one of them wanted to know.

Carlie focused on them and Luke was resigned. She couldn't resist entertaining Poppy Gold visitors and she quickly explained the history of how the Victorian buildings had been preserved during the Great Depression.

"James Connor's ancestor had moved to California in 1849 to find gold," she continued. "That was Seamus O'Connor, but he discovered the real money was in selling supplies to the miners. His original base of operations was in Glimmer Creek and he built a huge mansion here for his family. The townspeople wanted him to be mayor, but he refused until there was a scandal regarding the current mayor."

"That was Mayor Colonel Stafford, right?" Luke threw in, recalling the story of how the interior finishing had *actually* been funded. How had Carlie described it—paid for by the services of good-time girls?

The visitors' eyes gleamed.

"Scandal?" asked an older woman.

"Yes. They learned he owned a number of brothels and saloons. Colonel was just a nickname his saloon girls had given him."

Snickers went through her small audience.

"I don't want to keep you from registering, but be sure to read the historical markers around Poppy Gold and Glimmer Creek," Carlie urged, diplomatically bringing the history lesson to a close. "You'll get a schedule of events at the front desk, but as a heads-up, tonight there's a lighted parade of historic vehicles. Caroling will begin immediately after that."

The visitors moved toward the doors into Guest Reception and Luke followed Carlie back to her office. Though there didn't seem to be any employees at their desks, she closed the door and dropped onto the couch. He appreciated it.

"Sorry for the lecture," she said. "I used to do living history and tours of Poppy Gold when I was in high school and during breaks from college."

"No problem—I'm the one who started it. Nicole has developed a passion for Gold Country history, but especially anything to do with Glimmer Creek. Probably because of Dr. Cartwright," he added sourly, sitting down, as well. Being a protective big brother was a hard habit to kick.

"Glimmer Creek is an interesting town." Carlie wriggled out of her coat and tossed it onto her desk, then kicked her shoes off. "If it's any comfort, everything I've heard about Gideon is positive. He has outstanding credentials and was given high recommendations from the clinics where he worked before moving here. Also from his soon-to-be ex-father-in-law, who owns a posh veterinary practice in the LA area."

Luke's warning sensors shot to their highest level. "Soon-to-be ex-father-in-law?"

"Local gossip claims Gideon is in the middle of a divorce, or maybe already divorced, *which Nicole knows*. So as I said before, leave it alone."

"Fine. I'll worry about the girls instead."

Carlie instantly looked sympathetic. "They seem much more outgoing than when you first got to Poppy Gold."

"Yeah, but I'm not sure how much has changed between us. Annie came and talked to me about something the other night, which was wonderful, but most of the time they just don't seem to need me."

"I think change usually comes in small steps— sometimes so small it's hard to see."

"Perhaps."

Luke leaned over to pick up a card that had gotten knocked to the floor. He barely had time to read "It's a boy!" on the front before Carlie snatched it and tossed it in the wastebasket.

His eyebrows rose. "You don't seem the type to throw a birth announcement away."

"That depends on who it's *from*."

"Which is?" he prodded.

She glared. "If you must know, my ex-fiancé's wife. I was supposed to get married a year ago in July, but the morning of the ceremony, I found Derek in bed with another woman. We were both working for the same company, and the CEO's daughter had come with her father to attend the wedding. And apparently to sleep with the groom."

"Oh. Sorry."

"I don't love him any longer, but we'd planned to start a family right away and now *they* have a baby. It's revolting. I mean, imagine the kind of person who sleeps with another woman's fiancé, hours before they were supposed to get married."

Luke was starting to regret his curiosity. This was the sort of conversation that women had with one another.

"Not that they don't deserve each other," Carlie continued. "Derek likes money and Vicki has plenty. So basically, she got a fortune hunter who won't hesitate to cheat on her, while he got an amoral wife."

Luke nudged the wastebasket with his foot. "Surely Derek and his wife weren't tacky enough to send you a birth announcement."

"There's no end to how tacky they can be. Vicki also sent me an invitation to the wedding and went around telling everyone that I'd wished them the best. Not exactly the truth. At least the birth announcement wasn't a surprise. A friend emailed to warn me a few days ago."

"It sounds as if Vicki creates her own reality."

"Another reason to feel sorry for her baby. So you see? Annie and Beth are much better off with you as their father than having Derek and Vicki as parents."

Humor tugged the corner of Luke's mouth. "That isn't a reassuring standard of comparison. A pack of hyenas would be better than those two."

Carlie laughed and some of the tension eased from her face. "You're right. In all honesty, it's easier to focus my angst over that stupid announcement than to keep thinking about my father."

"Then things are worse than you let on at lunch."

"Mom and I hoped a few days of rest would do him good, but we should have known better. Dad is so stubborn. He refuses to take enough painkillers to genuinely help and he doesn't eat or sleep enough. His health is actually declining by being off work."

Luke debated again whether to tell her about the orthopedic specialist, but there was a chance the plan would fall through. Besides, Tessa McKinley was willing to pretend the doctor's visit was coincidental, saying it would be easier for Carlie to convince Mike if she didn't know. It was strangely reassuring to know that even a family member didn't think Carlie could effectively carry off a harmless deception.

CHAPTER SIXTEEN

"CARLIE, ARE YOU HERE?" called a voice from the outer office, making them both jump in surprise.

"Yes, Joan," Carlie called back.

"We're leaving for the day. Shall we lock up?"

"Sure—go ahead."

When silence had fallen again, Carlie gave Luke a troubled look. Telling him about Derek hadn't been appropriate and he certainly didn't need to hear about her father's health issues. He had enough concerns.

"I shouldn't have said anything about my ex-fiancé or my dad's health," she said softly. "You're here to celebrate Christmas."

"This isn't a pleasure trip for me, Carlie. I'm having a good time, but I came for the girls. Besides, I'm the one who asked about your father at lunch and wanted to know what that birth announcement meant. I'd like to think we're friends and I know Nicole feels that way, too."

It was easy for Carlie to see Nicole as a friend, but Luke? That required a much bigger leap of the imagination.

But maybe there *was* something she should say about his daughters.

"Luke, I've been thinking about what you said… that the girls rarely come to you for anything. Is there any chance Annie and Beth's caregivers are urging them not to disturb you with their problems? Especially since your wife died."

He frowned. "Why would they do that?"

"Think about it. The things that go on in a child's life are hugely important to them, but may seem trivial to an adult. It's a question of perspective. I'm just speculating, but let's say Beth is upset because a teacher made a small, unfair decision and Dacia tells her not to bother you with it. After all, you've had a hard day and she'll probably forget by tomorrow. Except what Beth learns is that her problems aren't important enough to bring to her father."

"Maybe, but I suspect it's something else." Luke's face was grim. "That is, I've wondered if Beth and Annie blame me for their mother not being here."

Carlie stared. "Why would they blame you?"

"Why wouldn't they? As much as Erika loved the army, it was difficult for her to go back after the twins were born. She might have resigned her commission if I'd encouraged her. Instead, I didn't say anything," he said with obvious reluctance.

"Do you *really* think she didn't know how much

you wanted her to resign?" Carlie shook her head decisively. "Trust me, she knew."

"But if I'd said something, things might be different now."

"Maybe, and maybe Erika would have just resented your making her decision that much harder."

"I'm not sure that makes me feel less responsible."

Carlie sighed. Luke missed his wife—that much was clear. But he was also dealing with a dash of survivor's guilt.

"What if Erika had wanted to be a police officer when you met her?" she asked. "Or fight fires? You can second-guess yourself forever, but in the end, you supported her lifelong ambition. It's admirable. I'm not sure that most men would have done it."

"That sounds awfully close to a platitude."

"Then I'll say something that isn't a platitude… but you won't like it."

He hiked an eyebrow. "Yeah?"

"Yeah. I think you're furious with Erika for choosing the army over you and the girls. You're angry that she left you alone to raise Annie and Beth and that she wanted to be a hero more than she wanted to be with you. That's what goes through your head at two in the morning when you can't sleep, isn't it?"

Luke's eyes flared. "How can I be angry with someone who's dead? She…"

Pain abruptly replaced the wrath in his face and he was silent.

"You're right," he admitted finally. "I *was* angry in the beginning."

"Not any longer?"

"Every now and then, mostly when things are tough with the girls and I don't know how to help them. And even though I know it isn't true, I can't help wondering if she expected to die in the line of duty the way her father died. Then I wonder how I could think any such thing about my wife."

"It's human nature, that's how." Carlie's heart ached for him, because no matter how much Luke had infuriated her since arriving at Poppy Gold, he'd lost so much more than she'd ever lost herself.

"How did you guess?"

"I dated a fireman for several months when I was in college and kept wondering what would happen if we got married and he died. But it's also because women have been asking those questions forever."

"Welcome to your world, right?" Luke's voice was filled with bitter irony.

"Actually, I'm pretty sure it's harder for men."

"How do you figure that?"

"You didn't grow up thinking you might have to face something like this one day. It still isn't part of a man's mental landscape. But now things are changing and you're caught in the middle. I'll bet most of your peers don't understand why you supported Erika's decision, which must make you feel even more alone. But it *was* her decision. You aren't responsible, whether you said anything to her or not."

LUKE COULDN'T BELIEVE he'd told Carlie the dark thoughts he'd never told anyone.

"Can I say something else you won't like?" Carlie asked.

"Hell, why not?"

"I know you have to work a lot of hours, but what do you do with Annie and Beth when you come home? I mean, do you spend time with the girls?"

"Is this the quality versus quantity argument?"

"It isn't an argument," Carlie said gently, "and I don't pretend to have the answers, but if they're in their playroom and you're doing something else, when do you ever talk? Even at Poppy Gold you're usually watching them do stuff with Nicole, not participating. Maybe your guilt has kept you from really connecting with them."

Luke frowned thoughtfully. "You might have a point. But I have to say, you aren't responsible for your father's stubbornness, either."

"I know. Still, I think I owe you a confession

in return." Carlie swept her long hair away from her neck, swirling it around her arm in a graceful gesture. "A year ago last July was really a lousy month. I was supposed to be on my honeymoon, but instead I was in Glimmer Creek, packing up wedding gifts to return them. My folks were upset and kept telling me they'd do it for me, but I wanted to handle it myself."

Her eyes seemed to be looking into the past and Luke waited for her to continue.

"We were in the middle of a hot spell and it wasn't cooling down at night, which was unusual for Glimmer Creek, so none of us were sleeping," she murmured. "One morning Mom and I were sitting in front of a large box fan, drinking iced tea and trying to cool off, when the phone rang. Dad's supervisor was calling to tell us Dad was being airlifted to the hospital." All at once Carlie shook herself. "Sorry—as they used to say at one of my old jobs, 'too much detail.'"

"That's all right. The morning I learned about Erika is as clear as if it happened yesterday—every detail, down to what clothes I was wearing and what I'd eaten for breakfast."

Carlie smiled sadly. "It's funny how the things we'd like to forget refuse to go away. And maybe I wouldn't remember so much if…"

"If?" Luke prompted.

"There's a part of my brain that questions whether

Dad's attention wasn't as sharp as normal because he was worried about me. I mean, maybe he was distracted and it cost him the split second he needed to get out that driver's way."

"You can't blame yourself."

"Come on, Luke, you know better—you've blamed yourself for Erika's decision to stay in the army."

They both laughed; it wasn't funny, but there was an inescapable irony to them both feeling responsible for something they would do anything to change.

"Another aspect of human nature," Luke acknowledged.

Carlie looked so exhausted that he reached down and lifted her legs onto the couch. She yelped a protest and pushed her skirt back over her knees, only to close her eyes with a sigh as he began massaging her feet.

The sun had set outside and the only light came from the Christmas tree in the corner. It was curiously intimate and Luke knew he should leave. He had a great deal to work through and being alone with Carlie wasn't going to help. Yet it was like a moment out of time, peaceful and quiet with the Christmas lights glinting off her golden-brown hair.

He'd never been involved with a woman who had such long hair. It was hard not to reach out and test its thick, silky length as it curled around her breasts...and to explore the feminine curves beneath.

Luke shifted the position of Carlie's feet on his thighs to keep her from noticing the way his body had responded. It was normal, he argued. He hadn't been with a woman in well over a year and she was extraordinarily desirable.

He looked down. Even Carlie's feet were attractive. She had nice ankles, neatly proportioned toes and high, slender arches that begged to be caressed. Tiny flecks of pale pink polish suggested she painted her toenails when she had time, which she obviously didn't during the holiday season.

Damn. It was bad when a practical man started getting hot over a woman's feet and it definitely wasn't helping to clear his head. He ought to be checking what Nicole and the girls wanted to do for dinner, but rational thought wasn't easy when a warm, desirable woman was so close.

"Carlie?"

She didn't answer and Luke was disconcerted to realize she'd fallen asleep. In the middle of his struggle with erotic images, the trigger for those images had drifted into dreamland.

Yet he smiled as he thought about it. Carlie didn't try to impress him. She wasn't like so many of the single women he'd met since his business had become successful—women who seemed as interested in the size of his portfolio as in him. Carlie and Erika were complete opposites as women, but that was one trait they shared—Carlie didn't give a hang about his money, either. In fact, he was fairly certain that it was a strike against him.

Luke debated what to do. He couldn't leave Carlie asleep in her office, but he hated to wake her.

Perhaps she sensed his tension because she opened her eyes and yawned. "Did I drift off?"

"'Fraid so. It's a good thing I have a healthy self-image or I'd be terribly wounded."

"Ha." She swung her feet to the floor, stretching in a way that made his mouth go dry. Suddenly it didn't seem to matter that he had things to sort out.

He leaned closer and cupped the nape of Carlie's neck. "For the record," he whispered, "that ex-fiancé of yours was a fool."

Her breathing quickened. "It all depends on what a man wants. What do you want?"

"A kiss."

ANOTHER KISS?

Carlie wasn't sure that was a good idea, but she wasn't sure it was a terrible idea, either. Even if Luke hadn't thought about that quick, hot embrace on the porch of the John Muir Cottage, she'd given it endless consideration, both waking and sleeping.

"How about it, Carlie? We barely got a chance to taste each other the last time."

No longer drowsy, she leaned toward him, the thought flitting through her mind that she'd always wanted to make love by the light of a Christmas tree. *This isn't sex—it's a kiss*, she reminded herself.

Luke's arms drew her against him and he dropped kisses at the corners of her mouth. Her lips opened and he deepened the embrace.

His fingers moved over her hips, leisurely exploring there before tugging her blouse from the waistband of her skirt. When he stroked her bare skin, it was as if electricity sparked between them.

She dragged Luke's shirt over his head. His powerful body matched his gorgeous face, belying his status as a man who worked behind a desk.

"Nice," she whispered, stroking the hard muscles in his arms before flattening her fingers over his chest.

Luke's eyes darkened and the bulge in his jeans grew more demanding against her thigh.

He buried his face in her shoulder, kissing, nibbling, tasting her skin, finding the pulse in her neck, resting his tongue against it as though counting her pounding heartbeats. As if reading her mind, he unfastened her bra and drew one of her nipples into his mouth, teasing with his tongue.

In the back of Carlie's mind a small, insecure

voice asked whether he was comparing her to the incomparable Erika, but the thought shattered as he brushed his thumb over her other nipple, teasing and coaxing.

She gulped.

This was a whole lot more than getting a better taste, but it was hard to object with the blood pounding through her head, discouraging coherent thought.

LUKE GROANED AS Carlie's fingers traveled over his back, knowing he'd felt like a cocky adolescent when she'd admired his muscles. Since when had he felt the need to strut his stuff? Yet her approval had undeniably excited him.

Even in the low light, he could see the flush of desire on her breasts and belly and it was driving him crazy.

Between kisses, he dispensed with her skirt and panties while she got busy with his zipper, easing it down and cupping his erection through his boxers.

Luke drew back long enough to shove his clothes away and search for his wallet, grateful the old habit of carrying a condom hadn't failed him. A moment later, he'd sheathed himself.

Carlie put her fingers around him again, tugging, guiding, and a second later he was buried in her warmth. For a moment he remained motionless, then withdrew and thrust again, the pace rising with each lift of her hips.

She climaxed a second after him.

They were both still gasping when Carlie abruptly pushed on his shoulders.

"What?"

"We're in my office," she hissed.

"You closed the door and your staff left for the day, remember?" Luke still felt too relaxed and satisfied to worry.

"They could have come back for something."

He craned his neck to look at the crack under her door. "You're safe—the lights are off out there."

Carlie made a sound of pure exasperation and Luke reluctantly sat up.

He'd never been big on afterglow, but it would have been nice to enjoy a minute or two before dealing with regret and recriminations. And when he thought about it, afterglow might be nice with Carlie; she was a lovely armful.

She hastily fastened her bra and hunted for the rest of her clothes while he reluctantly did the same. The condom was a problem—she wouldn't want it discarded in her trash can—so he stuffed it inside a few tissues and dropped the bundle in his pocket.

Carlie was dressed by then, but for some reason she was on her stomach, fishing under the couch with her hand.

"Something missing?"

She finally straightened, face flushed, and held up the condom wrapper. "Yeah, *this*. Half the employees at Poppy Gold are related to me. I don't want whoever cleans my office this week to guess what happened tonight."

CARLIE WAS READY to die with embarrassment. She'd made love with a guest on her office couch? It was such a cliché.

It would be easy to blame their actions on the storm of emotion from their mutual revelations, but that wasn't good enough for her.

Her office, for cripes' sake?

It wasn't even *late*. Employees were still coming and going. And that wasn't counting all the Poppy Gold guests who might have wandered into the back of the building, exploring.

Carlie tried to clamp down on her racing thoughts and bring her breathing under control.

It wasn't just *where* she'd been intimate with someone…it was with *who*. How many times had she warned herself about Luke?

"Uh, I think…" She swallowed and glanced at the clock and it was as if she'd been thrown a lifeline. "Heavens, you're going on the stargazing hayride tonight with Nicole and the girls. You've got less than half an hour to get to the parade staging area."

"Damn. I forgot about it. We'll talk later."

He rushed out, not waiting for an answer. Carlie locked the outer door of the activities area behind him and sagged briefly against its supportive surface.

She was quite sure he would have backed off if she'd suggested going to her apartment. He would have looked at her, realized she didn't come close to Erika in either beauty or sex appeal and made a polite excuse.

Carlie clenched her teeth. She hated doubting herself. Maybe it would be different if Luke had been divorced, instead of widowed. How could she compete with a memory that was as perfect and unique as Erika Forrester?

Carlie sank onto her office chair and looked at the condom wrapper still clutched in her fingers. The compulsion to find it hadn't been entirely to keep their activities from the cleaning staff. She'd also wanted to check the date on it. According to Nicole, Luke hadn't socialized much since his wife's death, so how old was the thing?

Carlie's pulse jumped when she saw that the condom had expired more than five months ago. As much as she'd love to have a baby, she didn't need the complication of getting pregnant under *these* circumstances.

They'd both been scrambling to get dressed, but she thought hard and seemed to remember Luke checking the condom to be sure it hadn't broken. Guys did that. They didn't like surprises, so even if she did get pregnant, he probably wouldn't believe the baby was his.

Belatedly she flipped the pages of her desk calendar and relaxed; the likelihood of anything happening was extremely low. So now she just needed to get rid of the remaining evidence. In the restroom, she watched the wrapper go down the drain and flushed a couple of extra times to make sure.

There.

Now they could pretend nothing had happened. *Again.* She just had to avoid being alone with him from now on.

NICOLE WAS LATE visiting Bandit at the clinic because of the hayride and she smiled when Gideon answered the intercom, rather than Allie or Peter. Initially things had gotten weird after they'd made love. She hadn't wanted to spend the night, so she'd left around midnight...only to have Gideon grumpily suggest she was acting like a guilty teenager.

"You're the one acting like a kid," she'd snapped at him. "A selfish one, at that. Or would you care to explain to my six-year-old nieces why Aunt Nicole was out all night?"

The next day, Gideon had called to apologize and they'd made up over lunch. She still felt proud when she stood up for herself. She was tired of being "timid Nicole Forrester." It was how she'd once overheard two women describing her at work; the sorriest part was that she hadn't faced them down. She might have enjoyed turning the corner and asking, "Timid *who*?"

She was changing and she liked it. Large animals still made her nervous, but the thrill of challenging herself was getting stronger. The process might have started by wanting to prove something to Gideon; now it had become important not to be so nervous and afraid.

"Hey," Gideon said as he opened the side door.

"Hey. Sorry I'm later tonight, but we—" A cat suddenly squalled loudly from down the hall, interrupting her explanation. *"What's wrong?"*

"Nothing." Gideon looked sheepish. "That is, I think Bandit recognized your voice and he's anxious to see you."

Nicole headed straight for the feline care area. Bandit was watching anxiously as she appeared. "Silly thing," she scolded affectionately. He began purring and leaped into her arms as soon as the kennel door was opened.

"I see you've dispensed with the cone," she commented to Gideon. Once Bandit had gotten strong enough to begin cleaning himself, they'd put one of the cone-like collars on him to prevent him from fussing at his wound.

"It was stressing him more than it was helping,

but the abscess is still healing well. He's going to be a gorgeous cat."

"He's already gorgeous."

She cuddled the kitten and walked him around the room. Part of her was anxious for Bandit to be released with a clean bill of health; the other part wondered if it would end whatever this was with Gideon. Neither one of them had said anything about the future, though she'd been giving it a lot of thought.

Moving to Glimmer Creek was a possibility, regardless of what happened between them, though it was difficult to think about leaving Luke and her nieces in Austin without a compelling reason. Basically, it would look to everyone, including her, that she'd moved there hoping Gideon would change his mind about them being together.

"Would you like to go out with me tomorrow evening?" Gideon asked, breaking into her thoughts.

Nicole pretended to consider the invitation, but inside she was thrilled. "Nothing fancy."

"There isn't anything fancy in Glimmer Creek. I was thinking about the steak house."

Nicole put a protesting Bandit back into his kennel. "That sounds nice, but I'd better go now. I told Luke I would only be gone a few minutes."

GIDEON SAW NICOLE out to her car.

He couldn't stop thinking about her, but didn't know what to do about it. He'd never earn an extravagant living as a country veterinarian and she plainly liked nice things. In his marriage, he'd tried to be "modern" and not object to the frequent gifts Renee had received from her parents, including expensive vacations and housekeeping services, but it had stung.

Now he was crazy about another woman whose brother was generous and fabulously wealthy.

Would Nicole consider staying in Glimmer Creek, particularly if he asked her not to accept so much support from Luke? She'd admitted she enjoyed the city, but that she wasn't opposed to small towns. On the other hand, Glimmer Creek was a really *small* community. Poppy Gold was the only reason they had as many services as they did. Then there was the question of Nicole's career—she was a computer programmer and Glimmer Creek didn't even have a computer store.

Frustrated with the circles turning endlessly in his brain, Gideon went back into the clinic and checked on his various patients, still thinking about Nicole. She was sweet, loving and trying to overcome her fears with a courage that astounded him. When she put her chin up and that look came into her eyes...

He groaned.

What if she fell in love with him, but didn't want to live in such an isolated place? Was staying in Glimmer Creek so important to him that he could give her up? He looked at Bandit, who was sulking because his favorite human had left him behind.

"You don't care where you live, do you, as long as Nicole is there. Right? You think I'm an idiot to even wonder what I'd do if she fell in love with me."

The kitten lifted a hind leg over his head and began licking the base of his tail. Though the gesture meant nothing—cats had to clean down there at some point—it still seemed to convey a measure of contempt.

"Right," Gideon muttered.

He *was* an idiot. Nevertheless, he'd seen how a marriage could fall apart when the partners were just too different.

CHAPTER SEVENTEEN

"I DON'T WANT to talk, Luke," Carlie said. She'd deliberately stayed away from Old City Hall the next morning, hoping to be hard to find, but he'd found her, anyway, near the sledding hill. "Aren't you supposed to be doing something?"

He shook his head. "Nothing at the moment. We need to discuss last night, but not around so many people. Stop procrastinating."

What was wrong with him? Women were supposed to be the ones who analyzed everything to death.

She tried to think of a place they could speak in relative privacy. Poppy Gold was such a hub of activity that aside from her office she couldn't think of anywhere, and they *weren't* going to her office or apartment.

"Fine. Let's go to the creek."

They walked silently toward the stream that had given her hometown its name. Frost still lay thick and white in places shaded by trees. Though it was beautiful, Carlie shivered. She'd wanted to help make Christmas wonderful again for Annie and Beth, but didn't know if she'd ever feel the same about it herself. The message of the day remained sacred, but would everything else just be a reminder of the mistakes she'd made?

"Okay, we're alone," she said when nothing else could be heard except the gurgling of water flowing over rocks.

"This is nice."

Carlie briefly closed her eyes, praying for patience. Why had he insisted on going someplace private if he wasn't going to actually start talking? "A lot of gold came out of this creek, once upon a time. Do you want to start panning for some?"

"There must be easier ways to make money."

"I doubt making money is something you need to worry about, but you're welcome to go for it."

He seemed to measure her expression and may have guessed she'd *love* to see him in the frigid creek as repayment for insisting they discuss something she would rather avoid.

"That's all right," he said. "I'll pass."

"So, what did you want to talk about?"

Luke hiked an eyebrow at her. "We made love last night—what do you think?"

"We didn't make love. We had sex."

He looked taken aback. "Okay, we had sex. I'm concerned about mixed messages. With the way things are with the girls, I just can't think about any kind of relationship."

"And I'm trying to make it clear there *aren't* any mixed messages," Carlie shot back, exasperated. "Honestly, I *know* we aren't compatible. Not to mention the whole thing with your wife."

Luke rubbed his face. "My wife?"

Carlie had regretted mentioning Erika the moment the words came out, but it was too late to take them back. "I don't want to come second to a memory. Besides, your wife wasn't just average beautiful—she was gorgeous."

He gave her a dark look. "I have a feeling this is one of those situations where I can't win, but I'm still going to try. You're beautiful, too, and I've *never* compared you to Erika."

"I'm sure it would happen sooner or later. On top of that, there's the totally arrogant, high-handed way you make decisions for people. That is *not* the kind of man I want in my life."

He threw up his hands. "For God's sake, are you talking about the SUV *again*? I've said I'm sorry—what else can I say?"

"No, I was thinking about the way you tried to poke into Nicole's love life yesterday. I understand you don't want anything else to happen to your family, but trying to run their lives isn't going to work."

"I'm not…" Luke stopped, obviously frustrated. She understood. He was probably torn between the desire to warn her off, be a gentleman and defend his behavior.

Carlie released a sigh. "To be honest, I'm embarrassed about having had sex with a guest on my office couch. It's never happened before, and believe me, it *won't* happen again. There's no need for more discussion. So let's just leave it alone."

LUKE WAS SILENT as he and Carlie returned to the more populated section of Poppy Gold. Her reaction should have reassured him that she wasn't expecting more than he could give, but instead it raised more questions.

He would always love Erika, but did that mean he couldn't fall in love with someone else just as deeply?

Carlie wasn't a memory; she was real. The two women were so different it was almost ludicrous to think of comparing them...though he was glad he hadn't said that to Carlie. She wouldn't have understood.

Erika had been like him, keeping her emotions guarded, declaring that restraint was the hallmark of a good officer. He'd respected that.

Carlie was the opposite. She was stubborn, hot-tempered and clearly had a poor opinion of him, but was softhearted enough to befriend his sister and daughters. Warning her off had seemed best, for her sake.

Still, he was starting to wish he hadn't been so hasty. That was the problem with operating on autopilot—it was too easy to do something without thinking it through. He also didn't know how to be single. It sounded crazy, but it was true. He'd been a married man for a long time and didn't know how to handle the intricacies of dating another woman.

And Carlie wasn't *just* another woman.

"I'm meeting some guests later to help with their costumes for the ball on Saturday, so I probably won't see Annie and Beth today," she informed him as they approached the sledding hill again. "Tell them hello for me."

"Sure."

Luke watched her walk away, recalling what the girls' grief counselors had said about "moving on." He finally understood. Now he just needed to figure out what moving on with their lives actually looked like…and whether he'd just torched a bridge he would regret.

THE REMAINING DAYS before the first dress ball passed slowly for Carlie. Despite her best efforts, she was distracted by thoughts of Luke. She was perilously close to falling for him.

The fact that he wasn't interested in a relationship with her wasn't a surprise. Of course, she'd made it equally clear that she wasn't interested, either, but the heart wanted what the heart wanted, and it refused to be sensible.

Finally on Saturday evening, Carlie closed the door and blinds in her office to put on her costume for the dress ball. She'd brought it to work in case she didn't have time to go home and change.

A knock sounded as she was putting the finishing touches on her hair.

"It's me," Tessa called.

Carlie unlocked the door and saw her cousin was wearing a black velvet gown that emphasized her petite frame. "You look terrific. Is something up?"

"I'm so excited I couldn't wait to tell you," Tessa exclaimed. "When I looked at the check-in list from last night, I saw a name I recognized. It's Teague Thornton. He's a famous orthopedic surgeon who practices over in San Francisco."

"You recognized his name?"

"Come on, Carlie, how often do you see someone named Teague? It really sticks out. He's the guy who operated on the baseball player hurt in the play-offs this fall. I remember reading about the case. Dr. Thornton is famous for innovative surgical techniques. He's saved several athletes' careers after everyone else gave up on them."

"Oh. Okay."

"Anyhow, I just got through speaking with him and he's interested in reviewing Uncle Mike's medical records. He's a maverick and likes challenging cases."

Carlie sucked in a breath, at the same time reminding herself that a different orthopedic specialist had claimed nothing more could be done for her father. Still, she and her mother had wanted a second opinion, and high-profile doctors who treated sports celebrities usually weren't available to the average patient.

"Dad will resist," she said slowly.

"I know, but this is an amazing opportunity. Uncle Mike *has* to agree. Guilt him into it if necessary. Tell him it's the only Christmas present that you and Aunt Leah want."

Carlie touched the antique cameo she wore. She didn't like the idea of badgering her father, but if there was any hope at all…

"I'll go talk to him right now," she decided. "The medical clinic has copies of everything, including all the MRI and CAT scans from the hospital. I can print a release form from the clinic website and Aunt Emma can send the records electronically once Dad signs."

Tessa grinned. "I'll give her a heads-up. I think she's on call tonight."

Tessa left as Carlie sat down at her computer and downloaded the form. She printed two copies, tucked them in a large envelope and rushed home. "It's me," she called as she opened the front door.

Her parents were in the den, where they spent most of their evenings, and smiled when she appeared.

"I wanted you to see how I look in the new dress," Carlie said, twirling around.

"You look lovely."

"Yes, but what's in the envelope?" asked her father.

Carlie had hoped to introduce the subject gently, but maybe a "shock and awe" campaign would work best, after all.

"Oh, well, Tessa told me there's a well-known orthopedic surgeon visiting Poppy Gold this weekend and he's interested in looking at your records. It's an amazing opportunity. You'd never get to see this doctor otherwise—he's far too busy treating famous athletes and other celebrities."

"No," Mike refused flatly.

"*Please* do it, darling," begged Carlie's mother.

He shook his head. "I'm done with getting poked and prodded. It is what it is."

Carlie planted her hands on her hips and glared. "Dad, Tessa broke one of her most important rules by talking to Dr. Thornton. He's here for rest and relaxation, but she told him about your case and asked if he'd consider giving us an opinion. She can't take it back now, so the *least* you can do is agree. It's also the least you can do for Mom."

"But—"

"No buts. Jiminy Christmas, all you have to do is sign a release so the clinic can give Dr. Thornton copies of your tests and reports. He won't even *do* an exam unless he believes he can help. I brought two blank releases with me." Carlie waved the envelope. "If you sign them now, I can go and enjoy the ball."

"You could still go, even if I don't sign."

"Except I won't. I'm *just* as stubborn as you are. More so, because I get it from both you and Mom."

She stuck out her chin, knowing she looked ridiculous standing there in a Victorian ball gown, acting as tough and pigheaded as her father.

Mike's expression was thoroughly harassed. *"Fine."*

Carlie grabbed a pen and book to use as a hard surface, ready to dance with glee. He signed the forms and handed them back. Though her father didn't have a roaring sense of humor, she checked to be sure he hadn't written something ridiculous like "Sherlock Holmes." He hadn't. Now she just needed to leave before he changed his mind.

"Great," she said. "I'll see you tomorrow."

Leah followed her to the front door and they hugged. "He won't back out now," she whispered.

"I'll get the release forms to Aunt Emma tonight. She should know about it already—Tessa was going to give her a call. Try to keep Dad focused on something else."

Her mother nodded. "I'll do my best."

NOTHING WAS FAR from anything else in Glimmer Creek and it was only a short distance to Aunt Emma and Uncle Daniel's house. Uncle Daniel opened the door and gave her a bear hug. "Carlie, you look lovely."

"Thanks. Did Tessa call about Dr. Thornton?"

"Yes," Aunt Emma said, ducking under her husband's arm. "Don't tell me you already got Mike to agree."

"You bet. I used a blend of outrage and guilt. It was remarkably effective. Anyway, before I talked to Dad I printed two blank releases from the clinic website." She held up the envelope. "Signed and ready to go."

"You're a miracle worker."

"No, just an obstinate daughter."

Carlie returned to her car after another hug and stuffed herself into the front seat again. In the ball gown it felt as if she was driving in a sea of velvet and lace. The days she wore costumes were probably the *only* times an SUV would be helpful.

She made a face and drove to Poppy Gold, determined to enjoy the dance. Regardless of her feelings about Luke and making the mistake of having sex on her office couch, she'd decided she wasn't going to let him ruin the holidays for her.

A HALF HOUR after the official start of the ball, Luke was still glancing around, hoping to see

Carlie. He knew Tessa McKinley had planned to talk to her about Dr. Thornton, but didn't know when or where.

Tessa and her husband were dancing on the other side of the room, and as if sensing Luke's thoughts, she looked his direction and gave him a thumbs-up signal.

Good.

That meant Carlie had been told about Dr. Thornton's interest. Knowing Carlie, she probably wasn't at the dance because she was talking to Mike.

Luke knew he had to come clean about it, even though it would undoubtedly mean digging himself an even deeper hole. But how else could Carlie start to trust him?

Over the past few days, he'd come to the inescapable conclusion that he'd been a fool. How else could he explain not recognizing earlier that he'd fallen for her so completely? It was different from what he'd felt for Erika, but no less powerful.

Carlie had made him come alive, forcing him to air out the old, dusty corners of himself that had kept him from being the man he wanted to be. She'd weathered the setbacks of her cheating fiancé and her father's injuries and still sparkled with life and purpose—champagne could go flat, but she never would.

"Aren't you going to dance with me?" his sister asked, breaking into his thoughts.

Luke glanced around. "What happened to your date?"

Pink brightened Nicole's cheeks. "Gideon left for an emergency call, but he'll try to get back as soon as possible."

"I see."

Luke extended his hand and they joined the other couples on the floor. His jaw ached from holding back the questions he wanted to ask his sister, but Carlie was right that he shouldn't interfere.

She was right about a lot of things.

He *did* get high-handed, exactly the way she'd said. Not that he'd thought of it that way. The impulse came from a lifetime of conditioning—first from the uncertainty of his childhood, spurred by the need to protect his little sister. Then later, with Erika away in the military, he'd *had* to make decisions alone. And after she was killed, all he'd thought about was keeping his family safe.

But Carlie was *also* right that if he'd asked his wife to resign her commission, she might have grown to resent him.

The truth was he'd been trying to make sense of Erika's death, but it was senseless, and feeling guilty and responsible wouldn't change a damn thing.

"Oh, look, Gideon is back," Nicole exclaimed

a few minutes later. "Maybe the case wasn't too bad. Do you mind? I should go check with him."

"No, of course not. He's your date."

NICOLE KISSED HER BROTHER, then hurried toward Gideon. His warm smile washed around her. "Is everything okay?" she asked.

"It's fine. The call was for a colicky horse, but the situation had resolved itself by the time I arrived."

She laughed. "I suspect that means something very messy that I don't want to think about."

"You got it." He pulled her close and they swayed to the music. "Thanks for not getting upset that I had to leave."

"There was nothing to get upset about. You're a vet and have to go when an animal is sick or hurt."

"You really feel that way, don't you?"

"Of course I do. I think you're wonderful," Nicole said boldly.

Gideon gave her a long, slow kiss. "I think you're pretty wonderful, too."

Just as she thought he was going to say something more, a couple stumbled against them.

"I'm so sorry! I tripped on my tail," said the woman.

Nicole blinked. Almost everyone was wearing period dress, but these two were dressed as cats.

"I'm a Victorian gentleman cat," announced the

woman's partner, "and this is my Victorian lady cat. We come to the ball every year."

"Oh. How nice," Nicole said, trying not to laugh.

The two "cats" danced away and she looked at Gideon, knowing the moment had passed. But that was okay. She didn't have any intention of losing him, even if it meant *she'd* have to be the one to propose. And she would, too, if it came to that. She was sure he loved her, and if he didn't know how she felt in return, then he was totally blind.

The question was whether he still believed there were too many barriers between them.

LUKE SIGHED AS he went to get a drink from the bar at the end of the ballroom. His sister was changing in front of his eyes; she sure didn't seem to need him any longer.

"What can I get you?" asked the bartender.

"Burgundy, if you have it."

"Certainly, sir."

Luke took his wine out to the gallery, hoping to avoid the single women who'd tried asking him for a dance. His custom was to freeze them out, but it hadn't seemed appropriate in the setting. Nonetheless, other than his sister, Carlie was the only woman he wanted to take onto the floor. If it hadn't been for the chance of seeing her, he wouldn't have even *come* to the dance.

Resting his arms on the gallery railing, Luke

gazed at the couples going up and down the sweeping staircase. There was a particular point on the steps where they stopped to have their picture taken. The photographer was dressed in a Victorian suit and took photos with an old-fashioned camera on a stand. There was a digital camera inside the prop, but it added to the ambience.

Luke would love to get a picture like that of Nicole and the girls. Maybe he could take them to the Old Thyme Pictures shop on the shopping street. Nicole had suggested they go on hospitality night, but he'd never liked mugging for a camera. Now it sounded like fun.

Fifteen minutes later, Carlie came through the front door of Old City Hall, flushed and smiling in a sapphire velvet gown with a low-cut bodice.

His body stirred and he gulped more wine.

Carlie looked up at the gallery and locked gazes with him. With that curious way she had of squaring her shoulders and sighing at the same moment, she climbed the stairs and walked toward him.

"No cloak? Aren't you cold?" he asked.

"Most of me isn't too bad, but my fingers are freezing. It was worth it, though. I just got my dad to agree to consult with an orthopedic specialist who's visiting Glimmer Creek this weekend."

"That's good news." Luke held out his glass of wine. "Spirits to warm the blood."

She smiled faintly and took a sip. "What are you doing up here?"

"People-watching and listening to the music." He gestured toward the ballroom. "The live orchestra is a nice touch and their Schubert is particularly good."

"We do our best."

"I, uh, have a confession," he said reluctantly. "I called Dr. Thornton and asked him to visit Poppy Gold. I wasn't trying to interfere. I just thought your dad deserved to have the best. It was before what happened between us," he added hastily, not wanting her to think he'd done it because they'd made love.

Carlie regarded him for a long minute. "I should be angry, but it's just what you do."

"I'm working on getting better."

"Oh?" She took a second sip of the burgundy, looking skeptical.

"*Yes*. I'm staying out of Nicole's relationship with Gideon Cartwright, for one thing. You have no idea how difficult that's been. Then she ordered a mixer and other equipment, just like yours. I tried to pay for it, but she said absolutely not and I respected her wishes. She's been laying down the law quite often to me since we came here."

A smile tugged at the corner of Carlie's mouth. "Small victories can lead to bigger ones. But don't backslide when you return to Texas."

Luke knew it would be easier not to backslide if Carlie married him, but it wasn't the right moment for a proposal. He was fairly certain she had feelings for him, though. There was a look in her eyes sometimes, caught before she could hide it, that sent both hope and heat surging through him. His best chance was convincing her that the two barriers she saw weren't barriers, after all.

"I won't backslide," Luke assured her quietly. "And you're right about small victories. I think that's how it has to be with the girls. Things have to be fixed with them, little by little. I'm trying. For one, they asked to go to the children's party tonight in the concert hall instead of having Mrs. Cabrera watch them in our suite. It wasn't easy, but we talked about it and I agreed. Maybe that doesn't sound like a big deal to you, but it was hard for me."

Carlie shook her head. "It sounds like a *big* step for a protective daddy."

"Thank you." Luke gestured toward the photographer in the lobby below. "How about getting our picture on the stairs? Something for memory lane. It would be fun."

She looked skeptical again and he grinned.

"Honestly. It's your influence. I've been thinking about the opportunities I've missed over the years and don't want to miss any more of them."

"From your childhood?"

"Partly. I stopped being angry with my parents a long time ago, but lately I've decided I should have appreciated them more. They didn't put us in boarding school. Instead, we did everything together. It's a shame I didn't let myself enjoy it."

Luke had the fleeting thought that his mom and dad hadn't been nearly as bad at parenting as he'd thought, and there were some things they'd done exceptionally well. Spending time with their kids was one of them. They'd certainly done a better job of it than *he* had with the twins.

Carlie returned the wineglass to him. "I think some children are born serious and take things more to heart."

"Like Annie?" Luke finished the wine and gave the glass to a passing waiter. "Do you really think my staff has been trying to keep the girls from disturbing me?"

"It's possible. Imagine how easy it would be to say, 'Don't bother your father—he's sad,' or 'Don't argue—you'll upset Papa.'"

It was all *too* easy to imagine.

"I'll have to talk to them," he murmured. "It isn't my daughters' job to protect me."

With their mother gone, Beth and Annie would never have the carefree childhood they deserved. The least he could do was preserve some of it.

He extended his arm to Carlie. "Come on, let's

get that picture. Here's your chance to give me another lesson on how to play."

Her expression was doubtful, but she put her hand on his elbow and they walked down to pose for the photographer.

CHAPTER EIGHTEEN

ON MONDAY MORNING, Nicole sat on the couch to make a list of things to do before going out to run errands. Chico instantly hopped into her lap, purring and arching against her. Like Bandit, he was a remarkably affectionate kitten.

"Tell you a secret," she said to him. "I'm bringing your brother home today."

She was thrilled that Bandit had been given a clean bill of health, and even more thrilled about how things were going with Gideon. He still hadn't mentioned the future, except to pointedly tell her that he'd chosen a resident to help at his clinic so he wouldn't have to be on call 24/7.

It seemed to be a good sign.

After Gideon had described his marriage, she'd stopped worrying about the hazards of rebound relationships and *started* worrying he'd think she was too much like his ex-wife.

Chico rolled on his back, his purr doubling in volume as she rubbed around his ears.

Gideon had specifically mentioned that he and his ex-wife had disagreed about where to live and about having children. Nicole frowned in thought. She might not be great with kids, but she wanted a family. What's more, she liked the country and didn't mind the limited services in Glimmer Creek.

As for housekeepers and cooks? They didn't appeal to her, either. And she could be a lot of help at the clinic, either by improving their existing computer system or designing a new one that worked better. She didn't care that it wasn't glamorous, just that she could have a real purpose. Much as Nicole adored her brother, he could hire any programmer he wanted. But Glimmer Creek didn't seem to have any tech-savvy residents. She could reach out to other businesses and offer her technical services.

Her cell phone rang and she saw it was Carlie. "Hey, what's up?"

"I wondered if the mixer and stuff you ordered had come, or whether I still need to bring my stuff for baking cookies tonight."

"Everything is here." Nicole glanced toward the suite's kitchen, where she'd unpacked everything, though she was still learning how to use the equipment.

"Terrific. But it'll be a lot of work getting everything back to Austin," Carlie said lightly.

"You know perfectly well I'm not planning to go anywhere," Nicole retorted and heard a laugh. "I'd rather have Gideon propose to me, but I'll do it if he doesn't. Oh, I'm bringing Bandit home today, so you'll meet him when you come."

"The pictures you've taken are precious. Uncle Liam has checked the live traps twice a day, but the only animals he's caught are pissed-off raccoons. I think it was just Chico and Bandit out there."

"That's great. I'd better go. I have your list of ingredients to buy before going to the vet clinic for Bandit."

"See you later."

Nicole hummed as she headed to the Argonaut Market. From there she went to the vet clinic, timing it just before the lunch hour. With luck she could snatch a couple of minutes with Gideon.

"Hi, Dorothy," she called as she opened the door.

The receptionist smiled back at her. "Big day, huh?"

"Yup." Nicole held up the animal carrier she'd gotten at a local hardware store. "No more cardboard boxes for the kids."

Dorothy chuckled and took her back to where Bandit was waiting, none too patiently. He purred under Nicole's chin for a moment, but was less happy to go in the carrier. "We're going home. You aren't staying in there for long," she scolded gently, and he seemed to calm down when she picked the carrier up and brought it with her.

"Is Gideon around?" she asked, taking out her credit card to pay the bill. There was no point in being coy when everyone on the staff seemed to be aware of their relationship.

"He's with a patient. Godzilla stuffed his nose in one of those large cans of chili."

"Poor boy. Will they be out soon?"

"Oh, yeah. He isn't hurt, just stuck." Dorothy handed her the credit-card slip to sign.

A loud bark came from one of the exam rooms and Nicole jumped. Her pulse still fluttered around the really, really *big* dogs, but she decided to put Bandit in the SUV and come back inside. No reason for him to get spooked while she was waiting for Gideon.

"I need more kitten food, Dorothy, so I'll be right back."

They were still chatting when Godzilla came bounding out. Nicole tensed, half expecting the loud woof he'd let out the last time they'd crossed paths. But Godzilla just whined and his tail swished madly.

"Uh, hello, Godzilla," she said with only a faint tremor in her voice.

"You were here when I brought him in the last time," exclaimed the dog's owner. "He's doing much better now that he's in obedience training."

Nicole swallowed, knowing Gideon was watching from the door of the exam room. Yet it didn't matter; she was proving something to herself, not to him. "I can tell."

The other woman beamed. "Thanks. We'd better get going, though. I don't want to tempt fate. Come, Godzilla."

GIDEON ADMIRED THE determined look in Nicole's eyes. Her fear of dogs was completely justified, making her efforts to overcome it even more admirable.

"Did you just get here?" he asked.

"No, Bandit is out in the SUV. I was just getting more food for him and Chico." Nicole held up the bag of kitten food. "I also want to invite you to dinner on Wednesday at our suite. Beth and Annie want to see you and it would be quieter than a restaurant."

"Sounds good. What can I bring?"

"Just yourself. Is five thirty too early? The twins hate missing the lighted parade and I thought we could all see it together."

"Five thirty is fine. I'll see you then."

Gideon went back to his office and dropped into the chair in front of his desk.

He'd fallen hard for Nicole. Now he had to figure out what to do about it. The money thing was still an issue, though he was getting the feeling that it wasn't that important to her.

Or was that wishful thinking?

Her admiration for Helga's quilt had been genuine, which was a good sign. And she didn't like her nieces' "snooty" school. She didn't put on airs or throw out the designer names for her clothes or draw attention to her jewelry. She seemed just as comfortable in sweatshirts and canvas loafers as she did in Vera Wang and Prada.

Ultimately, he just needed to have faith that she knew he wasn't rich and could live with what that meant.

THAT EVENING, CARLIE found Nicole was determined to be as hands-on as possible during the cookie-making process. As her friend grew more assured at measuring ingredients and mixing the dough, Carlie stepped back and let her take over.

It made her feel good to see Nicole getting closer to her nieces. They'd bonded at the skating rink, where Annie was showing a real ability. The other guests loved watching her skate, but she seemed oblivious to the attention.

Beth had sulked when she realized Annie was better, only to get over it when three jugglers from the Madrigal Players came to demonstrate their techniques. Beth had been fascinated and immediately began practicing, while Annie couldn't have cared less.

The balance between them might always be tricky, but Luke had begun stepping in when tensions arose. He also seemed much more comfortable with the girls as the days passed. Carlie wasn't an expert, but her mom had always said raising kids was a marathon, not a sprint. Luke would just have to keep plugging away.

The two rescued kittens were playing together, clearly happy to be reunited. But Bandit frequently ran to Nicole with a cry, seeming to want reassurance, and was picked up for a quick snuggle.

"You seem uptight, Carlie," Luke murmured, handing her a cup of the wassail his sister had made earlier.

"Not at all."

It was stretching the truth. Over the past forty-eight hours she'd gone through a roller coaster of hope and worry about her father. Her mom was just as bad, though they were trying not to let it show.

"I got a copy of the photo from Saturday," Luke said softly. "It's really good, even if we weren't smiling."

Carlie had received a copy, too, and the picture had startled her. She and Luke were looking at each other in the image, appearing to pass a hundred unspoken messages between them.

But was it just a case of photo hocus-pocus? Perry had been the photographer that night and he was gifted at finding the magic in ordinary moments. On the other hand, Luke had been trying to show he was willing to change and no longer be quite as domineering.

If he didn't have feelings for her, why would he be doing that?

ON WEDNESDAY EVENING, Gideon knocked at the Yosemite suite and heard a shriek of childish voices, each declaring, "I'll get it."

The twins opened the door together, giggling. "Hi, Gideon," said the one he thought was Beth. "Aunt Nicole has another kitty and she says you made him better."

"Let him come in," Nicole scolded. Her face was flushed and she wore a dish towel tied around her waist. She'd never been more beautiful.

Beth and Annie each grabbed one of his hands and dragged him inside.

"Hello, Gideon," said Luke Forrester.

"Hi, Luke." They nodded and shook hands, as if following a ritual. Maybe they were. He was "meeting the family" in the age-old ceremony of a man formally meeting his sweetheart's relatives.

"We're almost ready to eat. I just need to put the food out," Nicole explained. She returned to the kitchen and soon called everyone to the table. "I hope you don't mind something simple."

"Of course not."

Gideon had expected takeout, but it was obviously a home-cooked meal.

"I'm in shock. Is it safe to eat?" Luke teased before taking his first bite.

"Of course." Nicole looked annoyed. "I'm taking lessons from one of Carlie's great-aunts. She claims I'm a natural." She glared at her brother when he laughed. "It isn't funny, Luke. I've wanted to take a cooking class for ages but couldn't find the right one."

"Well, this is delicious," Gideon interjected. The baked chicken was juicy and lightly seasoned, the way he liked it best. And he found himself irritated with Nicole's brother for teasing her. Learning to cook wasn't easy. Helga had taught him the basics, but he couldn't claim to have a special knack for it.

The whole thing was making him think. When he'd married Renee, they'd both been young and convinced that love was all they needed. They hadn't worked at their marriage—they'd just gone along, making assumptions about the future. If he'd still loved Renee, he could have suggested they compromise by living in a smaller community that was close enough to the city to take advantage of its benefits. And if she'd still loved *him*, she might have agreed.

Being in love took effort and meant meeting halfway, whether you had everything in common or just a few things.

Nicole was patiently listening to her nieces tell a story about the sledding hill and Gideon smiled.

He was crazy about her. Now he just needed to find the right time to tell her how he felt and hope she felt the same.

ON THURSDAY MORNING, Luke walked over to Old City Hall for another useless attempt to get Carlie to talk over a cup of coffee. She'd practically thrown him out the day before, so he almost expected the employees at Guest Reception to bar him.

He was getting more and more frustrated. Outwardly Carlie was friendly and willing to do as much with the girls as before, but a wall remained between them. He didn't blame her. She had no reason to trust him and ample cause to think he was an arrogant ass who'd never listen to what she wanted.

One thing was sure, though—he wasn't returning to Austin until he'd convinced Carlie they belonged together. If necessary, he'd move to Glimmer Creek with the girls and camp out on her doorstep.

He'd talked very seriously with Beth and Annie, saying he wanted them to understand that he would always love their mommy, but it didn't mean he couldn't also love someone else. Beth had seemed a little confused until Annie told her, in a very solemn tone, that Papa meant Carlie. Both of them were in favor of her becoming their new mother *and* of living in California, though he'd reminded them that it wouldn't always be sledding and Christmas and baking cookies.

"We know that, Papa," Beth had said. "That isn't what we love about Carlie."

Anne had nodded. "We love Carlie because she's Carlie."

Luke had hugged them both, his heart so full he couldn't speak. Somehow his daughters had grown very wise. He loved Carlie because she was Carlie, too. She was bright, lively, determined and fun. She was also the most caring and generous person he'd ever known.

In the back of Old City Hall, he found Carlie talking to Joan Peters about the second children's party on Saturday. She looked exultantly happy and he hoped it was good news about her father.

"What's up?" he asked when Joan had returned to her desk.

Carlie smiled even more brightly. "Dr. Thornton has reviewed my father's records. He called last night to give us his opinion. Apparently surgery should improve Dad's mobility and strength. But the most important operation will be to correct spinal damage that the other specialist missed. The first surgery will be in San Francisco, probably in February."

Luke frowned. "Why so long?"

"Don't go meddling," Carlie warned. "Dr. Thornton would operate earlier, but he needs Dad to stay off work and get into better health first—rest, eat properly and get plenty of sleep."

"Mike is okay with that?"

"Yes, because now there's a purpose to taking it easy. Dad has even agreed to follow a pain-management program. So, even though you interfered by calling Dr. Thornton in the first place, I can't be too unhappy about it."

Luke felt enormous relief. "I promise not to do anything like that again without discussing it with you."

"It isn't likely to come up."

"You never know. I'm considering a move to Glimmer Creek, so I may be around more than you think."

Carlie rolled her eyes. "That hardly seems likely, either."

"Hey, I'm serious. Will you look for land with me?"

She regarded him for a long minute. "Why land?"

"Because I'm told there aren't many houses available at the moment and I may have to build. How about it?"

"I'm sure you don't need my opinion."

Luke tried to be patient. He had no intention of buying property without Carlie's full involvement.

"I'd rather look with you. The real-estate agent said she was free this afternoon."

Carlie glanced at her watch. "Sorry, but Mom and I are going to Stockton to shop. Dad has promised to sleep while we're gone and I think he really means it." She hurried out before he could suggest he take them in the SUV.

But it wasn't until later that he realized he should have first asked if Carlie even *wanted* to stay in Glimmer Creek. Obviously he had a distance to go when it came to making assumptions and decisions that affected other people.

AT THE SECOND holiday ball, Nicole wore a dark green velvet gown and felt like a fairy-tale princess as she and Gideon whirled around the ballroom to a Strauss waltz.

She didn't expect life in Glimmer Creek to be one continual party, but she had every intention of enjoying the excessively romantic moments, along with the more everyday ones.

After the music ended, Gideon cleared his throat. "It's warm in here. Do you want to step outside for a few minutes?"

"Sure."

She collected the cloak that matched her ball gown and they walked across to the park twinkling with thousands of tiny lights.

"This is so beautiful," she murmured. "Like a Christmas fairyland."

"I prefer looking at you." Gideon ran a finger under his high collar, appearing uncomfortable. She knew he'd rented a costume for the night and appreciated his effort. "As a matter of fact, I'd like to look at you for the rest of my life," he added.

Her breath caught. "Oh?"

"Yes. I'm not rich and never will be, but I love you and I'm praying you feel the same way about me," he said simply. "Please marry me. I knew we'd need to make compromises about where and how we live, but we can do whatever it takes."

"You haven't been divorced that long. How can you be sure?" Nicole asked, suddenly realizing she needed to know *why* he thought they could make it when his first marriage had failed.

Gideon sighed. "Nicole, my marriage ended a long time ago, way before it was official, and I'm just as much to blame as Renee. We should have recognized that we were *so* different we'd need to work extra hard at staying in love and building common ground. Instead, we drifted apart. But I promise that I will never let that happen with us. I'll love you forever, with every particle of my being."

Love and certainty overwhelmed Nicole and she threw her arms around his neck. "I won't let it happen, either. I love you and there's nothing I want more than to live in Glimmer Creek and be your wife."

"We don't have to live here. I meant what I said about making compromises. I also expect to do my share around the house, including cooking and changing diapers. That is, I mean, you *said* you wanted kids and I—"

She put a finger on his lips to stop him. "I do. And I know we'll have things to work out, but not about Glimmer Creek. I *want* to stay here. You simply have to be patient while I figure out how to do it all. There's just one thing…" She paused and looked at him seriously.

"What's that?"

"Even when we're sharing laundry duties, *you* have to wash your own work clothes because I'm not touching them. Cow manure may smell like money to some people, but I agree with my niece. It just smells like cow poop to me."

"Agreed." Gideon laughed.

He held out the velvet-covered box that had been burning in his pocket all evening and watched as Nicole opened the top. Inside was an antique ruby ring that had belonged to Helga's great-grandmother. Helga had given it to him a few months before after learning that he was getting divorced. She hadn't wanted Renee to have it, but he had a feeling she'd approve of Nicole.

"This came down through my foster mother's family. They thought it had been lost, but found it when they moved off the farm."

"It's perfect," she whispered as he put the ring on her finger. "Even the size is perfect."

The sound of people talking came from nearby but Gideon didn't care as he pulled Nicole close for a kiss. It was just the beginning, but what a great beginning.

"WOULD YOU DANCE with me?" asked Luke.

Carlie drew a sharp breath and turned. He looked unbelievably handsome. "All right."

She took his hand and he swept her onto the floor.

"Did you hear?" he asked after a minute. "Nicole and Gideon just got engaged. She isn't even going back to Austin. She's staying in Glimmer Creek and moving in with Gideon."

Carlie almost missed a step. "*That's terrific.* I mean, about the engagement."

"I'm excited for her. Concerned, too, but that's my natural state, as you well know."

"But you're resisting the urge to interfere. Right?"

"Right. I may learn slowly, but I learn."

The music ended, but Luke kept hold of her hand. "One more, please?"

It was the "please" that got to her, but she tried

to let her mind drift as they danced. She was thrilled for her friend and the holiday ball was such a romantic night for an engagement. She'd seen Gideon and Nicole posing on the staircase for a photograph and would have to get a copy of the picture specially framed for them as an engagement present.

"What will happen after your father's surgeries?" Luke queried, startling Carlie from her reverie.

"Meaning?"

"I just wondered if Glimmer Creek is in your future, or if you plan to move back to the San Francisco area."

"I'm staying," she said. "I enjoyed the city, but it wasn't home. We're close enough I can always go overnight to see a play or visit Fisherman's Wharf. Los Angeles is a little farther, but it's still doable for a long weekend."

For some reason Luke seemed pleased by her answer, but she didn't want to think about why. It was too easy to start reading meaning into everything he said and did, like his attempt to get her to look at property with him.

He couldn't seriously be thinking about moving to Glimmer Creek. The most likely explanation was that he'd guessed Nicole might be staying, and wanted to have his own place when he came to visit.

Still…there had been a strange look in Luke's eyes when he talked about moving. And just now he'd asked if she planned to stay in Glimmer Creek, as if he'd realized he should find out what her plans might be.

Sternly, Carlie reminded herself that Luke had warned her off after they'd made love, saying he was worried about mixed messages and that he couldn't think about relationships because of the girls.

But hope was irrepressible, especially at Christmas, and Carlie's heart soared along with the music as they danced.

CHAPTER NINETEEN

THE DAYS BEFORE Christmas Eve seemed to hurry by and Carlie did her best to stop thinking about Luke.

Now that her father was doing what the doctor had ordered, he was finally improving, so she ought to be content…except she was madly in love and didn't know what to do about it.

She even was starting to think Luke cared about her, as well, but it wasn't that simple. Sure, he was working on not being quite as high-handed, but could she trust that he wouldn't look at her someday and realize she didn't compare to Erika?

"Gideon has an apartment above the clinic, but we're going to look for a house," Nicole told Carlie on Christmas Eve morning. They were in the Poppy Gold library, drinking tea. "It won't be easy to find the kind of place we want in Glimmer Creek."

"What kind of place is that?"

"A good-size home, with enough land for rehabilitating injured wildlife. And raising kids."

Kids… A pang went through Carlie and she

swallowed. "Sounds like you've been converted to country living."

"Totally. But we have things to work out, especially about money. I'm going to sell my condo in Austin and want to use part of the sale to start a computer business here, and put the other part on a house when we get one."

"That sounds reasonable."

Nicole nodded. "Yup. Gideon is trying to have a modern attitude, but I can tell it bothers him. We'll get through it, though. Of course, he's also getting thrown in at the deep end when it comes to family. My folks are coming for Christmas. They usually spend December in the Bahamas, but they're arriving early tomorrow morning. I'll move down to the bedroom on the ground floor and let them use my room. Luke still has to let Guest Reception know they're coming."

Carlie wondered if she'd meet the senior Forresters. It might be uncomfortable, given what she'd heard about them. "That's nice. Are you cooking or attending the Poppy Gold luncheon?"

"Gideon and I are cooking. We've come up with a menu that isn't too challenging. Desserts will be from Sarah's Sweet Treats, but we're doing the rest."

Nicole's phone chirped with a text message and she looked down at the screen, smiling. "Speaking of which, he wants to meet so we can shop for groceries."

Carlie sighed as her friend left in a whirl. She didn't begrudge Nicole her happiness, but it was challenging to smile and pretend she wasn't distracted by her own love life.

Luke and the girls would be in Glimmer Creek for only another two weeks. That was, if Luke didn't move to California, which she still couldn't really believe he planned to do.

Finally, she went back to her desk. She'd considered taking Christmas Eve off, but had been too restless to stay home baking and cooking with her mother.

The rest of the day rushed by, and toward evening, Carlie decided to take a walk through Poppy Gold before leaving.

The air hummed with the energy she always associated with Christmas Eve. Costumed carolers walked the streets and frost was forming early on the grass, with the multicolored lights reflecting off the ice crystals. The only thing that could complete the festive picture would be snow falling in the park, but they'd decided it would be too complicated to bring any of the snowmakers over from the sledding hill.

Detouring to watch the skating rink for a few minutes, she saw Nicole and the twins on the ice, along with Gideon. They were laughing with Luke, who'd obviously just taken a tumble. So, he'd actually gone skating instead of just watching.

They're happy, she thought as she walked toward the employee parking lot. *All of them.* Christmas and Poppy Gold had finally woven its spell.

"Carlie, wait up."

She turned and saw Luke waving as he removed his skates at the edge of the rink. A moment later he sprinted toward her in stocking feet.

"You all seem to be having fun," she said, trying to sound bright and cheerful, the way a good activities director should sound.

"It's hard not to have fun here. I, uh… Could we go somewhere and talk?" he asked.

"It's Christmas Eve, Luke. You need to be with your family."

A slow smile curved his mouth as he stepped closer. "That's sort of what I want to talk about."

Her pulse jumped.

"You see, I've got this problem," he continued. "My family can't be complete unless you're part of it."

LUKE REACHED OUT and stroked Carlie's face, feeling like a teenager again, tongue-tied and awkward with a pretty girl, unable to say the things he needed to say the most.

"You warned me away, remember?" she said, her voice trembling.

"Guys say all sorts of stupid things," he breathed. "Please don't hold it against me."

"Luke, *stop*. Nicole and Gideon are watching. So are the girls."

"I don't care. You see, I'm in love with you," he whispered. "Completely and utterly. Is there any chance you're willing to take on a ready-made family?"

Her stubborn chin went up. "I'm glad your trip to California has helped you and the twins, but you're just caught up in the moment. After all, Christmas is a time when all things seem possible."

"*Listen* to me. I'm not caught up in a moment or confused by a haze of holiday spirit. *You* make everything possible, because you're wonderful and loving and challenge me to be a better person."

She shook her head. "I can't compete with your wife's memory. I wouldn't even know where to begin."

"Except this isn't about Erika. It's about you trusting me."

Carlie's eyes filled with tears, making Luke ache and hope at the same time. "Even if that's true, it doesn't mean we're right for each other."

"You're perfect for me. And even if I'm not perfect for you, I'll do my damnedest to try."

CARLIE SWALLOWED.

"Carlie, a million possibilities are waiting for

us," Luke said intently. "Please trust that I know my heart and will never intentionally do something to hurt you. You *can* trust me. And even if you say no, I'm not leaving. The girls and I are moving to Glimmer Creek and I'll wear you down eventually, because I love you, heart and soul."

"What about your business?"

"I'll get the right equipment to run it from here. Problem solved."

Carlie felt like a kid again, standing in front of the grandest Christmas tree in the world, with all the sparkling potential it offered.

"But are Annie and Beth ready for a stepmother?" she asked, wanting to believe him more than she'd ever wanted anything. It wasn't that she wanted Luke to forget Erika. She just wanted to have her own place in his heart.

This *was* about trust.

Luke gave her another heart-pounding grin. "I already talked to them. We drove down to the valley yesterday and they helped pick this out for you." He held up a ring between his thumb and forefinger. "It took negotiation—you know how the girls don't ever like the same things—but then I told them we should think about what *you'd* prefer."

The ring was lovely, with diamonds and sapphires. Yet it was what Luke had said that made Carlie melt. *I told them we should think about what* you'd *prefer.* It told her more than he knew. Relationships were give and take, with no one person coming first all the time.

He gave her his heart-stopping grin. "Please don't make me wait any longer—you don't want the father of your present and future children to get frostbite, do you?"

"Present and future children?" she asked, her throat tight.

"Beth and Annie are already the daughters of your heart and they want little brothers or sisters, which I think is a splendid idea. Say yes, Carlie. Say you love me."

Carlie desperately tried to hang on to her common sense.

Luke *had* been trying to show her that he could change. And for all his faults, she couldn't see him ever being deliberately hurtful. Of course, his stiff-necked pride was a pain, but she'd be able to deal with that...

She shook herself. Could she seriously be considering his proposal?

Yes.

Her smile grew. "Okay, I love you. And yes, I'll marry you. But don't think it changes anything. You aren't getting your way all the time."

He slid the ring over her finger and gathered her close. "Actually, I'm counting on you to keep me in line," he murmured against her lips.

Carlie was aware of excited voices nearby, but right now the only thing that mattered was the strength and certainty in Luke's arms and kiss.

Christmas just kept getting better and better.

* * * * *

Come back to Glimmer Creek with the next book in Julianna Morris's POPPY GOLD STORIES *miniseries, available in August 2017, wherever Harlequin Superromance books are sold.*

LARGER-PRINT BOOKS!

HARLEQUIN

Presents®

GET 2 FREE LARGER-PRINT NOVELS PLUS 2 FREE GIFTS!

PASSION GUARANTEED SEDUCTION

YES! Please send me 2 FREE LARGER-PRINT Harlequin Presents® novels and my 2 FREE gifts (gifts are worth about $10). After receiving them, if I don't wish to receive any more books, I can return the shipping statement marked "cancel." If I don't cancel, I will receive 6 brand-new novels every month and be billed just $5.30 per book in the U.S. or $5.74 per book in Canada. That's a saving of at least 12% off the cover price! It's quite a bargain! Shipping and handling is just 50¢ per book in the U.S. and 75¢ per book in Canada.* I understand that accepting the 2 free books and gifts places me under no obligation to buy anything. I can always return a shipment and cancel at any time. Even if I never buy another book, the two free books and gifts are mine to keep forever.

176/376 HDN GHVY

Name	(PLEASE PRINT)	
Address		Apt. #
City	State/Prov.	Zip/Postal Code

Signature (if under 18, a parent or guardian must sign)

Mail to the **Reader Service**:
IN U.S.A.: P.O. Box 1867, Buffalo, NY 14240-1867
IN CANADA: P.O. Box 609, Fort Erie, Ontario L2A 5X3

**Are you a subscriber to Harlequin Presents® books
and want to receive the larger-print edition?
Call 1-800-873-8635 today or visit us at www.ReaderService.com.**

* Terms and prices subject to change without notice. Prices do not include applicable taxes. Sales tax applicable in N.Y. Canadian residents will be charged applicable taxes. Offer not valid in Quebec. This offer is limited to one order per household. Not valid for current subscribers to Harlequin Presents Larger-Print books. All orders subject to credit approval. Credit or debit balances in a customer's account(s) may be offset by any other outstanding balance owed by or to the customer. Please allow 4 to 6 weeks for delivery. Offer available while quantities last.

Your Privacy—The Reader Service is committed to protecting your privacy. Our Privacy Policy is available online at www.ReaderService.com or upon request from the Reader Service.

We make a portion of our mailing list available to reputable third parties that offer products we believe may interest you. If you prefer that we not exchange your name with third parties, or if you wish to clarify or modify your communication preferences, please visit us at www.ReaderService.com/consumerchoice or write to us at Reader Service Preference Service, P.O. Box 9062, Buffalo, NY 14240-9062. Include your complete name and address.

HPLP15

REQUEST YOUR FREE BOOKS!
2 FREE WHOLESOME ROMANCE NOVELS IN LARGER PRINT
PLUS 2 FREE MYSTERY GIFTS

†† ‡† ‡† ‡† ‡† ‡† ‡† ‡† ‡† ‡† ‡† ‡† ‡† ‡† ‡† ‡† ‡† ‡†

HEARTWARMING™

‡† ‡† ‡† ‡† ‡† ‡† ‡† ‡† ‡† ‡† ‡† ‡† ‡† ‡† ‡† ‡† ‡† ‡†

Wholesome, tender romances

YES! Please send me 2 FREE Harlequin® Heartwarming Larger-Print novels and my 2 FREE mystery gifts (gifts worth about $10). After receiving them, if I don't wish to receive any more books, I can return the shipping statement marked "cancel." If I don't cancel, I will receive 4 brand-new larger-print novels every month and be billed just $5.24 per book in the U.S. or $5.99 per book in Canada. That's a savings of at least 19% off the cover price. It's quite a bargain! Shipping and handling is just 50¢ per book in the U.S. and 75¢ per book in Canada.* I understand that accepting the 2 free books and gifts places me under no obligation to buy anything. I can always return a shipment and cancel at any time. Even if I never buy another book, the two free books and gifts are mine to keep forever.

161/361 IDN GHX2

Name   (PLEASE PRINT)

Address   Apt. #

City   State/Prov.   Zip/Postal Code

Signature (if under 18, a parent or guardian must sign)

Mail to the **Reader Service:**
IN U.S.A.: P.O. Box 1867, Buffalo, NY 14240-1867
IN CANADA: P.O. Box 609, Fort Erie, Ontario L2A 5X3

* Terms and prices subject to change without notice. Prices do not include applicable taxes. Sales tax applicable in N.Y. Canadian residents will be charged applicable taxes. Offer not valid in Quebec. This offer is limited to one order per household. Not valid for current subscribers to Harlequin Heartwarming larger-print books. All orders subject to credit approval. Credit or debit balances in a customer's account(s) may be offset by any other outstanding balance owed by or to the customer. Please allow 4 to 6 weeks for delivery. Offer available while quantities last.

Your Privacy—The Reader Service is committed to protecting your privacy. Our Privacy Policy is available online at www.ReaderService.com or upon request from the Reader Service.

We make a portion of our mailing list available to reputable third parties that offer products we believe may interest you. If you prefer that we not exchange your name with third parties, or if you wish to clarify or modify your communication preferences, please visit us at www.ReaderService.com/consumerschoice or write to us at Reader Service Preference Service, P.O. Box 9062, Buffalo, NY 14240-9062. Include your complete name and address.

HW15

HILP15